To

Doug

from

Gayle
Honeycomb

23-10-2010

The author trained and worked as a nurse and social worker in England, later studying at Sussex University, graduating with a BA Hons in politics in 1984.

Her first novel 'Brown Sugar' published in 1996 was a sell-out.

Her second novel 'Mercy Farm' published in 2007 was featured on Meridian TV, ITV One, and entered for the MacKitterick Literary Prize.

Her third novel 'Three and a Half Hours to Go' is a crime fiction highlighting the case of 'Miscarriage of Justice' and the pain it inflicts on its victims.

Set in the Caribbean and England, (1950s–2003)... from rags to riches... prisoner and glory... it's a gripping, moving story not to be missed...

By the same Author

Mercy Farm
ISBN 978 184386 348 9 (Vanguard Press)

Praise for 'Mercy Farm' –

'It feels optimistic and life affirming in tone and some of the characters are well-drawn and empathetic.'
Phil Temple BBC Vision Productions

'Standing side by side next to top writers on the bookshelf at Waterstones bookshop.'
Martin Shaw, Meridian TV

'Remarkable, courageous, brave…'
Debbie Thrower, Meridian TV

Three and a Half Hours to Go

Gayle Honeycombe

Three and a Half Hours to Go

Vanguard Press

VANGUARD PAPERBACK

© Copyright 2010
Gayle Honeycombe

The right of Gayle Honeycombe to be identified as author of
this work has been asserted by her in accordance with the
Copyright, Designs and Patents Act 1988.

All Rights Reserved

No reproduction, copy or transmission of this publication
may be made without written permission.
No paragraph of this publication may be reproduced,
copied or transmitted save with the written permission of the publisher,
or in accordance with the provisions
of the Copyright Act 1956 (as amended).

Any person who commits any unauthorised act in relation to
this publication may be liable to criminal
prosecution and civil claims for damages.

A CIP catalogue record for this title is
available from the British Library.

ISBN 978 1 84386 478 3

Any characters, names and dates of legal acts/entities mentioned in this
publication are purely fictitious.

Vanguard Press is an imprint of
Pegasus Elliot MacKenzie Publishers Ltd.
www.pegasuspublishers.com

First Published in 2010

Vanguard Press
Sheraton House Castle Park
Cambridge England

Printed & Bound in Great Britain

This book is dedicated to the people of the world who were victims of 'miscarriage of justice' for crimes they did not commit.

Chapter One

Click! Clock! Click! Clock! Footsteps...

Clang! Clang! Clang! Clang! Noises... it sounded like... like... a bunch of keys rattling...

Click! Clock! Clang! Clang! The sound got closer... the bunch of keys rattling around the Warder's waist, her fat belly wobbling, her buttocks dancing as she marched along the dark, deserted corridor.

Click! Clock! Clang! Clang! The noise drew closer, then Slu-ss-h! The peephole opened – two eyes stared, searching... searching... along every corner of that stinking hell-hole, for God knows what. Searching for something...no one knew.

Eve jumped. She stared back, frightened, bewildered, confused – their eyes met – no sign, not a word – nothing... nothing...! Then Slu-ss-h! The peephole door closed again, as quickly as it opened and like a jiff, the big woman was gone, the keys rattling around her fat waist as she tramped back along the barren corridor.

Eve sat on the hard, cold, bare mattress, strategically placed on the stone-cold floor it seemed, to keep the inmate frozen. She went numb – in a state of shock – frightened, confused, dismayed, not knowing what was going on, not knowing what was going to happen.

She was cold. She was trembling.

Shaking violently, she stared around her – bare stoned walls, dirty graffiti words written all over it. She strained to read the words... her eyes wandered.

At the far corner, a dirty stinking toilet pan which never saw the light of soap or scrubbing brush – it stank to high heavens; the great big heavy iron door; the peephole; the whole place musty, airless, smelly, so small you could hardly swing a cat in it. She felt queasy. She shook rigidly.

It was a prison cell alright – Cell No 1 – this man-made monstrosity in which she'd found herself. She couldn't come to terms with it – she couldn't think straight.

Her state of shock intensified...

She picked up the papers which the police had given her – they'd let her keep her spectacles, she didn't know why. She pushed the glasses over her nose and began to skim through:

NOTICE OF ENTITLEMENT, it read, 'Cells should be clean, heated, ventilated and well-lit...'

She felt sick, the stench around her over-powering.

'You are allowed to make one phone call and inform someone of your arrest...' she continued reading...then she thought... 'Sam, Sam! Yes! I will phone Sam'... but then she noticed the words...

NOTICE TO DETAINED PERSONS, it read: 'You can speak to a Solicitor anytime, day or night...'

'Yes! Yes! I would phone my Solicitor'... she was so confused...her mind whirling, when Click! Clock! Clang! Clang! And Slu-ss-h! The peephole opened again, two piercing eyes stared.

Bang! Bang! Bang! Bang! "You fuc... son-of-a-bitch! Get me out of here." A distraught female prisoner from the opposite cell was screaming, shouting obscene words. Banging, banging at her prison door, the noise so deafening, Eve's eardrum was about to burst.

"Would you like a drink?" the Custody Officer shouted through the peephole, her words barely audible through the pounding, shouting noise opposite.

"No thank you," Eve whispered angrily, the papers she was reading having just dropped from her hands.

She was petrified.

Thirsty and badly in need of a drink – she hadn't even had time to have her breakfast when the police broke her door down and arrested her. But, in her current state of grief; of anger; of despair, she refused the drink which was offered her.

Slu-ss-h! The peephole closed again, as quickly as it opened and Click! Clock! Clang! Clang! The Warder was gone, as quickly as she appeared.

Eve looked around her, her eyes searching for? She did not know what.

Maybe she could find a way to escape…?

'Crazy! Crazy!' she thought, then, a set of graffiti words caught her eye.

'Jac de Rippa was 'ere…' it read.

She jumped. She went cold, her eyes froze, then wandered again.

'Martin Tunderbal…bals…Fu-c – Screws…headless chicken…fuc you…go get you…son-ov-a-bitch.'

She shivered as she thought of the distressed state those poor prisoners' minds were in when they wrote those words.

'Was Jack the Ripper really here?' Her mind was playing havoc.

She sweated. She went cold, hot, then cold again. She shook her head in disbelief.

"No it can't be," she heard herself saying. "No! I'm not in this hell-hole. No! No! No!" Then…Clang! Clang! and Slu-ss-h! The peephole opened again.

"Would you like something to eat?"

"No!" she shouted.

She was hungry really, but she hated the situation she was in so badly, that she refused.

'That son-of-a-bitch Warder.' Then, as quick as a flash… "Yes. Yes. I would," she squealed, her voice trembling.

"What would you like? Curry and rice or spaghetti?"

"Roast turkey," Eve bawled.

"This is not a hotel, you know?"

Angry, defeated, Eve's tone lowered…

"I would like spaghetti please and," remembering her 'Rights' from the papers she'd just read, she continued, "could I please phone my son?"

"Right!" the Warder blurted and off she went, the keys clattering around her waist.

Within a few minutes she was back, this time with a mobile phone. "Up! Up you get! Come! Come!"

Anxiously Eve jumped up.

"Now here is the mobile phone. You can phone your son, but do not get any closer."

She took the mobile from the Custody Officer, but in her disoriented state, she couldn't even remember the number. Then she remembered that she had written it on a piece of paper – just in case – but the police had stripped her of her belongings, all but her glasses.

She told the Warder so and off she marched again, quickly returning with the piece of paper with the number written on it.

Standing a safe distance from the Warder, she dialled…"Hello Sam, it's Mum. I'm, I'm in jail Sam. Brickwater Prison…"

She was shaking uncontrollably.

"What! What! I can't hear you, Mum?"

Bang! Bang! The distraught prisoner from opposite was banging.

Straining to speak, Eve repeated, "I said, I'm in Brickwater Prison, Sam, they…the police, broke my door down and locked me up." The tears were welling up inside her as she spoke.

"Brick? Jail? Those fuc...bastards!"

"Up! Up! Time's up!" the Warder shouted – all the time – listening to the conversation. Who knows, they may even had taped it from some secret location. Who knows?

"I've got to go Sam. I've got to go," she said and nervously, hesitatingly passed the phone back to the Warder, her mind in such turmoil, she forgot to phone her Solicitor.

Slu-ss-h and Click! Clock! Clang! Clang! The Custody Officer disappeared. Eve, slumping back onto the thin, cold, hard mattress, sobbed her heart out, the banging opposite continuing unceasingly.

Tired, hacked and dazed – she couldn't sleep but she could hardly stay awake either.

She sobbed and sobbed her heart away.

She was in Brickwater Prison alright and that was something she was finding hard to accept. Another half an hour passed by, then the Custody Officer returned – this time with some food.

Slu-ss-h! The peephole opened.

Eve jumped.

She could see the food through the hole and as she stepped forward, the Warder thrust the spaghetti straight into her hand.

"Your Solicitor will be here at 1.30pm to see you," she said, not a hint of feeling showing on her blank face.

Eve nearly dropped the spaghetti.

In her distraught state she'd forgotten to phone her Solicitor – that was the first thing she should have done – yet she'd forgotten. Then it came to her – 'Sam! Sam! He must have phoned her and now she is coming. At last! At last!'

She looked at the pack of ready-frozen microwaved spaghetti and thrust the fork straight into it. She couldn't eat.

Fatigued, the stench of that soul-destroying prison was suffocating her – her distraught mind working havoc ...'She is coming... at last! At last! At last! At last!'

It didn't dawn on her why this Warder was peeping at her every half hour or so; it didn't click that she was under 'surveillance' – 'suicide watch' they called it.

But they had given her, her spectacles – she could have done the job easily with those glasses.

She was too distraught to think straight.

She sat on the hard bare mattress on this cold day – June 3 2002, her mind playing havoc...

'How could dey do dis to me? Me, an old woman of 62, marched away so unceremoniously by de police, after dey had broken mi door down, den locked me up in dis stinking hell-hole, for a supposed crime...?

'An accident, it was... How could dey? All mi life I had worked hard, paid mi way, lived decently and now? Now? How could dey...?'

'A barefooted, penniless girl from de Caribbean – I came to England, struggled as a nurse; served de community; contributed to de economy; did endless rounds of tireless charity work an' even received a Damehood for mi groundbreaking work wit disadvantaged people an' now? Now...? Doesn't sacrifice, credibility and hard work count anymore?'

Her mind was wheeling, leaping in bounds – like the mighty waves on a thunderous day – thinking... thinking. 'Three and a half hours to go...' she thought.

'It was just gone 10am when they locked me up in this death trap. Soon, it would be 1.30pm and my Solicitor would be here, at last! At Last!'

Her mind was running riot, when...

Click! Clock! Clang! Clang!... footsteps... her Solicitor and the Warder were making their way to her prison door.

She heard the keys rattled then Bang! The prison door flew open.

Like a lost child, she rushed toward her Solicitor then Bang! the door slammed shut behind them, she following her Solicitor along the deserted corridor, her mind whizzing about, her thoughts drifting back to where it all began...

Chapter Two

"Wake up girl! Wake up!" Mah shouted at 10-year-old Eve, shaking her hard round the shoulders. "Time to get up girl! Time to get up!" she bawled, then hobbled back downstairs to the kitchen, where she continued with her cooking.

Eve moaned, rubbed her eyes, then rolled over and drifted off to sleep again. Not that she was sleeping on a comfortable bed. She was lying on the cold, hard floor, on a make-do mattress, made of flour bags and dirty old linen – so hard it was, that her young bones crackled as she tried to sleep, tossing and turning about on it, all night long.

It was 4am – so early, far too early – even the cocks were not crowing and so, tired and exhausted, the young mite Eve rolled over and fell asleep again.

Ten minutes passed and Mah was getting impatient. Up she trotted. "Come on girl! Get up! Get up! You got to help Mah wit de cookin, you kno," she bawled, shaking Eve hard, by the shoulders. She grabbed Eve's hand and tried to pull her up, only this time Eve did not resist.

Crawling up onto her feet, she pulled on her dirty old frock and followed Mah sleepily down to the kitchen.

"Now, look girl. Wach!" Mah asserted. "Remembar 'ow ah show you to cook dem roti yesterday? Look girl! Look!" Mah repeated. "You rol de roti (pastry) like dis, den put it on de tarwa (hot plate) an' turn it like dis. Quic! Quic! Den you go see it does cook. OK Eve! OK?"

"Yes Mah, OK!" Eve replied, rubbing her sleepy eyes, straining hard to keep them open.

Sitting on the cold mud floor in the makeshift kitchen downstairs, 10-year-old Eve began cooking. She rolled and pasted, turned and greased, in between piling more wood onto the mud-hole fire, trying to keep it alight. But she was having a tough time. For the more wood she piled, the more the fire kept going out. She persisted, nonetheless.

Sweating, tired, hungry and doing what Mah had told her to, on she toiled, struggling hard to keep awake, the heat from the fire taking its toll – until a whole heap of rotis were cooked – enough to feed the whole family of eight for the day.

Mah meanwhile, was busy elsewhere.

Pacing gingerly in case she trod on a frog, she visited the latrine (toilet) outside. She was petrified of frogs. 'Dem green tings,' she used to say, 'jumpin' on you, on two legs in de dark! So slimey…an ooh dey stinc! Ooh!'

She would shiver when anyone dared mention frogs.

Now, here she was – so early in the morning – washing herself down with a bucket of water in the backyard outside, after visiting the latrine. Then, moving with speed, she got dressed quickly in her dirty, old, flour-bag dress and was ready for the day's work.

She helped Eve wrap the rotis and fried potatoes (aloo) in pieces of cloths and gave her her instructions for the day.

"Now Eve, you mus' give de boy an' girl (Eve's younger brother and sister) dere food, an' get dem ready and take dem to scool. OK? An' don' foget! You mus' sweep de yard today girl, an' soak dem clodes in de tub, ready fo' mi to wash wen ah come home from work. An'… don' foget to wash dem plates an' cups too. You hear mi girl?"

"Y-E-SS Mah!" Eve hardly had time to reply when Mah grabbed the bundle of food and rushed off to work.

It was 6am and Mah had to hurry to get to the fields in time – to crop the sugar canes before 1 o'clock, when it would become too hot to work. For that was how it was in Trinidad – workers would start work in the sugar fields at 6am and finish at 1pm, before the hot, blazing sun got the better of them.

Eve however, having been given her tasks to do was busy. Here she was at 6am on this Monday morning, June 6 1950, hustling and bustling about the place, not really knowing how she would ever get through them and be at school by 9am.

She felt scared.

She rushed upstairs, woke up her 6-year-old brother Raja and her 5-year-old sister Sita and brought them downstairs in their shabby clothes. Then she thrust the yard broom into Raja's hand and said, "Come on boy, sweep de yard! You hear mi boy? Sweep!" She was so nervous.

Taking the broom from her hand, "Yes Sis! No Sis!" Raja teased. He shovelled the broom around slowly – backwards and forwards it went, barely touching the dead leaves strewn around on the ground. As far as he was concerned, Indian boys did not sweep yards – only girls did that.

'Indian boys went to college and became doctors and lawyers and Indian girls swept yards, cleaned homes, learnt to cook and wash and sew, so that they could make good wives and serve their husbands well, when they grew up and got married.' At least, that was what he was told. For, that was the custom – Hindu customs – drummed into him and the girls from birth; customs which became part of their lives; traditions which no one dared question or challenge.

That was why Eve was named 'Sabita' – a Hindu name – but because she was so cute and pretty, every one called her Eve. "Eve! Eve!" they would shout and soon she got stuck with that nickname.

And now here she was, a 10-year-old girl, late for school and not getting much cooperation from her little brother, Raja so she sought help from her 5-year-old sister Sita.

They swallowed their breakfasts and tea sweetened with lots of condensed milk, as quick as they could, then together, they washed the breakfast dishes – tin cups and enamel plates and scrubbed the iron pots and turned them over to dry on the wash-stand in the back yard outside. Then she gave Raja and Sita a bucket of cold water and told them to wash themselves down, she meanwhile, hurriedly soaked the dirty clothes in the wash tub. When she'd finished, she bolted back upstairs, made the beds quickly, then continued assisting the two children to get dressed.

She helped Sita into her cotton frock and Raja into his khaki pants and shirt, then she pulled on Marla's worn out dress – it hung over her like a sack. But she took no notice. Instead, with speed, she pulled on a dirty old flour bag pantie, grabbed their lunches which Mah had earlier helped her bundle into pieces of cloths and bare-footed, they headed for school.

On they raced, Raja and Sita skipping all over the place, the tropical sun blazing down on their bare faces, forming shadows on the parched, dry earth; wooden shacks and mud huts with holes for windows and grass-tops for roofs on one side of Carli-Bay Road; sprawling acres of sugar canes, bowing and bending their tall lean trunks, crackling to the tune of the winds – as if they were telling a tale – there they stood, clusters of them on the opposite side of the road.

Trotting and skipping along, the children soon reached Perseverance Village. Here, the road was wider and made of Tarmac. There were houses on both sides with a sign on the local postmistress's house which boldly read 'POSTMAN'.

On they raced, before long reaching Couva Cemetery – white tombstones scattered everywhere – a burial ground for the rich, it was rumoured – the poor being discreetly disposed of in the Pauper's graveyard, a short distance from Pah's house where Eve lived.

Scared of the cemetery, they bolted onwards as fast as their legs could carry them, Couva Anglican Church standing nearby, its tall spires shooting high above in the sky, like a cast iron carcass on display. There it stood, this church, the sound of its bells peeling regularly on Sunday mornings; so deafening it was, it woke the whole neighbourhood up – but most people didn't mind, for that church was the pillar of their community – Christians and non-Christians alike.

Skipping along now, Eve, Raja and Sita reached the three-way junction, traffic speeding in all directions, it seemed. Terrified, Eve grabbed the children's hands firmly and said, "Now. You don' cross until de cars stop. You hear mi!" and they nodded in agreement.

"Dey stop! Dey stop! Run fo' it! Run fo' it now! Now!" and they bolted across the road, one driver hooting madly, others following suit, swerving and swivelling, trying to avoid hitting the children.

It was a lucky escape. Because somehow, Eve and the children had missed their cue.

Breathless, they were still racing – the sun beating down on their bare scalps – and so before long, they reached St Andrews village, the Pitch Road getting wider now, pavement along on one side all the way to Upper Couva. The houses were painted pink or white with white front gates and well kept hibiscus hedges bordering them, almost hidden behind wooden half-walls.

Some of these houses had tall fruit trees in their front gardens – fruits like mangoes and sweet, milky, kimets and sometimes the children used to pelt them down with stones and sneak through the gates with the stolen fruits. Then, on other occasions when it was cooler, they would play hop-scotch and leap-frog, occasionally getting into a brawl. But today they were late for school, so Eve hollered to the children, "Com' on, we late. Run fo' it! Run! Run!"

She was getting frantic.

And so, like wild horses, they bolted along the pavement until they reached Couva Anglican School and just as they were about to cross the road, they heard the bell ringing. Bang!... Bang!... Bang!... it went as they raced across the road.

"Phew! We make it. Phew!" Eve went, nervous and sweating like a frightened child.

She knew if they were late they would have to kneel in front of the whole class and made to look like fools – a punishment it was hoped, would deter other children from arriving late at school. So, she breathed a sigh of relief...

"Phew!" she whispered to herself. "We make it!"

"We make it! We make it!" she whispered again, puffing and panting with exhaustion.

Chapter Three

Couva Anglican School was a remarkable building. Standing on tall posts with galvanised rooftop and pale green walls – its paint peeling off in places – it was a constant reminder of its colonial past. Bleak and gloomy underneath – its concrete walls cracked and un-kept in places – the children played leap-frog, hop-scotch and hide-and-seek there, whilst netball and rounders were played in the back yard; the front yard being taken over by the boys.

The boys always played cricket in the front, their shadows changing shape in the cool of the heat. Sometimes the ball would 'bolt' and land straight on the main road, the traffic screeching to a halt, the drivers cursing like mad, but that didn't deter them from playing there.

The teachers were proud of that school. Often at weekends, Miss Marshall and Mr Marshall would paint the flaking walls, because they said that the government did not have enough money to maintain the school and sometimes they would enlist the help of parents to assist them with the chores too. They were such caring teachers.

Miss Marshall was always well groomed. She used to look smart in her starch-white shirt, her well pressed navy blue or black skirt and black high heeled shoes, her hair always nicely combed back from her forehead and gripped at the top of her head with pretty little clips. She was so young and lovely, 21 or so and Eve was proud of her.

At 22, Mr Marshall wasn't one for dressing up, but he always managed to look good in his baggy flannel pants and striped shirt – it smelt so distinctly of Palmolive soap. He was so popular, most of his pupils liked him a lot. As for Eve, well she absolutely adored him.

Every morning during 'recess time', the teachers would take turns in dishing out the powdered milk to the children.

"Drink up! Drink up!" Miss Marshall would assert. "Go help you grow strong, you know."

She used to give Eve two helpings, "Drink up girl," she would assert. "Go help you grow prettier, you know and one day a statesman go come an' take you away an' you go be a great big States lady!"

Eve was so poor, her Mah and Pah couldn't afford to buy shoes or decent clothes for her to wear. But Miss Marshall saw potential in the little girl. She knew very well that one day Eve would go places… She knew… Oh how she knew…

One morning, whilst picking up mangoes from under a tree, some boys were busy pelting stones and one fell on Eve's head. It bled so profusely that Miss Marshall thought Eve had cracked her skull.

Unable to stand the sight of blood, Miss Marshall panicked and started to scream. She screamed so loudly, that one of the teachers rushed out to see what all the commotion was about. When she saw the blood, she bandaged Eve's head with speed – it being such a wide cut – they had to send her up to Couva hospital quickly, where the nurses put six stitches in… and Miss Marshall didn't get over the shock for a long, long time…

During teaching lessons, she would point at the blackboard with a stick and say: "A for Apple! B for Bat!" and the children used to repeat it after her. Then, she would call on Eve. "Come on child!" she would call. "Read it out loud!" And Eve would reel it off, all in one go.

She was only five then, but she was so bright for her class that the Headmaster had to move her up one class higher, where Mr Marshall would then teach her.

At drawing classes, Eve would draw dark green hibiscus hedges with beautiful red flowers peeping out, here and there.

It looked so real, that Mr Marshall had no choice but to give her a good 99% when he marked her papers.

Excelling in almost every subject: English, History, Poetry, Drama, Essays – essays being her best subject, she cropped 95 or 96% for every essay she wrote. The only subject she couldn't master was Arithmetic – she couldn't work out why $X+Y=Z$.

At 40, Mr Bagshot the Headmaster, was a stern disciplinarian. He loved to dress in his dark suits and brown ties. He had a Chinese wife and six children and the kids used to call them Chigroes, because he was a Negro and she was Chinese.

Being an ardent music lover, he taught it with ferocity.

At music sessions, he would strike the tuning fork on the table, put it to his ears and it would go, 'Ping!' and he would hum, "Doh, Ray, Me!... Doh, Ray, Me, Fah... So, Lah, Ti, Doh!" And the whole class would chant "Doh..." after him.

His second love was poetry and having found out from Mr Marshall that Eve was good at reciting poems, he chose her to recite a piece on Parents' Day, for secretly, he too had a twinkle in his eye for Eve – she was his prized pupil and he was determined to show the world that.

It was July 6 1951 and having grown up so fast (Eve was almost eleven) when Parents' Day came – the guests arriving in full force – from everywhere, it seemed.

Hot and humid, the women were fanning their faces with their hats, some drinking water from bottles, the men waving and chatting to their friends. Then, the show began.

One boy got onto the stage and sang; another read a piece from the history books – all about Queen Elizabeth and Captain Drake. Then, it was Eve's turn...

She got onto the platform and looked down at the audience. She was shaking...(Mah and Pah were not there – they didn't like the idea of their Indian daughter on stage, reciting some God forsaken poem) so they stayed away.

Combing the audience, Eve spotted Miss Marshall and Mr Marshall. There they were standing proudly; waiting quietly...waiting in anticipation...waiting...waiting...

She looked at them and she was overcome. Feelings of respect, of loyalty, of love, surfaced within her and she knew she had to recite that piece – if not for herself, but for them – they, her beloved teachers, they, who had taught her so much...She knew she had to do it...

Trembling at the knees and getting cold feet, she braced herself, took a deep breath and...started. She reeled out the words with a willpower...and veracity...she never knew she had.

"Ramped and roared, like a lion," she went and she stamped her feet and roared...like a lion and then took her bow.

The audience erupted...They stood up. They whistled. They hooted. They clapped...and she felt like a star.

She looked at Mr Marshall, standing there at the back, a proud smile on his face, a smile, not just for her, but for him too; for it was he, Marshall, who'd taught she, Eve, how to recite poems.

The thunderous uproar continued for some while – she, the poor girl from Carli-Bay Road standing there, proud, listening... basking in that moment of glory! She knew it was her day, but it was his day too... he, the teacher she called Mr Marshall.

Innocent days they were; school days, childhood days which she was enjoying. But, little did she know, that they would soon be gone; lost forever! Sacrificed by traditions – customs – Hindu traditions – which would one day, almost destroy her life...

Chapter Four

Carli-Bay Road where Eve grew up was rich in culture. But things hadn't changed for ages, it seemed. Its customs and traditions were so entrenched, that its way of life left an impression on her for the rest of her existence.

Sugar was part of the scene. For, on one side of the road, sprawling acres of sugar cane fields stretched for miles and miles – only the narrow dirt tracks divided them – the canes growing so tall and lean, bending and twisting as the tropical winds got the better of them.

During the crop seasons, the Foremen used to set fire to these canes, burning out the pests and bushes so that the workers could crop them without fear of attacks from snakes and insects, or any unseen prowlers. The fire used to rage like mad, shooting red tongues high up in the sky; the burning cane crackling like thunder 'Crack! Crack! Crack! Crack!' it went, the burnt out ashes flying around like black birds, settling inside the houses and yards, dead!

Almost daily, the occupants had to clean up the mess, but they didn't mind, for it was part of their lives.

And amidst all this activity, Pah's house stood proudly at the far corner of the road – waiting as if to tell a tale.

There it stood, on tall wooden posts, its silver-coloured galvanised roof shining under the sun, its wooden walls rotting in parts, stray dogs and cats hanging around below, waiting to grab the first bit of cast-off scrap of food, to feed their hungry, empty stomachs.

On the right side of Pah's house, lived two Negroes – Melvyn and his partner Alice. They lived in a mud hut with a grass rooftop. Melvyn used to catch fish down at Carli-Bay

Sea and sell it to the vendors. And sometimes he worked the fields too, just to make ends meet.

Every Saturday night, as regular as clock-work, he and his friends would drink rum and play cards – gambling for money, until late at night – sometimes winning…sometimes losing…And sometimes, in the heat of the moment when he got stinking drunk, there would be an argument and he would take out his belt from around his waist and beat the hell out of his partner Alice.

Alice would run for her life, often hammering on Mah's door, waking us all up, screaming, screaming, "Oh God, Miss Sam! Oh God, Miss Sam! De man is beetin' mi up again! Help mi, Miss Sam! Help me, Miss Sam! De man is beetin' mi up again."

Mah used to feel sorry for her and give her a drink to try and calm her nerves, but come next week, it was the same story all over again.

Poor Alice! Week after week, she tolerated the hiding and when it was over, there would be strap marks all over her body – her arms and legs. Rumours had it, that Melvyn belted her because she stank. No matter how much Bay-rum she dabbed on herself, she still stank of urine.

Melvyn was always up to his pranks. Sometimes he would climb over Pah's wire fence and steal Pah's money from under his mattress. And sometimes, when Pah's chickens – cocks and hens – flew over the fence into Melvyn's yard, he would entice them into his hut by feeding them with corn, then, once they got inside, he would put a wet towel over them to muffle their noises and catch them, either to sell to his friends, using the money to buy more rum, or cook them for his Sunday lunch.

Rumours soon surfaced and Pah became wise to Melvyn's escapades – his hordes – but Pah was scared of him – Melvyn was a big man and Pah didn't want trouble from him or the police. All Pah could do, was hide his money elsewhere, in the hope that Melvyn would not find it.

On the left side of Pah's home, was a pink painted house, its concrete steps adorned with flower pots. Miss Carmen, a flamboyant Negro lady who made her living as a seamstress, lived there. She used to sew clothes for people from all over Trinidad and would dress herself in the most colourful outfits and headscarves, that people used to say how rich and classy she was.

Every weekend, a Negro man used to visit her. He always looked so smart in dark suits and colourful ties, that rumours soon abound. The locals said that he was Miss Carmen's boyfriend and that he was rich and had a nice job at Pointe-a-Pierre, that's why he always looked so smart.

Miss Carmen used to make sweet bread, ginger beer and sugar cakes and give to Mah, Mah cooking darhl and roti and curried meat and giving them to her in return. They were really good neighbours – these two – Miss Carmen often teasing Eve, telling her how pretty and cute she was, sometimes giving her lots of sugar cakes to eat.

But the real gossip-monger in the street was Miss Dai. She lived at the back of Pah's house and was always coming over to Mah's, gossiping about everyone at Carli-Bay Road. Even when Mah was busy, she came and gossiped. A real page-turner – she knew almost everything, about everyone in the Road.

Sometimes, Mah would get so angry, but she never let on, because she didn't want to lose a friend.

The children too were up to mischief, sometimes playing under the beams of the moonlight, their shadows changing shapes as they pranced about. And sometimes, they chased the birds too, having so much fun in between the bushes, in their simple and innocent ways.

Eve enjoyed watching the birds, their red-green wings buzzing about a thousand times to the dozen, their colourful wings shimmering, as they fluttered briskly from one tropical flower to the next.

"Don't go near de birds girl," Mah used to scream. "Dey don' like you followin' dem, girl," Mah would assert. But Eve was so bewitched by the beautiful creatures, that she sneaked away when Mah was not looking and watched the birds anyway.

One day, she followed one to its nest and watched it feeding its young chicks, their little mouths opening as wide as cracked nutshells as they tried to swallow their meals. But when the bird saw her approaching, it flew away and never returned. She tried feeding the chicks with breadcrumbs, but not long after they were abandoned by their mother, they died.

Eve was so sad she never went near a bird's nest again.

A strange bunch of people they were at Carli-Bay Road; an amazing mix – all living together side by side – each following their own lifestyle, blending together like a jigsaw puzzle; a puzzle which, if one part was to go astray, the whole scheme of life would be lost, crumbled forever.

There they lived, these people, sometimes in harmony, sometimes in conflict; yet being able to diffuse situations, stopping disagreements erupting into race riots.

It was a life which was to leave its mark on Eve; a life which made Trinidad and the Caribbean so unique, so tempting, drawing people from all over the world to sample a taste of its uniqueness.

Chapter Five

Sport was one of the subjects in which Eve took a keen interest. So she enrolled for the Egg and Spoon race, which was to take place on Sports Day, July 4 1952.

She didn't have to wait long, before the Big Day came.

The teachers had worked very hard to make this day a success and now they were busy, buzzing around like bees, hurrying here, scurrying there. Ten to the dozen, they moved, trying their best to arrange the events: Tug-of-war, two-legged, running, sack race...They raced about with speed, some laying out prizes on long tables which were covered with large white cloths; others hurrying about, doing this, doing that. And high above, the Union Jack flew proudly – something to do with Trinidad being a Commonwealth Country – so the teachers said.

Scorching hot, not a sprinkle of breeze to cool the humid air, the spectators rolled in and the place was soon jam packed with people. Drenched with perspiration, some were fanning themselves frantically to keep cool, others drinking cold drinks from bottles, all waiting anxiously for the games to start.

Time pressed and before long...'Whif'... the sign went up... and..."God save our gracious Queen," they sang and 'PING!'... they were off...

A boy called Willy was doing the Short Distance. He was wearing 'yellow' shoes and his mother was going wild with excitement. "We want Willy! We want Willy!" she was shouting, jumping up and down like a wild cockatoo – so sure she was that Willy would win the race. But Willy came last and she didn't get over the shock for a long, long time.

Another boy was doing the Two-legged with his friend. They kept falling over and the crowd kept booing and teasing them: "Wats de matter Roy? You moder didn' feed you dis mornin', boy?" one man shouted. "Get ah grip Roy. Get ah grip, man!" they were shouting.

Then came Eve's turn. Face composed, she stood proudly in line, Egg and Spoon in her hand, the crowd hooting, whistling and making noise like mad. "Come on Eve! Come on Eve!" they went, Miss Marshall hollering in the background, egging her on.

She kept on and on... Miss Marshall, making so much noise, that as Eve neared the end, she got so excited that the egg tumbled, cracked and fell off the spoon – leaving a trail of yellow mass dripping down the front of her dress and a sprawling mess on the ground.

"Ooh!... Aah!" the crowd went in sympathy, Eve sobbing her heart out. She was used to winning and now that she had lost the game, she couldn't cope with it.

She sobbed her heart out.

Back at home, however, someone was waiting. Like a wild hyena, Rajkapur, her eldest brother, waited for the 'kill'. And so as soon as she returned, he went for her.

"So you break de egg girl! No silver spoon eh girl!" he taunted, laughing in her face, tears welling in her eyes.

He couldn't face the fact that Eve was liked by most people. He saw her as a threat to everything he stood for and so hated her so much, that he couldn't wait to humiliate her, destroy her – her very soul – if he could. And as luck would have it, he almost succeeded.

That night she cried herself to sleep, vowing secretly, that come next year – no matter what – she was going to win that game. But she didn't bank on the fact that come next year she would be heading for 13 and Pah and Rajkapur would not let a 13-year-old Hindu girl run the Egg and Spoon race.

In her child-like innocence, she was unaware of the complexities of the environment in which she was growing up; a nation so rich in culture, yet beset by traditional values – in her case – Hindu customs which was to suffocate her and almost destroy her life...

The naïve, innocent child however, continued her journey of life, and so, a couple of days later, Mah took her up to Auntie Nell to spend the rest of her holidays. And what a welcoming break it turned out to be!

What a shock to her system, it was. For Auntie Nell lived in a big white house amongst the rich in Upper Couva – so different to the atmosphere at Pah's home, in which she was growing up.

It had glass windows with lace curtains and flowerpots adorned its steps. The floor was so well polished, you could almost see your face in it. And brass spring beds, with crocheted covers, gave a comfortable feel to the place, with showers to bathe under and ovens to cook in, completing the fittings.

How they lived in such luxuries baffled Eve. She couldn't understand. But Auntie Nell's husband worked as a Bookkeeper at Texaco and his brother was a School Teacher at Waterloo. The fact that they had secure jobs and secure incomes helped them to live a more refined lifestyle – something which Eve was far too young to understand.

The family used to eat meat or fish every day and Eve was given great helpings of it. They used to bake fresh coconut cakes and give her lots of it to eat too. But above all, she treasured the fact that she was allowed to have daily baths under the warm indoor shower – a sharp contrast to home and the weekly baths under the cold stand pipe out in the busy street – passers-by staring at her naked body, her adolescent pubic hairs exposed for all to see.

She used to get so embarrassed and upset at bath-time and would cry out... but Mah took no notice. Instead she would shout at her.

"Don' be stupid, you silly girl. No one is lookin' man! Come on! Come on girl! No one is lookin' man!" she would holler and continue with the chore of scrubbing Eve's body down.

What a difference it was at Auntie Nell's home?

At Auntie Nell's home, the whole family would sit at the table and eat their meals together of an evening time and talk and joke about the day's events. Not so at Pah's house. There, Eve never sat and ate with the males. Instead, she sat on the cold floor and ate separately, surrounded by females only.

Such were the customs, Hindu customs – which held that males and females should be segregated; eat separately; do most things separately; divided by the sexes – a distinct contrast to that at Auntie Nell's home – where, the way of life which Eve was witnessing was so different; a pattern of family life, (a Christian life) a lifestyle which, until now, Eve didn't know existed.

She was happy there. Blissfully happy! But she knew full well that soon she would have to return home to Pah's – to a life of poverty, cruelty and drudgery. 'Home' to a life where the sexes were segregated. 'Home' to a place where males were regarded as superior beings. 'Home' to a life so different from the one she had come to know and love at Auntie Nell's.

Chapter Six

Cushioned by a wall of innocence and unaware that she was growing up so fast, Eve remained strangled by the vein of the Hindu customs into which she was born.

She was not allowed to mix with males. "If ah cach you kissin' a boy," Pah warned fiercely, "you see dis belt?" he pointed at the belt around his waist, "ah go beat de hell out of you!"

Eve knew very well that he meant what he'd said, so she vowed that she would not disobey him and so, sought escape in other ventures instead. She played, explored and tried to learn as much as she could – her sharp eyes taking in and storing...a lot of what she saw – and make no mistake, she saw a lot.

One venture she enjoyed took place on Saturday mornings. Every Saturday morning at around 5am, Mah used to go to Chaguanas Market to buy supplies to restock her parlour which was built underneath Pah's house. She would buy ground provisions, fresh fruits, vegetables and sweets... enough foodstuffs to sell for the whole week. And what a 'scene' Chaguanas market was. It was chaotic!

There were big trucks pulling in and out of corners, almost ramming into each other; cars hooting, their wheels rattling and taxis swaying here and there, to avoid being crushed. The atmosphere at Chaguanas market was like that of a mad-house! Eve taking in every bit of it.

Often, she would go there with Mah, getting up at 4 o'clock in the morning to sort out the rice bags etc., in which they would carry the goods. Then 4.30am sharp, they would dive into Mr Jaggernand's taxi, he, speeding like mad down the zigzag road, just to avoid the traffic and get there by 5am at least, well before the best provisions were sold out. For they knew too well that if they did get there late, the best bargains would have gone.

One day, Mr Jaggernand's taxi almost got hit by a truck. "Wach wey you goin' Man!" he screamed, the big truck swirling, tumbling, just missing the bonnet of his car by a fraction of an inch.

Mr Jaggernand swore and cursed like mad, his temper rising so high that he almost burst a blood vessel and he never stopped cursing and swearing for the rest of the day.

Once at the market, Mah would jump out of his taxi, Eve following suit, both rushing around like mad – mountains of yam, cassavas, eddoes, sweet potatoes…plantains, mangoes, sapodillas, kimets and loads of yellow corn were on show, piled in random heaps on the ground around them – tomatoes and red watermelons, adding a touch of variety to the scene.

The vendors used to shout, "Red melon – 50 cents! Come and get you watermelon!"

"40 cents… 40 cents!" Another would yell.

"Nice wite yam, $2.50 a bag!"

"$2.00 a bag!" Another vendor hollered.

And so it went, the crowd sweating through the sweltering heat, scrambling to grab the best bargains they could find.

Eve used to watch Mah as she bartered for her share of the goods. "Ah giv you $2.00 for dat bag of yam Mr Jack, $2.00!" she would assert, pushing the $2.00 right under his nose.

"No Miss Sam. No man!" Mr Jack would protest. "Dis here is de best yam ov de seeson man. Ah carn giv for less dan $2.50. $2.50 Miss Sam! $2.50…"

"$2.00 Jack! Oh no deal!" Mah would shout and walk away, flashing the notes in her hand, then reluctantly, Mr Jack would succumb and sell his goods at her price.

"OK Miss Sam. OK $2.00! You have it... A man is not makin' a livin', you know," he would protest, knowing full well that he was making a good profit, even at that price.

And so it went – that was how they traded – these market people – always asking a price much higher than the goods were worth, then under duress, they would drop the price, giving the buyers the impression that they were walking off with a bargain. But the buyers knew their game and played it accordingly. Eve, taking it all in, eyes glued to the scene, learning much about bartering.

When the bartering was over, she and Mah would carry the goods to the far end of the market, from where Mah would flag down a taxi to take them back to Carli-Bay Road. Then, once they arrived home, they would arrange the provisions in big heaps – yam, cassavas, plantains, watermelons – all nicely displayed on the parlour shelves in an inviting manner.

But sometimes, Mah hardly had time to unload the goods, when the customers flocked in to buy.

They used to pile in by the dozens, each picking the best foodstuffs they could find: anything from plantains to cassavas, fresh fruits and watermelons...and sometimes they paid their bills too – for Saturday was pay day.

They were so poor – these people – far poorer than Mah and Pah, their wages barely lasting the week. So Mah used to let them buy the goods on credit, then come the following Saturday, she hoped they would pay their bills. And true to form, they paid – sometimes in part; sometimes the whole – Mah's trust paying off as they did their best to pay their debts.

Saturday was indeed a hectic day for Mah.

One Saturday however, Mah had other business to do so, after returning from the market, she went to Upper Couva to buy some clothes for a forthcoming wedding, leaving Eve in charge of the parlour.

It was a good day for Eve, for she had done a lot of business and the cash box was filled with money. But Melvyn was lying in wait...

He came over on the pretence of buying cigarettes and told Eve that Marla, her eldest sister had had an accident, 'she fall and injure sheself bad' he asserted and the naïve Eve panicked.

With Marla living only a few houses down the street, the frightened child dropped everything and rushed out of the parlour, making for Marla's house. And so Melvyn didn't waste any time.

Noting the cash box was filled with money, he seized his chance. He emptied it of all its contents and scampered away like a sly fox.

The poor child Eve! Naïve as she was, when she returned home she didn't think of checking the cash box. And so, when Mah came home that day, she couldn't wait to tell her how much money she'd made.

"At leas' $200, Mah! Ah make $200 today!" she boasted with excitement. But when Mah opened the cash box, it was empty.

She looked at Eve. Eve went hysterical and started to cry.

"Ah didn' take it Mah! Ah didn' take it!" she pleaded, bawling her head off, Mah not knowing what to make of it. But then, when she had calmed down and told Mah about Melvyn's prank – how he'd said 'that Marla had an accident' and had her scampering off to her sister's, Mah knew straight away that he had stolen the money.

Melvyn was a thief and everyone but the innocent child Eve knew it.

Eve went into a state of shock...and it took her a long while to get over it.

It was her first lesson in the art of trust – a lesson about 'whom to trust and whom not to.' A lesson she was to learn the hard way. A lesson she was never to forget.

Naïve as she was, she didn't think twice about putting her faith in Melvyn, but she soon learnt from that experience.

She was growing up fast; learning the art of survival... learning the art of trust...an experience which – little did she know – she would draw on, in times to come.

After that episode, things went quiet for a while, but it wasn't long before there was to be further excitement in her youthful, eager life...

It came from a group of people they called 'The Shango People'. They had 'a bit of a reputation', these folks – a group of Negroes who lived on the opposite side of Pah's house – and so, the locals kept their distance from them.

They used to have Shango dances once a year – a kind of spiritual, religious, come Voodoo celebrations, inherited way back from their ancestors in Africa. These celebrations went on for weeks and weeks and people from all over Trinidad would attend. But Pah strictly forbade Eve ever to mix with them, or go anywhere near them.

"Bad for you girl! Bad! You hear mi?" he warned fiercely. "If ah cach you goin' anyway nere dem, ah go beat de hell out of you! Beat you so bad, you go carn walk! You hear mi girl?" he bellowed, pointing to the belt wrapped firmly round his waist.

Poor Eve! She shivered at the thought. But the sound of the Shango drums were too tempting. She couldn't resist it.

And so, one evening about 6pm she sneaked away, when no one was looking and hiding behind some bushes, she watched the commotion going on.

Some Negro men were beating drums in front of a raging fire and some Negro women dressed in white dresses and wearing white headscarves, were dancing ferociously in front of it. They lifted their skirts high up in the air, so high, Eve could see their white panties; their dark bodies shaking so rigidly, as if going into some kind of frenzied fits – some kind of trance – the drummers blasting away. Louder and louder, it went, the noise deafening. Then all of a sudden, the women dancers fell to the ground, unconscious, only to be carted away and replaced by others.

A few women were standing behind these dancers, grunting… chanting to the sound of the deafening drums.

Then after the first group of women fell, the men brought out a live goat, chopped its head off, its dying body trembling rigidly, as if in fits; trembling…trembling…blood spurting all over the place. Some of the men were catching the blood and drinking it raw, after which they roasted the carcass on the blazing fire.

Later that evening, they would feast on the roasted goat and peas and rice, so 'rumours had it', but Eve was too terrified, to wait to see.

Scared out of her wits at such a gruesome sight and shaking like a leaf, she belted home as fast as her weakened, trembling legs could carry her, puffing…panting…gasping for breath, hoping that no one had seen her, but she was wrong. A neighbour saw her and told Pah.

Poor Eve! She was all done in!

The next day Pah gave her such a hiding. "Ah warn you not to go girl, but you stil' go. Now, you go turn bad girl, bad! An' no Indian man go marry you. You hear mi girl! You hear mi?" he bellowed, Eve bawling her head off, as he whipped…and whipped…the hell out of her.

Beaten to submission, Eve sobbed her heart out. That night she cried and cried until she finally fell asleep.

Yet another lesson in Pah's Hindu Code… a lesson which Eve was to learn with pain.

She was growing up alright; growing up fast and learning… learning the hard way – or so it seemed…

Chapter Seven

Growing up through childhood experiences, Eve was 12 years old, when one day whilst playing hop-scotch, she noticed blood seeping down her legs. Terrified, she screamed and Mah rushed out to see what the commotion was about.

"Wats de matter girl, why you bawlin' so?" Mah enquired, anxiously.

"Look Mah, look!" Eve squealed pointing at her legs.

It was no surprise to Mah. She took her indoors, cleaned her up, padded her with some old rags and explained.

"Look girl! You menstratin' girl, you menstratin'. You gone 12 now and every mont, dis go happen. Is normal girl! Is normal! Wen dis happen, you mus' pad youself up wit de cloth, den wash dem an' hang dem to dry in the back yard. Den you mus' fol dem up ready for de nex time. OK girl? An' don'n tell nobody about dis. OK Eve?"

"OK Mah," Eve went, trembling with fear.

She didn't really understand much about it, nor why she had to keep it a secret, but she was given her orders and she knew she had to obey.

Time moved on and back at school, Eve had now reached the 7th standard class. She had no further to go in her Elementary education, for the 7th standard was the highest in that form of teaching. So, she hoped she would attend college like all the other rich girls from Couva did and become a teacher one day and wear nice clothes and live in posh houses and give her parents plenty of money, from her wages.

But she was poor and she knew Pah would not let her go to college.

"Over mi dead body!" Pah always said. "Pay for mi Hindu daughter to go to college? Never! Not in dis house? No man!"

Such a privilege was accorded to his sons only and nothing was going to change that. 'Hindu girls must learn to cook, wash, sew, get marry and serve dere husbands well, when dey grow up' – that was the custom – and nothing on earth would shake that. Pah was adamant.

So Eve devised a plot.

She knew Mahadaye, her best friend was attending evening classes, getting extra lessons to prepare her for the 11+ exam and college, so she decided to steal her notes and copy them.

'If ah could get dese extra notes, ah could study hard and pass the 11+ too,' she thought, 'den ah could go to college free – Pah wouldn' have to pay a single penny.' And so, one evening, she sneaked in the class when no one was there, stole Mahadaye's notebooks and started copying.

Poor Eve! In her one-track, child-like mind, she just wasn't thinking straight. For she hardly had time to copy one paragraph, when Mr Marshall walked in and caught her in the act. For a moment he stood there, staring at her, the expression on his face stony, hard and as cold as ice.

Then suddenly..."Who's book is dat Eve? Let's have a look," he bellowed – the name 'Mahadaye' clearly written all over the front cover.

He went mad!

"You steal a pupil's book Eve. Steal! Steal! A thief Eve, a thief!" he shouted, reaffirming his anger. "In this school Eve, dat is not accepted. I cannot believe it girl. I cannot believe it!" he barked, red in the face.

"You must be punished Eve. Punished!"

Scared out of her wits, Eve started to bawl, crying her eyes out; ashamed of what she'd done; ashamed that she was found out – and by her favourite teacher too. She tried hard to explain her reasons, but Mr Marshall just wasn't listening. He fumed with rage.

Angry and disappointed at her behaviour, he ordered her to go to the front of the class and kneel there for half an hour, she sobbing and sobbing her heart out, he being too angry to hear her plea.

That evening, when she returned home late, Pah was waiting.

"Ah tole you girl, ah tole you! How meny time ah tole you not to mix wit dem bad girl Eve, but you stil' do, you stil' do girl!" he warned, fuming with frustration.

He was so convinced that she was late because she was hanging around with bad girls, that he took out his belt from around his waist and gave her a good hiding – no amount of pleading and begging for forgiveness from Eve, appealed to his conscience.

He simply refused to listen to her explanations. He had no time for such excuses...

But, that evening, something else was happening. After Eve left for home, Mr Marshall felt guilty and did some swift thinking...He thought...a lot about Eve – the apple of his eye – and the predicament in which she'd found herself.

He knew she was poor, always barefooted, with no decent clothes to wear and he knew too, of the strict environment in which she was being brought up – the Hindu codes which Pah had for his daughters. But he also knew that she was a decent child, bright and clever: a child who loved education; a child who excelled in classes.

'If only she was given the chance to achieve further education,' he thought, 'she would work hard and become somebody... someone important... one day...'

'She'd be a shining example for all the world to see.' He was sure of that.

'Any child, who goes to such an extreme as to steal another's notes in order to better herself, deserves a better life.'

His mind was working overtime.

That night he thought and thought...for hours, until he finally fell asleep. The next day, he made up his mind – that come what may – he was going to see Pah, down at his home in Carli-Bay Road and put it to him.

He was going to put his case to Pah, put it straight to him, no matter what...

Chapter Eight

It was July 13 1953, during the school holiday, when Mr Marshall set off on his bicycle to see Pah, the rain drizzling slightly, sprinkling the parched earth as he pedalled down Carli-Bay Road. He was soaking wet.

From behind a post in Pah's back yard, Eve watched nervously as Mr Marshall got off his bicycle and leaned it against Pah's wire fence. She was nervous.

She knew why he was there to see Pah – because he had told her so – but she also knew that Pah would go mad, even give her a good hiding, once her teacher had gone. She was shivering.

"Good afternoon Mr Sam," Mr Marshall greeted, stretching out his hand to shake Pah's.

"Well hell! Is Mr Marshall, de teacher. Dis is a surprise Mr Marshall. Wat you doin' here, sir?" Pah replied, taken by surprise.

Pah shook his hand then, "Sit! Sit down sir," he commanded, pulling a chair forward. "Cole drink? Mah! Bring a cole drink for Mr Marshall – Eve, teacher. He here."

Mr Marshall sat apprehensively on the wooden chair underneath Pah's house, Mah racing out within seconds with a glass of Coca-Cola. She greeted him politely, then dived straight back again, leaving the two men alone, as was customary.

Bracing himself, Mr Marshall began, "Well...well you see Mr Sam, I actually..." he stuttered, then... "A've come to see you about Eve, Mr Sam...You see Mr Sam, Eve is a bright girl at school and ..."

"Ah no dat sir, ah no dat!" Pah stopped him in his tracks. "So wat you come to say, say it."

Mr Marshall cleared his throat, then, "As I was saying Mr Sam, Eve has done very well at school, always coming first in class, you know…" He was sweating.

"Yes Mr Marshall. Yes sir! So wat you wan' from mi sir? Wat you wan'?"

"Well Mr Sam, the girl has reached the 7th standard class and there is no further for her to go in her education at Couva Anglican School. Soon, she will have to leave that school and that would be a shame. She is bright, Mr Sam, bright. She could take the 11+ and go to St Luke Convent, but…" he paused, "in order to prepare for this exam, she must attend evening classes, have extra tuition, extra classes Mr Sam…"

Pah shifted in his chair.

"It would only cost $1.50 a month, Mr Sam. $1.50…"

Losing what little patience he had, Pah shouted, "A'm a poor man, Mr Marshall. A poor man! Car'n do it sir, car'n do it. Car'n waste mi money on de girl, sir. Car'n do it."

He shifted in his chair, then continued, "Ah got mi boys to tink of, sir. Mi boys! Ah got to pay bookkeepin' lesson for Rajkapur. He go be a bookkeeper one day, you know…a bookkeeper…a big boss at Texaco!"

Mr Marshall was beat. Stunned by Pah's steadfastness. He was just about to give in, get up and go, but…He had to do some swift thinking…

He'd heard a lot about Pah and Rajkapur's treatment of Eve – their 'Hindu codes' – their suppression of females and now he was hearing it straight from the horse's mouth. He hoped that as her teacher, somehow he would be able to persuade Pah to change his mind. But now he wasn't sure.

He knew that Rajkapur was a dunce – would never make it as a bookkeeper, but he couldn't tell Pah that, not now. He was here on a different mission and that was Eve's education. He must not lose track of that. He must give it all he's got, come what may.

He took a deep breath, then continued. "But the girl is the brightest child in your family, Mr Sam. If she make a good pass in the 11+, she could go to St Luke free! It wouldn't cost you a penny, Mr Sam, not a penny!" (He knew full well that Pah would have to pay for school books and uniforms, but he wasn't going to tell him that, not now.)

Pah sat there, his face expressionless. It was as if he wasn't listening. He just wouldn't budge. A Hindu man with Hindu codes and values about women's position in society, he was seething with anger.

Then all of a sudden, he burst out. "No daughter ov mine go, go to college, sir. You hear mi sir? Ah 'ave no money to spen' on all dat female college nonsense." He stood up, moved closer, then warned, "Eve head gettin' too big, Mr Marshall, too big! All dat fancy college talk, huh!" He moved back a little.

Aware that he was getting nowhere, Mr Marshall's mind was working ten to the dozen…he must plead, cajole, beg if he must. He pleaded…

"Listen Mr Sam, hear me out, please! Mr Sam. If Eve get the chance to go to St Luke, she would pass all her exams, become a teacher and you will be so proud of her Mr Sam, so proud. I know that."

"You makin' mi mad, sir, you makin' mi mad," Pah shouted, "no daughter ov mine go ever make mi proud Mr Marshall, only mi sons go do dat sir, mi sons. Mi daughter, dey cost mi money sir, money!"

"Money? Mr Sam, money?"

"Yes sir, money!"

Shocked at what he'd just heard, Mr Marshall shuffled a little, then looked Pah straight in the eye. Eve was always running around barefooted, dressed in rags, with hardly enough food to eat and now Pah was saying that she was costing him money? He was puzzled.

Baffled, his mind working overtime, he fixed his eye on Pah, as Pah continued unabated… "Yes sir money, Mr

Marshall, money! Ah 'ave to pay out big dowries to fine husban' for dem sir, husban'! Is de law! sir, Hindu law. Eve go 'ave to learn to cook and sew, so ah could fine a good husban' for she sir, a good husban'. Ah need de money to pay for a dowry sir, money! Eve go 'ave to leave school now, Mr Marshall, leave school now, so we go fine she a good husban'."

Mr Marshall was beat – beaten to a pulp by Pah, this Hindu man bound by Hindu traditions, customs brought to Trinidad by his ancestors – Indians from India who came there almost half a century ago, bringing with them values – values so deeply entrenched in Pah's soul, he couldn't break away from it, even if he tried.

Hacked, Mr Marshall did not say another word. Instead, he jumped on his bicycle and quietly cycled away, thinking... thinking... deeply of how he would break the sad news to Eve.

Chapter Nine

That afternoon, Pah didn't waste any time. As soon as Mr Marshall left, he summoned Eve. "Eve who tel' Mr Marshall to come and see mi?" he bawled. "Is you girl, is you... Ah know dat girl. Ah know dat. Too much damn college stuff in you head girl. Ah feel like beatin' de hide out of you. You hear mi girl! You hear mi!" he warned. "Now you go 'ave to leave school and learn to cook and sew. You hear mi girl! You hear mi," he howled, mad as a bull.

That night Eve cried herself to sleep, knowing too well that her fate was sealed. And there was nothing she could do to change it – she knew that.

Two weeks later, when she attended school, Mr Marshall broke the sad news to her.

"Ah know Mr Marshall, ah know. Pah tel' mi so. After you leave, he was goin' to beat mi. He say ah go have to leave school now and Mah is fixin' up wit Miss Ramdaye for mi to have sewin' lesson."

Eve was crying; her eyes red with tears.

She was happy at school. There, she felt secure, loved. All she ever wanted was to continue her education, become someone one day. But Pah would not have it.

She started to bawl, crying so loud that Mr Marshall was at a loss as to what to do. Feeling helpless and not quite sure what he should do, he did what he thought was best. He put his arms around her shoulders and tried hard to console her.

"Never mind girl. Never mind," he whispered. "One day you will make it girl, you'll see... One day you will make it so big girl, really big... I know that Eve, I know that..." he tried to console her, the pain in his heart unbearable.

As her teacher, he saw hidden talent in her that no one else saw. He knew that somehow, one day, she would break out of that poverty trap and make it in the big wide world... he knew that. But Eve couldn't see it. All she knew was that she was a poor Hindu girl hitting 13, having to leave school, learn to cook, wash, sew and get married.

She was in a distraught state.

'Wat was Mr Marshall talkin' about?' she thought. 'How could mi, a poor Hindu girl, make it big in dat great mystry world?' As a mere child, she couldn't see beyond the dark clouds that now surrounded her.

That September 1953, was the last term Eve was to attend Couva Anglican School. Two weeks before Christmas, she packed the few books she had and said her last farewell to her beloved teachers and friends.

"Come and see us sometime," Mr and Miss Marshall said, trying hard to console her desolate spirit.

"Yes Miss Marshall, yes Mr Marshall," she replied, sadly, unaware that she may never see her beloved teachers again. Overwhelmed, she couldn't hold the tears back; it just poured out like a fountain – a feeling of desolation, emptiness, overpowering her, as she walked away choked.

She looked at Couva Anglican School for the last time; that old antiquated building, so reticent of Colonial days; that school which she learnt to love so much; that place which she almost called her home; a sickening, pounding feeling thundering inside of her; she knowing full well that she will never ever be a pupil there again.

Then, slowly... she walked away... clutching her few books, faintly hearing the voices of her favourite teachers... as they said their last 'Goodbyes'.

Chapter Ten

It was all arranged. Eve was to start sewing lessons at Miss Ramdaye's as soon as the school holiday was over. God didn't answer her prayer...it seemed.

Dressed in her yellow cotton frock which Auntie Nell had given her and carrying a cloth bag with a few pieces of cotton thread in it (left over from Mah's) it was January 12 1954, when Eve set off on the quarter mile trip to Miss Ramdaye's house for the first time, the tropical morning sun just starting to heat up. She arrived there, 9am sharp, just in time and she was sweating.

"Good mornin', Eve," Miss Ramdaye greeted her warmly, pleased that she arrived so promptly.

"Mornin', Miss Ramdaye," Eve replied politely.

"Hope de walk wasn' too hot for you?"

"It was OK Miss Ramdaye, OK," Eve replied, nervously, anxiously.

"Sit Eve, sit!" Miss Ramdaye asserted, pulling up a chair for Eve. "Ah go fix up a nice milkshake for you girl, go calm you down nicely." She laughed.

Looking around at the décor which surrounded her, Eve felt overwhelmed. Even though Miss Ramdaye's apartment was built within tall posts below her sister's house, an aura of opulence, progressiveness, seemed to prevail.

Floral chairs adorned the living room, two settees on either side, embroidered cushions strewn everywhere, the wooden floor polished to a sheen, a white rug flung in the middle; a glass table in one corner; a sewing machine and pieces of bric-a-brac materials and sewing threads in the other.

In the bedroom, a brass bed took centre stage, a pink wardrobe, dressing table and easy chair, on one side and an Indian rug at the foot of the bed. Lace curtains adorned the windows.

Eve sat there, mesmerised. Apart from Auntie Nell's house, she had never seen a home looking so beautiful – a sharp contrast to Pah's house, where the rotten wooden floorboards creaked; the mattress was hard and filled with holes, stiff fibres sticking out in places and insects crawling on the floor where she slept.

"Here you go girl," Miss Ramdaye interrupted her thoughts, "a nice banana milkshake, go cool you up nicely."

Frothing at the top, the drink was so tempting but Eve's mind continued to work overtime. She swallowed it slowly, thinking... thinking... 'if only ah could have a home like dis, one day...if only.' But she knew deep down, that learning to sew and cook would hardly provide the opportunity to fulfil such a dream – she knew that.

"You like mi house Eve?"

"Yes Miss...Oh yes! A do."

"Well a'm glad girl, glad! 'Cause one day you go have one just like dis, you know, just like dis."

'Never!' Eve thought. 'How could mi, a poor Hindu girl? Hindu girls could never be rich – only boys do dat' – Pah once told her. And now...? Miss Ramdaye was bluffing? She was sure of that.

Here, at Miss Ramdaye's house, they lived a different lifestyle. Her husband was a bookkeeper at JT Allum, the super food store in Upper Couva. And she came from a wealthy family in McBean – acres and acres of farmland they owned and lots of cattle too. They were unorthodox Hindus, never allowing Hindu customs to dominate their lives. They encouraged their daughter Miss Ramdaye to have freedom, leverage, in order to make a better life for herself and so she and her husband did. Their lifestyle was testimony to that.

"Well, come on Eve, let's get you started, girl," Miss Ramdaye asserted, as she positioned Eve in front of the sewing machine.

That day, she showed her how to do running stitches, join up the seams of a skirt, the sides of a bodice and seams of two sleeves. Eve made many mistakes that day, but she was learning fast and mistakes were inevitable.

At lunchtime, Eve used to sit under the shade of the tree in Miss Ramdaye's back yard and eat her lunch – plain dry roti and curried aloo, which she had brought with her in her cloth bag. Then she would drink some cold water to wash it down and before long, it was time for her to return to sewing.

Daily, she stitched and sewed, cut and stitched and by 3.30pm, it was time for her to go home – home to the cold bare floorboards; home, to a brother and father who tortured her; home, where they drilled it into her that her position as female in society was lowly.

She hated going home.

But time passed quickly and she soon learnt to sew a whole dress, to embroider cushions and make curtains and bedspreads too. She looked forward to going there – every day, Monday to Friday, five days a week. She lived for it, that atmosphere of homeliness. She had no qualms about going there to sew.

It was such a relief from home, where the atmosphere was dead, stone cold, empty, nothing. There, everyone had either gone to work in the sugar cane fields, or to school and she didn't want to be alone in an empty house.

Here at Miss Ramdaye's home, there was so much family life and she was happy.

Every day, Miss Ramdaye's husband used to come home for lunch. He used to horse around, sometimes picking up his 6-month-old baby boy, hugging and kissing him, Miss Ramdaye breast-feeding the baby, at times.

There was so much love and fun in that house.

Sometimes Miss Ramdaye would give Eve fresh milk and sometimes (dahi) stale milk mixed with rice and plenty of sugar. And occasionally, she gave her a cooked hot meal – rice and darhl and fried salmon. Eve loved the food and enjoyed being pampered.

Miss Ramdaye's husband used to feel sorry for her. He knew she had talent and was wasting her time learning to sew, so one day he found her a job in the cosmetics department of JT Allum. What he didn't know was, that Pah with his entrenched Hindu beliefs, would nip it in the bud.

"Only bad girl work in a shop or anyway," he told Eve firmly. "Good girl stay home, do 'ousework an' go get marry." He was adamant about that and so without further ado, he put a stop to that job.

Depleted, Eve cried herself to sleep that night, unable to erase the dark clouds which surrounded her.

She was enjoying her sewing lessons so much though, going to Miss Ramdaye's house five days a week and paying her $1.50 a month for the privilege, that she hoped it would never end. But, as luck would have it, something was to happen that would change all that...

One Friday morning, Miss Ramdaye was waiting for her. She was happy as a lark. She gave her a cold lime punch from the icebox, then said, "Eve, ah have some news for you girl, good news girl, good news!" She looked at Eve, her face beaming with joy, then continued. "Mi husban' buy a Rum an' Goods shop in Upper Couva by de Anglican church girl. He go buil' a Beer Garden dere girl, a Beer Garden...Excitin' news Eve, excitin' news, girl..."

She was so excited, she didn't stop to think what effect such surprising news would have on Eve, so she babbled on. "We go busy fixin' it al up, Eve, so ah won' be givin' you sewin' lessons no more..."

Eve stood there numb, her distressed body unable to react to what she'd just heard.

"Tel you Mah" she concluded, "you go finish sewin' lesson at de en' of de mont, so you won' be owin' mi no money, Eve."

Eve's body went cold. It was a blow which hit her like lightning. Here, at Miss Ramdaye's house, she had found love, comfort, happiness and now it was being wrenched from her, so suddenly, just like that? She tried to hold back the tears, but it came tumbling down, Miss Ramdaye desperately trying to console her, comfort her, but to no avail.

She just didn't realise that Eve would take it so badly...she just didn't understand.

Drying the tears from her wet eyes, Eve looked at her, a blank expression on her face, as the message hit home hard and fast – there would be no more going to Miss Ramdaye's house; no more sewing lessons for her, ever again.

It was July 16 1954 when Eve packed her sewing bag and left Miss Ramdaye's house for good. She was never to return there again.

Chapter Eleven

At 14, with no sewing lessons to occupy her time and Pah not letting her go to work either, all Eve could do was wait and wait and wait until Pah could find her a husband. Then she would get married and start a new life, she hoped.

It was during one of these boring waiting periods, that her elder sister Marla had gotten into trouble with a boy from next door. She was caught red-handed in the act of making love and Pah went mad.

"No dauter of mine go bring disgrace to mi, you hear mi girl!" he shouted, roaring like a bull. And so, Marla was made to marry the boy who had destroyed her virginity, for that was Hindu custom and Pah wasn't going to forget it.

Eve didn't want to repeat the mistakes Marla had made. She was a considerate and honest girl and didn't want to bring disgrace to her family's name. But she was growing up fast, getting prettier by the day, blossoming into a real beauty – ready for the picking – and so the young men used to hang around Mah's parlour like flies.

They flocked around to buy anything, just to get a glimpse of pretty little Eve, just to talk to her, if they could.

A Moslem boy called Ali, who lived in the next street, adored her. He wanted to marry her, but Pah wouldn't have it. '...a Moslem boy, marryin' mi dauter? Never!' So Ali used to hang around the street corner, sit on the archway there and watch Eve's every move. He was 21 years old and just crazy about her.

Winston, a Negro boy from down the road, also fancied her. He used to come into Mah's parlour and buy any old thing, just to get a chance to speak to her. At 15, his adolescent body longed to touch hers. He burnt within.

Eve liked Winston. He was such a quiet boy. Whenever she and Mah took Rajkapur's shirts to his mother for ironing, she noticed he was always so polite, so kind, always offering them cold drinks from the icebox.

One day, he came into Mah's parlour to buy something... he didn't know what... and it wasn't long before he and Eve started eyeing each other up. They were smiling, giving out the 'come and get me' signals – puppy love – the kind boys and girls did when they fancied each other. Then Winston started to peck her on the lips...

Like two little birds, they pecked away at each other, Eve's newly-formed breasts, hard as apples, heaving up and down, her heart beating, thumping, as he pecked and pecked into her, almost eating her.

Sweating like mad, his hands, his whole body trembling as he groped at her, his hands trailing slowly towards her heaving breasts, her heart pounding like thunder. Then he held her breasts firmly in his hands, fire ranging inside his hot teenage body.

He was just about to take his pants off, when someone called out. It was Ali. He was watching them from the archway outside...Good old Ali. He had saved the day!

"Ah wan' a pack ah cigarette," he shouted and Eve jumped, scared out of her wits, her hungry body going numb as she let go of Winston, he recoiling... frustrated.

Poor Winston! He was just about to do his first manly act, when he was disturbed, harpooned... so untimely, by Ali.

Seething within, he wanted to hit Ali, punch him in the face, but he knew Ali would beat the hell out of him – Ali was a big man and he might well kill Winston. So all that was left for Winston to do was walk away sheepishly, fear in his heart, fear of what Rajkapur and Pah would do to Eve when they found out.

And found out they did. Word soon got around about the whole episode – a touch of spice added here and there to heighten the gossip and Pah went crazy. He raged...

'A Negro boy kissin' mi Hindu dauter? Murder...! Murder...! Out of de question...' He went crazy.

That evening, he took out his belt from round his waist and gave Eve a good hiding. She cried and cried until she fell asleep, wondering when this nightmare would ever end. She was 14 now, but still being beaten like a dog. 'Would it ever end?' she cried...

She woke up the next morning only to learn that the search had intensified. The heat was on to find her a husband, as quickly as possible. No holes barred... no stones left untouched.

Chapter Twelve

Five weeks later, Eve's first marriage match was arranged. Toleram and his family were coming to see her, check her out, delve into her character, screen her profile, do everything to see if she would make a suitable wife for Toleram – their 28 year old son.

It was Sunday August 23 1954, when he and his entourage arrived. They arrived sharp, very much on time and ready to make the picking.

Eve had to look her best, so early that morning she had a bath under Pah's standpipe in the back yard outside. Then she dressed herself in a white cotton frock which she'd borrowed from her sister Marla – having mended and pressed it well, the day before.

She tried so hard, did her best to make a good impression, but when she saw Toleram, who looked almost as old as her father – so neat in his crisp well-starched white shirt and tight fitting black trousers, his well cropped jet black hair and moustache neatly trimmed – she was shocked.

His neatness threatened her and she felt uneasy. But he was a rich man with a thriving Rum and Goods shop down at Penal. 'He would give her a good life,' so Pah's sister had told them, when she'd arranged the match.

Within minutes, the entourage was positioned in the most comfortable seats Pah could find – as was the custom. They had to be fed first, before any Marriage Deal could be executed and so, Mah and Marla dished out the best food and refreshments which they had scrupulously prepared the day before.

They served them with vegetable soup for starters: darhl and rice and curried chicken (a fresh hen killed and cooked the day before) as the main course; jalleybi (Indian sweetmeat made from thick syrup and flour) served for sweet and sour-sup flavoured ice cream (homemade from a pail) to finish the meal off. There was lots of rum and cold drinks on offer too, with homemade ginger beer galore to refresh their hungry souls.

This meal, carefully organised with precision and thought, was offered, partly as a means to help the marriage plans along – and so Mah and Pah kept their fingers crossed.

The scene was set and now that the entourage had stuffed their stomachs to the fill, they were ready to see Eve, put her under the spotlight, suss her out, analyse her every move, till their empty brains were filled with gloating.

And so, draped in a white silk orhini (head cloth) over her head, almost covering her face – like a funeral procession – Mah and Marla marched her in. Slowly…slowly…they trotted, the men staring from the distance, straining to see her as she approached…head bent…so serious, not a smile on her face. She looked like a ghost!

There she stood, lost, forlorn, more like a spirit having just risen from the dead, than a bride to be, the men peering, staring, not a word being uttered as they scrutinised her.

Toleram looked at her, this innocent girl standing in front of him and a painful smile came over his face. She was beautiful alright, just as they'd said – he could see that – but she was a mere child. A teenage doll. He was shocked – shocked to the core of his bone.

He was a man of the world; experienced, grown and mature and so he was looking for a woman to match his standing.

'How could dey present mi wit dis chile, a mere teenage puppy?' He was angry! Mad! Furious! He was seething within. He didn't want to look at her anymore and so without saying a single word, he just turned his head away quickly, a hard, anxious, crazy look on his face – a look which was hard to describe – but one which remained with Eve, as they shepherded her back to her lonely, empty bedroom.

His father, watching his son closely, saw the expression on his face and realising that his son was boiling within, got the message. They didn't even have to say a word to each other.

And so, within minutes, Toleram, his father, his fat uncle and his big brother jumped into their cars and sped away as fast as they could, their fat stomachs bulging with the good food they had just consumed; they, no doubt, burping out the wind as they made their way back to Penal and the red watermelons which they'd left behind.

Eve never saw them again.

Shocked, distressed, disappointed, amazed, Eve's family were left sitting there, 'holding the baby' as it were, trying hard to seek solace in their own predicament.

No explanation was given by Toleram's family as to their swift departure and Mah and Pah just couldn't get the 'covert' message – that their daughter Eve, was far too young.

And so with that escapade over and having been left firmly in the lurch, Pah began to get frantic. He wondered whether he would ever find a husband for Eve.

The pressure was on – relatives and friends from all over Trinidad were put on the alert to find her a husband, as quickly as possible.

But the scheme didn't go down well with everyone though – one Negro friend, Norma, objected strongly. She protested bitterly.

"Dat girl Sam," she warned Pah, "is make for better tings man. She is bright an' pretty Sam, so don' spoil de chile by marryin' she to some God-forsaken Coolie man, boy!"

She was angry! She was furious!

But, tried as she did, her protests fell on deaf ears. Pah had his sons Rajkapur and Raja to think of. His money was for spending on them only and only he knew what was best for his daughters.

'Wat busines is it of she to intafere? How dere she? Dis Creole. Ah wish dis Creole woman shoud stop meddlin' in mi business,' he barked to himself madly.

He went raging mad, totally ignored her pleas and continued on his mission.

The heat was on, more than ever now, to find Eve a husband...

Chapter Thirteen

Feeling a little lonely and isolated, Eve soon made friends with a Moslem lady called Shara. She used to give Eve lots of cast off lipsticks and powder to make her face up and Eve felt as proud as a queen, when she wore them. But she had to remove them quickly, before Pah returned home from work, for she knew that if he saw her wearing make up, he would hit the roof.

Finding solace in her newfound friend at last, she felt happy, but it was not long before that happiness was to be shattered – Rajkapur, her eldest brother had found a woman.

It was at a neighbour's wedding that Rajkapur met a woman called Lola. And within minutes of meeting her, she was in his bedroom where he screwed her unashamedly, Eve listening nearby.

It was a scene which shocked Eve to the core, as she witnessed the unabashed ruthlessness of Rajkapur's behaviour, totally disregarding and paying no respect to her presence. But she didn't dare tell anyone, because she knew that if he found out, he would ring her ears, kick and beat the living daylight out of her. He hated her so much.

And so, about a month or so after that episode, on October 24 1954, he married Lola and moved her into his bedroom for good. He'd found a wife now and he was set on removing Eve out of his life forever.

At 18, Lola had been around. She'd slept with many men and knew well how to please them and their family.

Every evening, she would feed Mah and Pah with the best food she could cook: curries or rice and darhl and stewed fish and lots of fruit juice too. And so, before long she became 'the apple of their eyes', Eve once again, being pushed out into the cold – the 'Cinderella of the family' – unloved and unwanted by them.

Every evening, Lola would dress in her best outfit, put on make up and perfume in readiness for Rajkapur's return from his job at Point-a-Pierre. She used to serve Mah and Pah first, then she would take up the best food – nice hot Darhl and rice and sardines or stewed fish or salmon – upstairs to her bedroom, where she and Rajkapur would have a good feast. Then the rumpus would start.

They would screw each other shamelessly, talk and laugh and make so much noise, not showing the least concern about other people's feelings in the household – their feelings didn't matter – only Lola and Rajkapur's counted.

That bedroom was their haven – theirs and theirs alone. He, Rajkapur had the right to screw and be screwed all day, all night, if he so wished. For being the eldest son, only he was granted such privileges. He was supreme!

Mah and Pah liked it. They watched the glow on their son and daughter-in-law's faces and they felt happy. For when Rajkapur screwed, he was procreating and so, soon they would have a grandson to inherit the family's name and fortune.

They wallowed in it.

Not so for their daughters though; according to customs, they must barely be seen and certainly not heard. After all, their offspring were not meant to inherit the family's name and fortune?

In consequence, life for Eve was sad, lonely and empty. How she would have liked to have some fun too. But she knew that was not possible. If she as much as made one false move, she would be kicked out. So, all she could do was listen to Rajkapur and Lola having fun and hope that one day when she got married, she would have as much fun too.

Sometimes when the vendor called on the corner of Carli-Bay Road, Rajkapur would rush out, buy two ice creams or snowballs (crushed ice-balls with think red syrup sprayed all over it) or two packets of hot pistachios and dive straight back into his bedroom – the Den. He used to walk past Eve, the ice creams dripping along the side of the cones, she watching, her mouth watering, longing for a taste of it. But never, ever, did he once buy her one. Instead he would shout, "Don' stand 'ere wachin' girl! De man go tink you don' get food…" Then he would laugh and race back to his bedroom, his hive, where Lola would be waiting – the ice creams dripping cold.

Her stomach rumbling, Eve used to stare at the vendors as they did their rounds on their bicycles, she, licking her lips, trying hard to imagine what an ice cream on cone would taste like. But she never did get one and it was not until she was 18 when she tasted her first ice cream.

One of her jobs was to clean Rajkapur and Lola's bedroom and make the beds with clean sheets. So every morning, she would get up at 6am sharp, clean the room, wash and dry the sheets, press them and remake the bed before Rajkapur came home from work. And what a job it was. For daily after their frolicking, the place would be a ramshackled mess – empty cans of Coca cola strewn all over bedroom floor; empty peanut packets everywhere; the bed in a tumbled state, sheets hanging on the floor; seamen stains all over it.

Daily the bed had to be revamped; made crispy clean for he and Lola to frolic.

Eve used to sweep all the rubbish, strip and make the beds, wash the dirty linen outside in a wooden tub, clean the rest of the house and help with the cooking too – even though the cooking was Lola's task.

Every day as regular as clockwork, Eve slaved over the whole family – all seven of them. So it was such a relief, when occasionally, she was sent up to Mr Ming's food store at Carli-Bay Junction to buy sardines or salt-fish, when they ran out. These trips gave Eve a welcome break, relieving her, albeit temporarily, of the burdens, misery and loneliness which she endured.

Sometimes on those trips she used to bump into her Moslem friend Shara. "How is you Eve? You lookin' good girl." Shara would say, so pleased to see her. "Ah hope you sista-in-law is treatin' you good girl," she would continue, smiling.

"Yes...Yes! Tank you..." Eve would reply nervously, knowing full well that she was not telling the truth. She had to put on a front, hide her feelings, or else she would be punished, beaten to a pulp, driven out by Rajkapur and Lola.

As for Pah, well, he never spent money on his daughters, especially Eve. His money was for his sons. 'To buil' a big house for Rajkapur one day,' he boasted. He gloated on Rajkapur – the heir to his fortunes. And Mah? Well, most of her income was spent on housekeeping or stocking up the parlour.

Rajkapur and Lola had the best that money could buy; whilst Eve spent her days slaving and her nights sleeping on the hard wooden floor on a bed made of flour bags and dirty old rags; insects crawling all over the place, as she tried and tried to sleep.

One day Mah decided to give her a treat. She bought her a pair of lovely red shoes, a pink floral dress and a gold chain, in readiness for her to attend a cousin's wedding at McBean. Then, on the day of the wedding, they all remarked how pretty and grown up she was. She looked a picture!

But time was pressing. Everyone but Eve was getting married, it seemed, and it was proving hard to find a husband for her.

Lola soon became pregnant and so Rajkapur wanted all the attention for his wife and his heir to be. Pah's money must be spent on them and them only – he was adamant about that.

And so in desperation and his determination to drive Eve out, he devised a plan.

He would persuade his best friend Ram-Ram to marry her and rid the family of that useless female Eve, once and for all...

Chapter Fourteen

It was Sunday. It was the 20th. It was 1954, the day when Ram-Ram's mother arrived at Pah's house to suss Eve out. It was pelting down with rain outside and when she arrived she was soaking wet.

A tall matronly woman in her mid-fifties, she looked more like a widow – so stern in her long black dress which almost covered her toes. She was wearing a white orhini, which covered most of her face and a pair of old black canvas sandals (through which her long stiff toes protruded), completed her prim garb.

Positioning herself carefully opposite Eve, on the wooden bench underneath Pah's house, she looked at her searchingly, scrutinising her, analysing her every move. She appeared so fierce. She never smiled once.

Wearing a pink chiffon orhini which her cousin from McBean had loaned her and the new dress which Mah had bought her, Eve looked a doll, but Ram-Ram's mother was not impressed. She was looking for a daughter-in-law, a hard-working woman to serve her and her family – not a pretty little maid. She knew straight away that this child did not fit the bill which she had in mind.

She stared at Eve hard, then blurted, "Youu no dres' like dat wen youu marry mi son!"

"She go dress proper for you Bahin (sister)," Mah intercepted, sensing the mood of this matronly woman. "She does wear long dress al de time, but dis is a new dress, Bahin. De seamtress, she make mistake, she cut it too short, Bahin. Dats all."

Mah's heart was beating fast now, but she couldn't lose the chance of finding a suitable suitor for Eve, now that the opportunity had arisen. So she swallowed her pride and tried hard to be polite; anything to persuade this daunting woman – Eve standing there all the time, shaking like a leaf.

Undeterred however, Ram-Ram's mother continued, "Youu 'ave to wear stron' clodes Miss. No dresin' up like dis 'cause youu go 'ave to work hard – cook and wash de clodes, clean de house fo' mi family, clean de cowshed and milk de cows too."

Those last words nearly knocked Eve over.

This horse-faced woman was not beating about the bush. She was looking for a hard-working daughter-in-law who would serve the whole family, like all Hindi daughter-in-laws did – a servant really – and this child, 14-year-old Eve did not fit the bill. She'd made no bones about it – she made her position quite clear. She meant business and she was straight to the point.

Stunned at what she'd just heard, Eve went cold. She shivered at the thought of cleaning cowsheds and she was scared out of her wits. But Mah however, was not put off. She had her beloved son and his pregnant wife Lola to think of. Her home was far more needed for them now – and at 14, her Hindu daughter Eve was becoming quite a burden. Finding a husband for her was not only hard, but proving impossible.

'She could sew a little – sure! Do embroidery – yes! But dat was not enough to earn a livin' an' subsidise her husban's wage. De teacher say she was bright academic – sure! Could write good essay – witout doubt! Recite poetry an' act – Well! Well! Do her sums – OK! But wat good was all dis as a Hindu wife? Dese was not skills – housewife skills – as is expect of all Hindu wifes. Dey were born to serve dere husban' and his family wen dey get marry an' Eve certainly do not have dose skills.'

Mah's mind was working overtime and so blinded by traditions, she just could not see through Rajkapur – his ploy to marry Eve off to his best friend and get her out of their lives for good. In her eyes, he could do no wrong! After all, Ram-Ram was his best friend. A good enough reason for the marriage to take place. She must therefore, do all she can, negotiate, crawl if she must, to try and fix up this deal. There was no time to waste.

But no amount of coercion could persuade Ram-Ram's mother. This indomitable woman could see right through Mah's ploy. And to make things worse, she just could not take to the child-bride-to-be, Eve. So she piled on the pressure.

She looked at the cracked dirty earth floor and said scornfully, "De groun' is crac Bahin. Dirty an' crac like a tortose bac'. In mi house Bahin," she continued, "de groun' is smoode an' shinin' like a lookin' glass." Her face about to crack, the veins around her temples protruding as she uttered those words.

But angry as she was, Mah tried to conceal her feelings. She would do anything; lie if she must to try and appease this daunting woman. She must not lose this opportunity, whatever the cost; she must do all she can to milk the consent of this marriage.

"Eve does dab de floor every week Bahin, every week. But is de sun Bahin – de sun does crac' it," Mah appealed, knowing full well that she was telling a lie. In fact, Mah used to use a piece of old rag soaked in a mixture of cow dung and mud and dab the earth floor every six weeks or so and not weekly, as she claimed. It was a procedure which would keep the earth's surface smooth and dry, so it could be swept clean and kept free from dust and insects.

But Ram-Ram's mother was not easily fooled. She could tell when an earth floor was dabbed regularly and she knew Mah was telling a lie. And so, for the first time since she came, her face broke into a smile.

Although Mah could sense the falseness in her smile, nonetheless she continued on her mission of appeasement. "Eve go do it for you every week Bahin, every week," (knowing full well that Eve did not know how to dab earth floors). "She is good girl Bahin. Good girl."

"Ah 'ope so Bahin. Ah 'ope so," Ram-Ram's mother replied coldly, "'cause if she no do it she be no good fo' mi son."

Those words struck Eve like lightning. It hit her as sure as a tornado struck a tree and she was petrified. 'Dis imposin' woman was makin' too many demand on mi,' she thought. 'It would almos' be impossible to live wit she...' Eve was thinking, the bones in her body almost crackling, as she stood there trembling with fright. And Mah knew that too, but she had to strike now; strike whilst the iron was hot.

Serving her the lovely meal which Lola had prepared – nice darhl pouri (Indian pastry) and curried aloo (potatoes) with thick tasty darhl and nice boiled rice to go with it, Mah told her that it was Eve who had prepared the meal – a stark, raving lie – and Ram-Ram's mother knew it, so seething with in, she continued her attack.

"Food is good Bahin. Good. But de girl go 'ave to cook better food Bahin, better food; karhi (ground peas) and rice and channa (chick peas) and aloo (potato) pouri an' she go 'ave to fix de dahi (stale milk) from de cows too..."

Turning her nose up, she picked fault at everything, reeling off a list of Indian meals which she expected Eve to prepare, many of which Eve had never heard of before, Mah's spirit meanwhile, beginning to deplete.

Mah was by now, having her doubts, but she wanted a husband so badly for Eve, that she dismissed her fears. She would tow the line; creep if she must; do anything to bring this foreboding woman round. So, she bit her tongue and replied, "Oh yes Bahin! Oh yes! Eve go cook anyting you wan' Bahin. Any food you wan'," she knowing full well that Eve could not cook – she hardly knew how to fry an egg.

Mah was almost crawling on bended knees.

However, no amount of begging, managed to persuade Ram-Ram's mother. For she had long decided that Eve was not a suitable match for her son. Ram-Ram, on the other hand, had made up his mind too, and he wasn't going to change that now. For he liked the very things his mother opposed in Eve – her innocence, her beauty, her naivety and from the conversation they had, he liked the fact that she was academically bright too.

He was determined to marry her.

A simple man, brought up in the cane farming village of Esperanza, he had no interest in analysing her too deeply. Young, pretty and a virgin – that was good enough for him – and as the eldest son of that Hindu family, his word meant law. His mother would have to agree to the wedding, no matter how she felt – for that was the Code.

Eve on the other hand, was getting the creeps. From the daunting and cutting remarks made by Ram-Ram's mother, she was left flattened; an uneasy feeling creeping up her spine when his mother left that day. Eve knew she was going to be a wicked mother-in-law and so she brooded for weeks afterwards. But she had no say in the matter. Her destiny was cast!

Always being chaperoned by family members and never being allowed to touch Ram-Ram, her deep emotions and feelings were never tested and stirred, so she did not know how she felt about him. And now she was going to marry him?

She was almost suicidal...

But Mah and Pah were delighted. At 14, she was as much a cast off piece of garbage as rubbish itself. No one wanted to marry her and she was too costly a commodity for her family to maintain. At last they had found a suitor for her and no one was going to change that now...

They must hurry. There was no time to waste. The marriage date must be set. And so, within a month, the wedding date was arranged.

As for Rajkapur and Lola, well they were over the moon. Soon, their carefully hatched plans would be perfectly executed and they would get that simpleton Eve, out of their lives for good – or so it seemed…

Chapter Fifteen

It was all fixed up. Sunday May 12 1955 was the day Eve was going to get married. And so, a few weeks before that, Mah and Eve spent the day trailing the hills of Sanfernando's shopping precinct, trooping in and out of shops, looking for suitable materials with which to make Eve's wedding outfit.

For the wedding dress, Mah bought white floral lace. For the petticoat – white slipper satin. For the veil – white embroidered net. For the wreath and bouquet – white organza and silver trimmings; a pair of white cord shoes completing the wedding outfit; the handbag and gloves being supplied by Auntie Nell.

They bartered and bargained, hassled and cajoled and after refreshing themselves with nice mouth watering Caribbean foods from the street vendors, they made their weary journey back home.

By the time they arrived home, they were exhausted.

It was agreed that Cousin Lorna from Laventille would make the wedding outfit and so the next day, Mah took Eve to visit her.

Lorna's father was the local headmaster, her mother the headmistress and they greeted them with such warmth that they were overcome. They joked a lot about Eve's youth and her intended marriage and they laughed so much about it that the whole place buzzed with joy.

Hoping that Lorna would take the necessary measurements and Eve and Mah would return home that day, Eve was surprised when Lorna insisted that she took on-going measurements – Eve must remain there for a week or so. For when it came to dressmaking, Lorna was a perfectionist. And so it was decided that Eve remained there for a while, so that Lorna could get her measurements and trim the gown to perfection.

For the next few days Lorna was busy, buzzing around like a bee – fussing, musing, measuring, trimming, pinning and altering, stitching and hemming, until she was sure she'd got it right, Eve taking it all in with great amazement.

The days soon went by and Eve was really enjoying her stay there. Lorna's two brothers used to make such a fuss of her. "Come here Queen Evita, you pretty little ting," they would tease. "You too young to get marry girl. Wat? Yoo fader don' like you or sometin girl?" they kept teasing and they would laugh so much that Eve couldn't help but join in the laughter too.

Her intended marriage baffled them. For a start, Lorna couldn't understand why Eve – a mere child at 14 – was getting married, whilst she was 24 and had no intentions of marrying. But the puzzle laid in the fact that Lorna was a Christian and Eve a Hindu. For in Trinidad, Christians lived a different lifestyle to Hindus, as Eve had discovered when she'd visited Auntie Nell during her school holidays.

She was having a wonderful time at Lorna's, really enjoying the hot meals which were being served – meals such as paratha made with butter, hot spicy beef or lamb curry and rice, delicious coconut cakes and sweet bread and homemade ginger beer was offered, to wash it all down.

She was allowed warm baths daily, under the hot indoor shower, which was positioned next to Lorna's bedroom. And on the one Sunday she'd spent there, they took her out for a stroll down Savannah park, where they had a picnic, watched the birds buzzing about and the people too – some playing cricket; others just strolling around, having fun.

She was so happy, having such a great time there, that she didn't want to return home to Pah's house. But, she had no choice – she had to – for she was getting married!

Back at Pah's house they were also busy. They too were making preparations for the wedding.

Great big canvas tents were being erected and a large amount of food would have to be prepared the night before the wedding in order to feed the guests. And so it wasn't long before Saturday May 11 – the day before the wedding came – and the final preparations were being put in place.

Large pots and pans were borrowed from Couva's Hindu Temple, to be used as cooking utensils; great big holes were dug in the far end of Pah's back yard, which would be utilised as cooking fires and hundreds of banana leaves were cut, washed and stacked in piles to drain, in readiness for serving the meals on.

They carted and carried, hustled and bustled, sweating their guts out in preparation for the big day.

They fixed the canvas tents overhead – sprawling across like umbrellas, from one end of Pah's yard to the other. Then they hung lanterns, in readiness for the preparations to start. And, as dusk approached, the men started to arrive, some dressed in loincloths and shirts; others wearing Khaki trousers; the fires being built with piles of wood, waiting to be set alight.

All night long these men prepared and cooked – curried aloo, rice, darhl, karhi and channa – mouth-watering Indian foods – with which they would feed the guests the next day.

Not far away, another group of men sat, singing Hindu songs and beating drums; 'TRAA...! TAAH...! TAH...!' it went, the noise so loud, deafening. Whilst, in a further corner, a few more men were playing cards and drinking rum – enjoying the festive mood.

Meanwhile, the ladies too took to their chores. On the opposite side of the tent they sat on long white sheets which were spread out on the hard ground. They too were singing to the rhythm of the drums, as they rolled out and cooked the pastries – tons of soft, buttered paratha, to feed the guests the next day. For, it was tradition that the women always cooked the rotis at weddings.

There they were these women, some dressed in saris and wore orhinis which almost covered their faces; others wearing dresses. They were gossiping and laughing and making rude jokes about the bride and groom's first night together. And when they laughed, their gold teeth glittered under the bright gas lamps, which hung precariously from the tents above their heads.

There they were, these people, segregated – men on one side, women on the other, singing, joking, cooking all night, preparing for the next day – the Big day – the day when Eve, the child, would get married.

From her bedroom upstairs, Eve stared in awe at the paraphernalia, the noise, the preparations that were taking place down below and she felt scared...

Lorna too was busy, putting the finishing touches to Eve's wedding gown, pinning it here, pinning it there, stitching it to perfection over Eve's body. So occupied she was, that she didn't even notice the sadness on Eve's face.

When she'd finished pinning, she fixed the wreath on Eve's head and pinned the veil too, then she gave her the bouquet of Anthurium lilies which she'd made from organza and silver trimmings – it looked exquisite.

Staring at Eve, Lorna could hardly believe what her eyes were seeing. "Oh my! You look so beautiful girl. Oh my!" she declared, Eve staring at the mirror amazed at her own beauty, dumb-founded, but not at all happy. For, deep down in her heart she didn't want to get married. She knew very well that she was only a child of 14 and she felt miserable.

Then all of a sudden, she could control her emotions no more and she started to cry...Lorna having to pull out all the stops to try and pacify her.

According to Hindu customs, Eve had to undergo certain preparations of rituals in order for the marriage to take place. And so, on the night before, two women rubbed her whole body down with saffron paste, dressed her in an old frock and left her like that all night, so that the saffron could soak into her youthful body. Then, at 6am on the morning of the wedding day, they would wash her body with cold water and sing rude songs about her virginity and her first night with the bridegroom.

Similar wedding preparations were taking place at Ram-Ram's home too, but with one marked difference. He was not pasted with saffron and his naked body was not exposed for all to see, because he was male and according to Hindu customs, males did not have to undergo such degrading rituals.

Upset by the barbaric tones of these ceremonies, Eve cried a lot that night. She was so distressed, she couldn't stop thinking... thinking 'of her suffering...' thinking of 'why Pah was spending so much money on her wedding, whilst her Christian friends got married simply and cheaply at the Registry Office and used the money to go away on honeymoon and buy nice houses in which to live.'

She just couldn't understand?

In the early hours of the wedding day however, things were getting hectic at Pah's home. Long wooden benches were being placed spuriously under the tents, the tasty mouth-watering foods stored in one corner, ready for consuming. On they worked and by 10am, the scene was set. Then, at 11am sharp, the guests started to arrive.

Smartly dressed now, hardly any of the men wore loincloths. Some wore white shirts and different coloured trousers, whilst others were dressed in heavy linen suits, mainly cream or brown – some Negroes, some Indians – on they came, ready for the feast to begin.

Group by group they were fed to the full with mouth-watering tasty Indian meals and using their hands to feed themselves, they raked it off from the fig leaves, licking their fingers bone dry, as they demolished the tasty morsels.

The women and children were there too. Now, nicely dressed – the Indians in colourful saris; the Negroes wearing colourful dresses; the boys in white shirts and short pants; the girls wearing knee-length colourful dresses, ribbons gathered round their waists and tied in bows at the back, their black hair platted or looped in ponytails, held up with clips or pretty ribbons. They looked a picture.

In an organised manner, they too were being fed – one lot at a time – and so by 12 noon, they were fed and watered and ready waiting for the wedding procession to arrive.

Dressed in a yellow sari, Eve too was waiting upstairs … waiting quietly… waiting patiently, waiting for the bridegroom to arrive.

The clock was ticking… the guests were getting excited… the sad and tearful Eve was getting more anxious as time ticked away…

But it was nearly 2pm and there was no sign of the bridegroom.

Chapter Sixteen

It was pelting down with rain outside and the impatient guests were busy speculating as to whether the bridegroom would ever turn up. "Ah don' tink he go come!" one Negro lady said to the other. "Ah hear he moder don' wan' him to marry de girl – she don' wan' a chile bride," the other replied. And so it went, the air bubbling with intrigue and hot gossip.

Upstairs the distraught Eve was panicking, tears streaming down her cheeks; tears matching the raging storm waging outside, her wedding presents – glass dishes and decanters, crystal glasses and cutlery sets – all lying in boxes in the far corner of the room, as if forever abandoned, waiting, waiting to be claimed by she, the bride and he, the groom – but he was nowhere to be seen.

It was unusual to see so much rain in May and Eve felt sure that it was a 'bad sign'. So distraught was she, that all of a sudden she screamed out – bawling like a demented child, Lorna and Auntie Nell doing their best in desperation, to try and comfort her.

They were almost ready to give up, when all of a sudden they heard a noise – a loud deafening noise – pounding into their eardrums. It was the sound of hooting cars.

They were hooting like mad, the wedding procession, all five cars cruising down Carli-Bay Road, Ram-Ram sitting proudly in the first one, his entourage following suit. And Eve breathed a sigh of relief when she looked out of the window and saw them.

The speculation could have been put to a halt because no one knew the real reason why Ram-Ram was late. His sister was getting married too (a double Hindu wedding) and since he was the eldest brother in that Hindu family, it was his duty to supervise his sister's wedding, see that everything went well first (even at the cost of his own marriage) before he could attend his own wedding and claim his 'child-bride'. Hence he was late.

As the cars approached Pah's house, some of the guests started flocking around his car, peering at him; reaching out to touch him; questioning with their eyes. It was as if they wanted to pinch him, just to make sure he was the real bridegroom and not some make believe one.

He looked like a prince, almost regal in his pink silk gown, a homemade crown shimmering on his head, lovely pink floral tassels hanging down and drooping round the sides of his handsome face. Some of the Negro guests had never seen a Hindu bridegroom before, so they stared in wonder, hemming him in, peering, touching as he scrambled out of the car and made for the tent as fast as his legs could carry him.

The Hindi priest was ready and waiting, waiting anxiously to start the ceremony. There he sat, cross-legged, this ghost-like priest – in his white loincloth and white shirt; a white turban wrapped firmly round his head; a garland of yellow flowers draped precariously round his neck; a look of wisdom in his age old face.

There was a makeshift earthen pyramid in front of him, decorated with garlands of yellow and white flowers; a variety of powders and scents placed on this pyramid. And spread around the middle area was a concoction of fluids in bottles and other paraphernalia; a brass lotar (jug) of water placed strategically in the centre, ready for the purpose it was to serve.

Some of the Negroes were gazing mysteriously at this strange set-up, when Ram-Ram and his brother suddenly whizzed past them and seated themselves firmly, next to the priest.

In the bedroom upstairs, Lorna and Auntie Nell were busy too, getting Eve ready. They covered her face with a white orhini and looking forlorn in her yellow sari, they marched her through the crowds slowly... slowly... seriously... head bent... the spectators gazing in awe, at this child-like bride.

Solemnly, they seated her carefully opposite Ram-Ram – her head still bent, a sad look on her face – the audience segregated: males on one side, females on the other; all waiting anxiously for the action to start. Then, the priest rang his little hand-bell and the ceremony began.

"Ram-Ram! Sita Ram!" the priest chanted in his Hindi tongue. "Join dis man an' woman togeder in holy marriage. Ram! Ram! Sita! Ram! Bhagwan (God) bles dem wit riches of many, many chilren, so dat dis woman go serve dis man well fo' de res of she life," he concluded, sprinkling some water and scents over the bride and groom's head, tinkling his brass hand-bell as he did so, the crowd sitting dead silent, spellbound, watching in awe, the every move of this ghost-like priest.

So mesmerised they were, they couldn't hear a pin drop, even if you dropped one.

The bridegroom was serious and quiet too, staring a lot at Eve throughout the ceremony, she, never raising her eyes once to look at him, following faithfully, the strict 'code of silent behaviour', that Hindu brides were supposed to maintain – as was drummed into her from childhood.

The priest chanted another Hindi prayer, then they spread a white sheet over the bride and groom's heads – almost covering their faces. Then Ram-Ram dipped his finger in a jar of red paste and placed a mark (tikka) on her forehead – straight in the middle of it – along the parting of her hair. He smiled.

It was the first time he'd smile since he came, for he knew full well that according to Hindi practices, that mark represented the 'seal of marriage' – the 'tie' which bonded them together for the rest of their lives; the child-bride Eve on the other hand, sitting there frightened, bewildered by it all.

She just did not understand.

With precision, the priest sprinkled a few more scents, jingled his hand-bell and Pah, now dressed in white, handed over the dowry to Ram-Ram on a red cushion – $1,000 in cash – Ram-Ram immediately passing it over to his brother. His brother then handed Pah some jewellery – a pair of gold earrings and chain, worth $100 – a consolatory gift to Eve for marrying Ram-Ram – a far cry from the cash dowry which Pah had just given him.

That over and done with, the stern-faced priest hastily chanted a few more words, tinkled his little hand-bell for the last time and BANG! The ceremony was over.

She, Eve – the child-bride and he, Ram-Ram were now man and wife and nothing it seemed, could ever change that.

Slowly… slowly… Lorna and Auntie Nell marched Eve back to her bedroom, her head still bent, her distraught face covered with the white orhini.

She was in a state of shock.

With the rains still belting down outside, Eve had a funny feeling deep within her that this was not going to be a happy marriage; feelings which almost crippled her – but the celebrations went on in full force downstairs, nonetheless.

Crown off his head, Ram-Ram and his entourage were fed to the full with channa and aloo, kharhi and rice and paratha and loads of rum and lime punch to wash it down with; the drummers beating vehemently in the background; Indian music blaring from microphones, which were fixed high up above on the tent.

Meanwhile, in the bedroom upstairs, they were busy too. Lorna and Auntie Nell were fussing about, getting Eve dressed in her white wedding outfit, in readiness for her departure to Ram-Ram's house, back there in the outback estate of Esperanza.

With her clean knickers already in place, they helped her into her white slipper-satin petticoat; then the white floral lace wedding gown, which fitted perfectly around her tiny waist, the skirt hanging in flares down to her feet; the long sleeves, a perfect fit stretching along her arms and finishing with a V-point around her tiny wrists.

They powered and rouged her face; put her red lipstick on; fixed the floral veil and homemade wreath of white roses with clips, gripping it firmly onto the widow's peak of her head. Then, she put on her gold chain and earrings and slipped on her white shoes, they finally sprinkling toilet water over her. They stood back in excitement, staring.

She looked and smelt beautiful.

Now, here they were, these women, standing back in the bedroom spellbound! Gazing at this child-bride, her white wedding outfit, showing the shapely contours of her youth-full body, she looking so innocent, so serene, so beautiful!

Overcome with pride at the beauty she was seeing, Lorna declared, "Oh my! Eve! You look so pretty girl. Pretty as de Queen, girl! Oh my! Queen Eve!" She chuckled and kissed Eve on both cheeks, the other women going, "Ooh and ahh!" and kissing her in turn too.

It was all too much for her. She couldn't take it. Deep down in her heart she was almost dying with pain about her marriage and here they were making such a fuss of her and that wedding outfit. All of a sudden she broke down in tears and started to bawl. She cried so much that they had to mop her eyes and powder her face all over again.

The business of marriage had to go on, however. So speedily, Lorna packed Eve's few worldly belongings – one new panty, the dress Mah had bought her, some powder and lipstick in a pull-string handbag and she was ready to depart. But there were no shoes in it, for she didn't have any.

Fully dressed in her bridal garb and looking so radiant, they marched her to the wedding car, slowly... slowly... head bent, her veil covering her face, the crowds cheering, whistling, hooting at the beauty they were seeing, Ram-Ram sitting in the car spellbound, unable to believe the transformation, the beauty he was beholding, Lorna supporting her on one side, Auntie Nell holding up the long veil, which stretched behind her for miles and miles it seemed; Eve clutching the bouquet of Anthurium lilies, her fingers trembling.

Gently they helped her into the car and fixed the veil neatly at the back and they were ready to depart. But Ram-Ram kept on smiling to himself – the expression on his face telling a tale – 'he was hungry as a wolf; hungry for one thing only…'

Head still bowed, hardly able to hold back the tears now, the sad Eve sat there thinking. She was thinking…'how at only 14 she was leaving Pah's house for good, to a destiny unknown; to live with a mother-in-law who told her she had to clean cow sheds.'

A throng of people were gathering around her car now, peering, whispering, smiling, having a last peep at this sad but beautiful, bewildered, child-bride. "Princess! Princess! Youu look like de Queen, girl!" they shouted; others hooting! whistling! Mah bawling her head off in the background.

It was customary that Indian women cried at their daughter's wedding and so Mah was almost going demented. As for Lola and Rajkapur, well, there was no sign of them. They had made their appearance only once, briefly, then disappeared quickly, clean out of sight.

In the background, Eve could hear someone shouting, "Good luck! Good luck, girl!" then a yellow flower was thrown at her. It was Shara.

The commotion continued… the excitement prevailed… and it was nearly 5pm when the wedding procession finally decided to depart; the cars hooting their horns, the microphones blaring Indian music in the background; the spectators waving their last 'goodbyes', the doleful Eve sobbing her heart out.

She cried all the way to Ram-Ram's home.

It was all over! It was one of the grandest weddings Carli-Bay Road had ever seen. And so, for months after, people were still talking about it – only, no one had bothered to take a photograph –'no snap shot, no keepsake for the family to look at.' Now all that was left was emptiness... as Pah and his friends tried to clean up the mess.

The trimmings spent; the feastings over and now the child-bride Eve was on her way... to spend her first night with a man she had never known – a man she'd married by arrangement.

Chapter Seventeen

As the wedding procession made its way through Esperanza Estate, the silence and bareness of the place overwhelmed Eve. Small mud huts with grass rooftops and holes for windows were dotted here and there on either side of the narrow winding dirty pitch road. There was no movement of people. Not a soul in sight.

Like sentinels, they stood – these mud huts – no curtains in their windows. Tiny patches of worn out black pitch, peeping here and there along the mucky unkempt track; miles and miles of sugar cane fields sprawling at random at both sides of it, their leaves as sharp as knives, ready to cut through anyone who dared trample them. And like a mirage amongst them, the local shopkeeper's house stood, its paint gleaming white in the distance.

So different it was from Couva – the whole scene – no visible signs of human activities; no children playing in the streets; no adults standing about gossiping; no fun – a far cry from the liveliness and spirit of Carli-Bay Road where Eve grew up – the only sign of human beings was Ram-Ram's mother, standing steadfastly in the front yard of her house at the bottom of the street, its white paint glistening like an iceberg.

She was so serious, her face looked as if it was about to crack!

Disturbed by what she was seeing, Eve started to cry again, but Ram-Ram kept shouting at her. "Wat you cryin' for girl? Is you weddin' day, you kno, not you funeral. You shood be happy, not bawlin' like dat!" he barked. "Wipe you face girl, wipe you face!" he ordered. "You don' wan' you moder-in-law to see you like dat! Do you girl? Do you?"

She tried hard to control the crumbling feelings within her.

As the car neared the house, she could see Ram-Ram's mother still standing there, still as a fortress, waiting to greet them.

"Bisundai go take yoo to room," she commanded, moving forward as they got out and with that, Ram's Ram's sister, 10-year-old Bisundai raced out towards them and ushered Eve straight up the stairs, leaving Ram-Ram talking to his mother.

Upstairs, the bedroom was spotless, so neat, it looked as if no one had ever lived in it. There was a white dressing table with a shining mirror and a white straight-backed chair placed in front of it; a brass bed, its mattress so thick and high, that Eve would have to stand on a step to climb onto it; the glass-louvered windows glistening like mirrors – all so prim and proper that it scared the living daylight out of her.

She felt uneasy, but she knew that there was nothing she could do but accept things as they were, so she began to get undressed – change from her wedding dress into the one cotton frock she possessed. But she hardly had time to get changed, when Ram-Ram entered the room, followed sharply by his sister Bisundai again, who offered them some food.

Utterly disturbed by what was happening, Eve couldn't eat and Ram-Ram didn't touch the food either, for his appetite was wet for one thing and one thing only...

He kept looking at Eve and smiling – a wry devious smile – which she, innocent as she was, didn't understand; his mind so filled with one thought, that he could hardly wait for his sister to depart. Then, as soon as she left, he bolted the door shut.

Still smiling, he didn't bother to take his clothes off, he just pushed Eve straight onto the bed, thrust his tongue inside her mouth thrusting... thrusting... squeezing her breasts with both hands, harder... harder... his whole body now on top of her, almost crushing her. Then, as quick as a flash, he pulled up her dress, pushed her knickers down to her knees and WHAM! Within seconds, it was all over. Then he crashed onto the bed like a ton of bricks and groaned like an animal.

He had in fact raped her, but she, being only a child, didn't even realise that she was raped. She lay there in a state of shock.

That night, he had a sexual feast and every time Eve made a noise, his mother who slept next door, kept banging on the wall. He screwed and screwed her to his full, and by next morning, she was so exhausted that when she got out of bed she could hardly walk.

Being only a child and having had it drummed into her by her family that 'she must serve her husband well and do what she was told,' she believed that that night's experience was 'the norm'.

'She must tolerate his treatment of her, try and make a go of things, whatever the cost,' she thought.

She simply didn't know any better.

The poor girl! Little did she know that her sufferings were only just beginning. For, as soon as Ram-Ram left for work at the Sugar Mills at 5am that morning and she hoped that she would be able to get some rest, his mother stormed in, ordered her to get dressed and go down to the kitchen to help her with the cooking.

Rubbing her sleepy eyes and groping her weary way to the mud-hut kitchen downstairs, she nearly fell down the stairs. Then, when she saw the kitchen itself, she was overcome... A large hole dug in the corner (a cooking fire) stacked with wood, ready to set alight; large pots, pans and other cooking utensils piled in random heaps about the place – the kitchen so small, there was hardly room to move.

"Nead dat ready fo' cook de roti," his mother ordered, as Eve entered, she pushing the half-prepared dough over. And so, barely able to keep her eyes open, Eve began to knead, kneading... kneading... the dough remaining as stiff as chewing gum, no matter how hard she tried. Her mother-in-law went mad!

"You car'n cook roti wit dat! Hard as iron!" she barked, grabbing the dough from Eve's hand and ripping it to pieces. Then almost frothing at the mouth, she kneaded it, again and again, until it became softer. Then she shouted, "Put water in de pan...make tea."

Nervously, Eve fetched some water from the barrel in the backyard outside, poured it into the pan, put some sugar and tea leaves in and set it to boil. But, within seconds of it boiling, the tea was as black as foul sewage – she had put in too many tea leaves.

"Look! Blac! Blac!" her mother-in-law barked. "Useles girl! Useles girl! No evn carn' boil tea. No good fo' mi son! No good! He go 'ave to leeve you!"

Trembling and shaking like a leaf, the shouting continued, Eve trying her best to please this woman.

She tended the rotis, replenishing the burning wood and poking the fire as best she could, when all of a sudden, a few burnt out pieces of wood split and landed straight onto the floor. Her mother-in-law went crazy.

"Go! Go! Go! Get broom an' sweep!" she bawled.

Terrified, Eve grabbed the broom and started to sweep, her mother-in-law laying on the curses. On... and on... she went, Eve thinking it would never end, but before she knew it, it was 6am and time for her mother-in-law to depart for work, leaving her with 'strict instructions' – a roster of housework for her to do. Then she departed swiftly.

She made no bones about it – Eve was to eat from tin cups and enamel plates and stay downstairs for the rest of the day. This is how the roster went: First, she must make the beds upstairs and sweep and scrub the wooden floor. Next, clean the kitchen, wash the dishes with a bucket of water and paste the kitchen floor, smooth to a sheen. Finally, she must scrub and wash the clothes with carbolic soap on a piece of stone in the back yard, rinse them with buckets of cold water and hang them out to dry on the wash-line outside.

She was allowed to have a break at 12 noon, eat her lunch of plain roti and aloo and wash it down with plain water – no milk to drink, for milk from the cows was reserved for male members of the family only, because they needed their strength to work. In their eyes, housework was not considered as work.

After lunch, she had to sweep the backyard and refill the water barrels from the street taps, a quarter of a mile down the road, by which time, her back would begin to give way.

There was no respite for her.

She barely had time to sit down and rest when it was time for her to start cooking the evening meal: darhl and rice, channa and aloo, roti and aloo pies too. They had to be hot and spicy, cooked in time and kept piping hot, ready for Ram-Ram and his mother to eat when they returned home from work at 4pm. Or… there would be hell to pay!

Day after day, she struggled to meet the demands of this wicked woman, but being barely a child of 14, with little or no experience of housework – tried as she did – she could never get it right, her mother-in-law on the other hand, cursing the hell out of her.

"You f…bich! Nigger! Nigger! You no dab de kichin! Go crac! Crac! You car'n cook! Creole! Creole! Dey no teech you…! Nigger! Nigger!" she cursed.

Distraught as she was however, Eve had to tolerate the cruel treatment dished out on her daily, for that was the custom (Hindu custom) which held that daughter-in-laws must honour and obey their mother-in-laws in all things. Daughter-in-laws were not allowed to answer back, fight back or stand their ground.

And so, Eve lived her life daily in fear.

The days went by and the cursing got worse. "Go to hell! Youu f…in bich! De devil go come an' get youu!" she would swear and curse, Eve going out of her mind in distress, unable to fathom out why her mother-in-law was torturing her; not knowing how to cope; not knowing what would come next.

As it transpired, Ram-Ram's mother was a possessive woman, bent on making Eve's life hell; bent on driving her out of her son's life because she wanted to have him all to herself.

Chapter Eighteen

Unable to cope with the misery of her life, three months later, Eve discovered that she was pregnant. Every morning her stomach heaved from morning sickness. And so retching like mad, she would dash out of the kitchen to vomit, but rarely ever making it in time. To make matters worse, Ram-Ram's mother couldn't accept the fact that Eve was carrying her son's child and so the cursing just got worse and worse...

Whore! Whore! Dat not mi son chile you carryin', es anoder man chile you carry. Whore! Whore!" she cursed, Eve getting so distressed at the garbage being spewed at her.

She knew she was a virgin and not pregnant when she got married, but nothing on earth could persuade her wicked mother-in-law of that. For, what she believed she stuck to and so her mind was set.

Sometimes, when Eve was cooking in the early hours of the morning, she used to faint, but Ram-Ram's mother showed no mercy – all she did was shout and shout. Not being allowed to rest and having to cope with the cooking and all the household chores as well, Eve was nearing a state of collapse.

On and on it went – this abuse – cursing by day and banging on the wall at night. And Mah didn't visit either because she didn't know it was happening. In fact, no one knew the hell Eve was going through. Any mistakes and there was hell to pay. "Bhagwan (God) go get you. Bhagwan, drive dis bad woman from mi son life," her mother-in-law cursed and cursed.

Tortured and terrified, Eve shook with fear, almost reaching the end of her tether – the turmoil never ending –

only to find that there was more bad news to come. One day, Ram-Ram returned home from work, face like thunder – it was as if the earth had just cracked and about to swallow him up.

"Ah loss mi job Eve. Ah loss mi job girl," he cried, in a state of shock. "Dey don' wan' two telephone operator no mor' girl. Dey say one is enough. So how we go live, girl? How we go live?" His eyes were filled with tears. "Ah go have no money to pay Mah now girl an' she go sure chase we out. Ah kno dat Eve. Ah kno dat girl." He burst into tears.

With no Social Security system in Trinidad and no more wages to come, Eve knew full well that Ram-Ram's mother would not feed them for free. So she started to cry too, bawling her head off, like a tormented soul.

They cried and cried and after he'd calmed himself down, Ram-Ram did some swift thinking. He had to try and find work. He had to, somehow. He knew that.

And so, every morning he would get up at the crack of dawn and go to different venues, hoping that some Foreman or other would hire him – give him some kind of labouring job – anything, just to feed his family. But everyday he returned home jobless. There was just no work going.

Consequently, he became more and more distraught.

With no money coming in to keep them now, his mother was getting more and more bad-tempered, more and more erratic, cursing the life out of them. She just couldn't control herself anymore.

"Youu f...arse-kisserr," she cursed, "Go get job! Now! Now! Ah no keep you an' dat creole woman in dis house no more. Arse-hole! Arse-hole!" she swore.

But distraught as they were, they didn't dare answer back for fear that she might put them out in the street. All they could do was retreat to their bedroom, taking with them what little food and drinks they had, desperately trying to isolate themselves from her. But the more they retreated, the more she went crazy, banging on the door shouting, "Pigs! Pigs. Dirty stinkin' pigs! Pigs! Rats go come and get you…"

As the pressure mounted, it began to tell on Ram-Ram's nerves, then one day, he lost control of himself and beat the hell out of Eve. He got so mad (she didn't know why). He just took out his belt from around his waist and whipped the hell out of her. He punched her so hard in the face that her nose began to bleed. Then, when he'd calmed down, he pleaded and pleaded…said 'he was sorry,' said 'he wouldn't do it again,' but it wasn't long before he lost control of himself and gave her another hiding.

On and on, the turmoil continued, until Eve reached a state where she could take no more. She wanted to run away, hide anywhere from the torture she was experiencing but she was six months pregnant now and no one would have her.

All she could do was cry and cry… for she knew that it was his mother's abuse of them which was making Ram-Ram snap. So, after doing a lot of thinking, she pleaded, begged him to run away with her; run away – anywhere – away from this wicked woman.

In her distraught state, she just wasn't thinking straight. Of course, he blatantly refused.

However, the threats, torture and cursing continued, until one day, his mother cursed him so badly that he could take no more. And so, he made up his mind that he would run away with Eve, come what may.

Determined to leave, they decided to make the break at night, because they knew that if Ram-Ram's mother saw them running away, she would put a 'curse' on them, and that 'curse' would bring them bad luck. And so, six months pregnant, homeless and penniless she Eve, and he Ram-Ram, waited till everyone was asleep, then at midnight November 13 1955, they slipped quietly out into the silent moonlight.

Slowly… slowly… they tiptoed down the front steps, he carrying the few belongings they had in a brown paper bag, they, knowing full well they had nowhere to go.

They were so distressed, they just couldn't think straight.

They thought of Mah and Pah, but they knew very well that Rajkapur and Lola would not let them stay there. They would make their lives hell... and chase them out.

Finding themselves at a loss, they sat under a Poui tree, thinking... thinking... then, like a flash of lightning, it came... Ram-Ram remembered his sister Sumin.

'They would go to his sister Sumin,' he thought. 'Sumin, who live in a big house down Point-a-Pierre way. Sure, she would take pity on we and take we in?' he was thinking.

He was certain of that.

Chapter Nineteen

Half asleep, they made their way along the narrow winding mud-beaten road, which would take them to the border of Esperanza Estate, then on to California and finally Point-a-Pierre. Being the dead of night, the place was deserted – apart from a few dogs barking here and there – and by the time they reached Esperanza Sugar Mill, the pitch blackness of the still night unnerved Eve, the moonlight having long faded into the dim background.

At the Sugar Mill, the pond into which the mill's dirty sediment flowed, was still – not a ripple on its black water – the foul smell of molasses drifting in the air and that of the sugar cane juice, churning within its mill, was nauseating; the sickening smell of these deposits so unbearable that Eve's stomach began to retch, her distressed mind tumbling, leaping in bounds at the predicament she was in. She could go no further. She simply had to rest.

They sat under an Immortal tree, its broad branches sprawling above them like a canopy, tent-like, the cold dirty ground so hard that they had to nestle into each other for comfort. Exhausted, before long, they fell asleep.

They must have slept for hours, it seemed, for when they woke up it was 6am. Cold and hungry, they dragged themselves up and continued on their journey. They walked for hours it seemed, miles and miles, until they reached the main road, which would take them from California to Point-a-Pierre – the journey seeming endless; the hot tropical sun now beating down on their bare arms and faces; the sweat pouring from their aching bodies; Eve's six months pregnancy weighing heavily on her.

It was nearly noon when they finally reached Sumin's house, just beyond Point-a-Pierre (a big white house standing tall at the end of a narrow dirt track) and spotting her sweeping her front yard, they doubled their paces as fast as they could – but then she saw them.

She recognised Ram-Ram and this young girl limping towards her, then all of a sudden, she saw the young girl collapse in a heap in her front path, right in front of her.

Quick as a flash, she bolted towards them, picked the girl up and laid her on the bench under her house. Quickly, she loosened her bodice and started fanning her, every now and then, putting the smelling salts under her nose to try and bring her back to life again. Then, after a few minutes, the girl recovered, lying there as limp as a dead fish.

Distraught at the dishevelled state this girl was in – barely a child, six months pregnant, pale, worn out, malnourished, her dirty clothes hanging from her like a sack – Sumin knew instantly that something was wrong. And so, wasting no time, she quickly questioned Ram-Ram, who spilt out his version of things.

He told her, 'how he and this girl, his wife Eve, had run away from his mother's home, because he'd lost his job and had no money to pay her for their keep, so she started harassing them. She treated them so badly, that they had to run away… and now they were homeless and had nowhere else to go.' He pleaded with her to allow them to stay there.

What he didn't tell her was, that he often beat his wife Eve, mercilessly.

Moved by their plight, Sumin didn't have the heart to turn them away, so she told them they could stay there, at least until they'd sorted their lives out. Then, she took Eve upstairs to her bedroom to rest.

Standing proudly in the middle of this room was a brass bed, so well polished that it shone like a mirror. There was a thick mattress on it, covered with lace covers; a few chairs positioned here and there; a dressing table in the far corner and a white rug at the bottom of the bed.

Sumin helped Eve into the high bed in spite of her dishevelled state – so clean, so warm and so comfortable it was – that within minutes, she was fast asleep, snoring away in her dirty garb.

Meanwhile, Sumin cooked some nice hot darhl and rice and fried a whole tin of salmon to go with it. Then, when Eve woke up, she fed her and Ram-Ram with the appetising meal and gave them a drink of ice-cold orange juice from the ice tub.

It was the first hot meal Eve had eaten for a while and after trailing the streets, homeless, penniless and very much pregnant, she was to remember this meal for a long time to come.

When they finished eating their meals, Sumin gave them buckets of water from the barrel and soap with which to wash themselves and Eve lapped it up. Washing her dirty body from head to toe, she laid into the cold fresh water like a magpie, then she got dressed in an old cotton frock which Sumin had given her and she felt much better.

Now that she was in a more relaxed mood, Sumin decided it was time to have a talk with her. She probed and questioned so gently, that before long, Eve began to open up and poured her heart out.

"Bahin," Eve said, her eyes wet with tears, "ah use to 'ave to get up 4 o'cloc in de mornin', cook dere food, clean de house an' wash de clodes for de wole family. Den, wen dey come home from work, ah use to 'ave to dish out dem food an' wach dem eat it, Bahin. Den, only wen dem finish eatin' Bahin, ah could eat mine – de left over from dem – an' drink plain water to wash it down wit. Ah use to get so hungry an' so tired Bahin...an den if ah didn' do de housework good, she (moder-in-law) use to curse de devil on me... Oh Bahin! Oh Bahin!" Eve started to cry.

Moved by this sad tale, Sumin put her arms round Eve and tried to comfort her, mopping her wet eyes with a piece of cloth, listening earnestly as Eve continued:

"It was hell Bahin. Hell! Den, come nite-time, if we talk, she go bang de wall, bang de door so hard, ah never get much sleep Bahin. Oh Bahin! Oh Bahin!" Eve was bawling now, tears streaming down her face and Sumin, unable to control herself, started to cry too.

Like two children they cried and cried, each hugging the other; each comforting one another; like mother and child, they clung to each other and cried for a good few minutes. But for fear however, of what Sumin might do to Ram-Ram, Eve did not let on that he used to beat her up.

Heartbroken at the plight of this 14-year-old pregnant girl, Sumin knew too well the demon in Ram-Ram's mother, for she too had suffered a similar fate from this wicked woman when she lived there. Now, she was determined to help Eve out, no matter what.

And so, come the next day, following Sumin's orders, Eve and Ram-Ram moved into her old wooden ramshackled second home, a few doors away. Worn by the elements and badly in need of repair – its cobwebs and dust now cleaned away by Sumin – it was ready for occupation.

Like a deserted fortress it stood, propped up on bent posts, leaning so badly to one side, that if a strong wind blew, it would surely tumble down. It was as if it was just waiting for onslaught by the oncoming monsoon.

Formerly occupied by Sumin's gardener, who had now moved to a room underneath her own house, this tumbledown building seemed a perfect place for a desperate homeless couple who had nowhere else to go. And so they set about to make it their home.

Chapter Twenty

It was not by accident, but by sheer hard work that Sumin and her husband acquired these two homes, and were now enjoying a reasonable standard of living. For, never afraid of hard work at the fruit and vegetable plantation which they owned – they would get up every morning at 6am at the crack of dawn, to tend their crops – yellow corn and peas, aubergines and tomatoes, cassava, eddoes and plantains and oranges, guava, plums and mangoes in the adjoining fruit section.

They watered in the evenings and hoed in the mornings. And sometimes under the blazing sun, they ploughed away. Then, come harvest time, they would reap and sell these crops to the local vendors, thereby earning a decent living for themselves. Consequently, Sumin always wore nice clothes and they lived and looked well.

Their way of life was so respected by Eve that before long she too was joining in.

Every day, after finishing her housework, she used to take hot lunches (cooked in Sumin's kitchen) out there to them, in the fields where they worked.

"It's darhl an' rice an' fry ochres today," she would call.

And the gardener would reply, "Oh yeah! An' ah hope de ochre is as sweet as you girl!" and they would laugh their heads off and Eve giggled too – so happy she was.

Even though it was hard work, working out there in the fields, they were having so much fun, that Eve used to look forward to helping out sometimes. She enjoyed herself so much.

And now that she and Ram-Ram were settling in nicely, they were determined to make a go of things. She had made some curtains and a tablecloth from cast off materials which Sumin has given her and with the few pots and pans which they now owned, the ramshackled house was beginning to look like home, as she and Ram-Ram pressed on with their lives.

Every morning at the crack of dawn, Ram-Ram would get up and cycle down to Point-a-Pierre or Sanfernando to look for work, only to return home jobless. But he never gave up. Instead, he made himself useful by helping Sumin and her husband out in the fields.

He would trim the banana leaves, plant and mould the crops, the sweat pouring from his body and those of the other workers too; the hot tropical sun burning down on them, their old worn out hats fading; the sun leaving its trail – classic sunburnt marks on their tired aging faces. But they were having so much fun, what with all the joking and larking about, that they didn't mind the hard work at all.

Often, Eve would visit Sumin at the 'big house' during siesta time. They would chat for hours, it seemed – she seeing Sumin as a mother and Sumin viewing her as a daughter, whilst Ram-Ram on the other hand, continued his plight to find a job. Then, one day his luck changed, or so it seemed. After two months of searching, he'd found a job at Point-a-Pierre – he was hired by a Foreman to build roads and he was so happy!

Saturday was payday and he would get paid cash. He would then pay Sumin the rent, buy some food and cod liver oil for Eve (to nourish the unborn baby) then buy a shirt or two for himself. And so, for the first time in his life, he felt a sense of security, a strand of hope to which he and Eve clung. But their luck was not to last. Something was to happen which would change all that.

Sumin was having an affair with the gardener and things would never be the same again.

It had been going on for a while – this affair – and when her husband found out, quarrels soon erupted. He warned her – in no uncertain terms – that the gardener must move out of his house or else she would have to go. But Sumin was not prepared to give up her lover, come what may. She chose instead, to give up her half-brother Ram-Ram and his wife Eve, regardless of the consequences.

Like a crazed woman, she was – her hungry middle-aged body yearning for and lapping up the hot sex she was having with her lover – and she was not going to give that up. Sumin had changed so much, it seemed, not at all the person Eve had come to know and love.

Eve was eight months pregnant now, but that didn't matter. In pursuit of sexual pleasures Sumin defied all conventions. It was as though she, Sumin, had undergone some kind of transformation and in the process, lost all sense of being.

Ram-Ram and Eve had to leave, she was sure of that. But neither he nor Eve must ever know the real reason – it being, that she preferred to choose her lover at the expense of her homeless and penniless brother and his young pregnant wife, regardless of the consequences.

And so, adamant that she was making the right move, she concocted the perfect alibi. Then, one morning, she summoned Ram-Ram to her house.

Bracing herself, she said, "Bhy (brother), Eve is near to give birt' now an' she mus' be near de 'ospital Bhy... She mus' be wit she Mah and Pah Bhy, near to de 'ospitol in Couva."

Taken aback by such sudden news and what he'd just heard, Ram-Ram sat there in shocked silence. Clearly, he knew nothing of the 'love affair' with the gardener.

She cleared her throat, then continued, "We 'ave no 'ospitol or midwive 'ere Bhy... an' is she firs baby. We carn' take no chance Bhy! She carn' 'ave de baby 'ere!"

Her cold, harsh words launched so unexpectedly left him stunned.

'For de first time in dere lives they were beginning to feel settled; feel a sense of hope; and now, she was more or less tellin' dem that they had to leave. And what about Eve? How will she take it?' Thoughts... thoughts... like a volcano whizzing through his mind. He couldn't think straight.

For a moment, he sat there, lost for words... not knowing what to do...but somehow he felt he had to try, give it all he had, try and appeal to her maternal instincts... her conscience... if he could.

"But sis," he pleaded, "de baby go due now an' we 'ave no way to go. No one go 'ave we. Were we go go sis? Mah an' Pah donn' wann' we. Were we go go sis? Were we go go?"

Sumin couldn't take it, but she had to put on a hard front, put on a show to protect her own interests and that of her lover. For right now, the only person that mattered in her life was him.

Like a tormented woman, a woman who was just about to lose everything, she snapped. "You go an' see you Mah," she ordered. "She dauter is 'avin she firs baby an' she mus' be care. She 'ave Couva 'ospitol near she. She go 'ave to keep you an' Eve. You hear mi boy?" she barked angrily, waving her fist at him.

Paralysed by her remarks, he stuck to the chair like glue, shocked out of his wits. He couldn't believe it – couldn't believe the change which had come over his half-sister.

The onslaught continued however. She attacked, "Mi no 'ave no 'ospitol 'ere. She carn' 'ave de baby 'ere. She mus' go 'ave de baby in 'er Mah house..." her voice heightening in intensity.

Then, with ferocity, she delivered the final blow. "You can no stay 'ere no more. You an' Eve mus' leave nex' week." And with that, like a tornado ready to explode, she marched straight into the kitchen and started throwing the pots and pans around. Bang! Bang! Bang! it went, as she attacked the kitchen utensils.

That last sentence hit him like a bulldozer. It was as if lightning had just struck.

He stood up, almost frozen... lost for words... trying hard to compose himself... unable to believe that she, his beloved sister Sumin, who was once so kind to them, could turn, become so ruthless, and so suddenly too.

He didn't understand.

It was as if he had just woken up from a bad, bad nightmare and he didn't know where to turn.

That evening, he broke the news to Eve and she went hysterical.

Young and still naïve, she took people at face value. It didn't dawn on her, that there were two sides to a person's character, two sides to Sumin's personality and so she considered Sumin's insensitive action as an act of betrayal. She simply didn't understand.

She didn't know how to handle the situation. She just didn't know how. All she knew was that she and Ram-Ram had to leave and the only place they could go now was to Mah and Pah. For, when Pah had been to visit her at Sumin's house, he'd told her that they could come and stay with him at his home. Now, they had no other choice but to go there.

What else could they do?

Feeling betrayed, they didn't want to stay at Sumin's house a day longer. So that very evening, they packed what little clothes they had in a brown paper bag, leaving everything which Sumin had given them behind. Then, at 7am the following morning, they said their last farewell and left Sumin's house, never to return there again.

Chapter Twenty-One

Homeless and penniless once again, Eve and Ram-Ram were on their way to the only person whom they knew would offer them shelter and that was Pah.

They walked the dirty mud track for miles and miles, it seemed, their aching feet threadbare, finally reaching the main road at Point-a-Pierre at 9am, from where they would journey onwards to Couva.

On they trekked, the early morning tropical sun beating down on their shabbily clothed bodies, traffic hooting as it sped past. Eve's pregnancy was bearing down so heavily on her, that she reached a point where she could walk no further. Hence, with the little money they had, they flagged down a taxi to take them to Couva Junction from where they would walk the rest of the journey to Pah's house at Carli-Bay Road.

Tired, hungry and parched, it was nearly midday when they finally reached Pah's house, the hot midday sun burning their worn out aching faces, Eve so exhausted, she was just about ready to collapse.

Lola was standing at Pah's front gate, her eyes wandering idly about the place, when all of a sudden, she spotted them. She went into shock and nearly passed out.

Aghast, she greeted them icily.

"Well, well Eve! Is it you girl? An' you pregnant too! My! Oh my…!" she went, sarcasm in her voice, "an' oh my! Is you Ram-Ram? Is you man?" she was so cold you could almost feel the ice within her.

She led them swiftly to the room below Pah's house – the room where they were to stay – then without saying a further word, disappeared quickly, clean out of sight. No hospitality, nothing! Nothing! She didn't even offer them a drink.

They laid the brown paper bag on the cold iron bed, its worn out mattress with its torn sheets sagging, the whole place smelling of damp, Eve being so exhausted, she immediately slumped onto it like a ton of bricks.

Looking around her, she was amazed at the dilapidated state of the place. There was a wooden table in the far corner; a wooden bench on which to sit; a wooden box in which they could store the few clothes they had; a few tin cups and enamel plates scattered here and there. The whole place stank of rot but at least they had somewhere to live.

Being destitute, they tried to settle down – make ends meet, and not having much money, they had to survive on dry roti and boiled tea sweetened with condensed milk.

Strict instructions were soon laid out for them – Eve was allowed in Pah's kitchen for 1 hour only – where she would cook her sparse meals quickly and take them back to her rat-hole of a room to eat. For that kitchen was Lola's domain and she did not want Eve there at all.

Hoping they could stay at Pah's house till they find their feet, Eve and Ram-Ram tried their best to rebuild their lives. And so, unable to find any other jobs, Ram-Ram started working in the sugar cane fields to try and make ends meet.

He used to work long hours cutting and cropping the canes, often doing overtime to try and save some money to build a home of their own; sometimes coming home tired and worn out. So tired he was, that at times he would lose his temper and shout at Eve over petty little things. One day he got so angry, lost his bearings and knocked her to the floor, punching and kicking her so hard that she thought she was going to abort – poverty and its consequential lack of human dignity, it seemed, was taking its toll.

But that was not the only abuse Eve had to tolerate, for Lola persisted in harassing her – accusing her of leaving the kitchen dirty; telling the neighbours how she and Ram-Ram were dirty and how they stank; hence stirring up no end of troubles for her.

Lola had her own axe to grind. She thought she had seen the back of them and now that they were here again, she Lola, the venomous female, was determined to get them out of Pah's house for good, this time.

Nine months pregnant now, life was becoming unbearable for Eve. Then one day on February 6 1956, she suddenly went into labour.

In agony with labour pain, her back aching and aching so much, the base of her spine getting so weak that she screamed with fright. And even though she was only a child of 15, Mah didn't seen to understand.

Every time she screamed, Mah accused her of putting on an act in order to gain attention.

The poor, distraught girl kept bawling out in pain. "Please God, help mi. Ah wan' to die. Oh God, ah wan' to die. Ah wan' to die!" she screamed, the little old lady (the local quasi-midwife) popping in every now and then to check for the baby's head.

A kindly lady, she did her best to comfort and help Eve but alas! Her knowledge of midwifery was limited. At least she was kind though – for she was the only person who showed Eve any mercy, any sympathy.

Because it was her first baby, the local District Midwife also called in to see Eve. "Everyting OK?" she enquired, then disappeared again, having assured Eve that she would call again the following evening.

Even she, didn't understand why Eve was screaming so much with back pain. She just couldn't comprehend.

In fact, Eve had some weak discs at the base of her spine and since there were only three hospitals in Trinidad, the x-ray facilities therefore were based at Port of Spain and were too costly to run. Consequently, it was used for emergencies only and so no x-ray was taken of Eve's spine.

The reality was that 'anyone suffering from back pain had to either find a doctor to treat them privately or learn to put up with it' – and that was what Eve had to do, because she had no money to pay for private medical treatment.

Now, the baby was bearing down so much on her damaged spinal disc, causing her such excruciating pain and no one understood.

As promised, the midwife returned the following evening, but she was in a state of flux and so every time Eve screamed, she shouted, "Don' bawl girl. You havin' a baby you know, not dyin'." She just didn't understand.

She refused to give Eve any painkillers as the little supply she had was for emergencies only and Eve's case was not seen as an emergency. And so, Eve continued to suffer in agony.

Each time Eve bore down, she couldn't help but urinate, the nurse shouting, "You peein' in mi han' girl. You nasty little girl. You pissin' all over de place!"

She got so angry that she left Eve lying there in pain and disappeared, Eve panting and pushing, puffing and pushing when, all of a sudden, the baby's head started to pop out.

"Nurse! Nurse! Is comin'!" she screamed, the nurse rushing in, in a state of panic.

She pulled on a pair of gloves as quickly as she could and ..."Push! Push!" she shouted, Eve pushing and panting, pushing and puffing with all the strength she could muster, the nurse holding the baby's head. Then WOOSH! Like a volcano, it plunged out... a pool of blood gushing all over the place.

And so, on February 8 1956, after two days of agonising labour pain, the teenage Eve gave birth to a bouncing baby boy weighing 8lbs and 1oz. They called him Sam, after his grandfather.

Eve was bleeding a lot so the nurse cleaned her, padded her up well and left her to rest. 'She'd be back on Friday of dat week to give her a check up,' she assured her. "And if, in de meantime you 'ave any problem, you should contact Couva 'ospital," she added and departed as swiftly as she came.

Apart from the midwife, there was no one else present at Sam's birth. Mah was too busy tending the parlour to hang around for long. And according to Hindu customs husbands were not allowed during childbirth, for it was too dirty a business for men to witness.

And so, with the exception of the nurse, the child Eve had given birth to her first-born, more or less alone.

But when it came to rejoicing, Ram-Ram didn't waste any time. For when he came home from work that day and learnt that his first-born was a son, he was over the moon, happy because (according to Hindi protocol) Bhagwan (God) would now shower down his blessing and bring good fortune unto himself and Eve – all because their first-born was a son.

On hearing the news however, Rajkapur and Lola raged with fire. Their first-born was not a son and so they went green with envy. 'A son would have speeded up dere inheritance.' They knew that. So they couldn't take the shock.

Mah too was not happy. For she wanted her first grandson to be born to her son Rajkapur, whereby he would inherit the family's name and fortune – carry on the family's tradition.

But somehow it seemed, Bhagwan did not grant her that wish.

And so, Mah kept her distance. She didn't express any joy. She didn't even kiss the baby – not even once. She just couldn't hide her feelings.

It was customary that on the sixth day of a birth, Hindu women should celebrate. They would cook and feed and pamper the mother who had just given birth –a special Indian concoction would be prepared and fed to her– ground saffron cooked in milk and sweetened well, which they claimed would help heal the mother's womb.

Then, they would prepare parched flour, cooked in ghee (Indian butter) and mixed with sugar and raisins called parsaad – an Indian sweet supposed to have religious connotations – an offering to Bhagwan for the blessing of the baby's birth.

At the ceremony, the women would eat, sing and dance, offering presents to the baby – new clothes, made mainly of silk and they would make a fuss of the newborn child.

Quite a set-up it was – the whole business, representing a process of cleansing – a purification of the mother who had just given birth. Then on the 7th day, she would be proclaimed clean and allowed to venture out and meet anyone who dared offer to meet her.

But utterly disappointed that Eve had given birth to a son, Mah flatly refused to have any such celebrations. And so, Eve felt betrayed. She felt so alone.

With no rejoicing, no fun to be had and no visitors either, Eve was sad, for all she had for company now, was a baby who seemed to cry endlessly – a baby who was proving difficult to care for and she began to despair.

Though an extremely healthy baby, Sam cried a lot. The more she breast fed him, the more he squealed, sleeping during the day and squealing most of the night, she being kept awake either breastfeeding him or changing his nappy. And so, within a week of his birth she became so distressed and worn out that she was barely able to cope.

But then, one day, as if by miracle, her Moslem friend Shara turned up to visit her...

Chapter Twenty-Two

"You lookin' well girl!" Shara remarked, smiling, the sad Eve knowing deep down in her heart, that she was not at all well.

She was sick – very sick – bleeding heavily from her womb, but she didn't want to allay Shara's fears.

"What a pretty little baby?" Shara continued, touching and caressing baby Sam's face.

"Look! Ah brin' he a present – a little hat – a nit it miself. Ah hope you like it girl."

Eve took the present from her, her face beaming with joy. For it was the only present Sam had received and she was overcome with emotions.

She offered Shara some Coca-cola and together they drank and talked and talked...then, before they knew it, it was time for Shara to leave – leaving Eve lonely once more – with no one to talk to; no one to lean on; no one to comfort her.

With baby Sam crying so much, Mah thought he was suffering from the wind, so she bought him some gripe water and suggested that Eve fed him with it. 'Anyting to stop he from cryin',' she thought. And so, following the instructions which Mah had given her, Eve fed and fed...endless bottles of gripe water to no avail.

He just kept on crying.

Whenever he cried, she offered him her breasts, but he just squealed, tugged and guzzled at her nipples so much that they became sore and drained of milk. He squealed and screeched most of the night, Eve hardly getting any sleep at all.

And so, life for her was becoming unbearable. With baby Sam crying endlessly, Lola piling on the housework and Rajkapur shouting whenever the baby cried, Eve had almost reached breaking point.

"Shut dat baby up oh ah go shut it up for you!" Rajkapur would shout. "Carn' you heer de chile is cryin'? Get up! Get up and feed it, oh ah go come down an' shut it up for good!"

Terrified of his threats, Eve used to drag her sleepy, aching body up and allow baby Sam to suck and suck until her nipples went dry, but still he kept on crying. And the more he cried, the more the shouting continued, Rajkapur wanting to put a stop to it, once and for all.

And so every evening when he came home from work, he would curse Eve...

"You lazy son-of-bitch! Lazy bitch! You carn' look after you own chile," he would scream. "An' you don' help Lola wit de housework too. Sick! Sick! Ah don' wan' you here no more. Ah go chase you out of dis house," he warned, shaking his fist vehemently at her.

But, try as she did, she became so worn out that she just couldn't cope. Then one evening, Rajkapur came home from work stinking drunk. His face rigid, his eyes rolling, he went bananas.

"Youu... did' ant...'elp Lo...la wit de...'ousewo...rk today!" he drawled. "Bit...ch! You bit...ch! Ge-t out ov d-is 'ou-se noww...!" he exploded and Eve shook with fear. But scared as she was, she didn't dare answer back and she didn't dare tell Ram-Ram about it either, for fear of what he might do to Rajkapur. Instead, that night drowning her sorrows, she cried herself to sleep.

Working hard under the hot blazing sun in the sugar cane fields in order to save enough money to buy materials to build a home of their own, Ram-Ram laboured on. They had planned to ask Pah to let them build their house on the plot of land which he owned down the road and they hoped he would let them have it.

It laid a mile or so away from Pah's house and was used to plant rice, tomatoes and other tropical vegetables, but most of the time it laid to waste. And Pah was always moaning how close it was to the cemetery – so they hoped he would let them have it. And so, bracing herself one day when he returned home from work, Eve approached him.

Shaking like a leaf, she appealed, "Pah, we have no way to go Pah. If you go let we 'ave de piece of lan' by de burial groun', we go only use a small piece to buil' we house Pah," she paused for breath as Pah stood there, looking at her motionless.

Feeling uneasy, she swallowed, then continued. "Pah, you go have de rest of de lan' to plant rice and tomatoes Pah. We go be no trouble to you Pah. No trouble at all!"

But for all the begging in the world, Pah did not budge. Like an unshakable rock, he just stood there rigid... lifeless... It was as if he had just been hit by a bolt of lightning and Eve seeing the anger in his face, shook uncontrollably.

'How dere she ask?' He was seething. 'Mi property was for mi son only, not dauters. She nows dat. Ah wouldn' break mi Hindu code – allow mi son-in-law to 'ave mi piece of lan'. Never! Never!'

He was just about to froth at the mouth when sensing his feelings and trembling to the core of her bones, Eve got down on her knees and started to beg. "Please Pah," she begged, "we go give you no trouble Pah. We go be good to you; good to you Pah," she cried unable to hold the tears back.

But no amount of tears could shift Pah from his unshakable stance. Her tears fell on deaf ears. He just stood there a stoic look on his face. He refused her blankly.

"De lan' is fo' mi son. You go no have de lan'. You hear mi girl! No mo beggin'! You hear mi!" he shouted.

Eve went numb, for she knew well that Pah meant business. There would be no going back on his word now...she knew that. And so, like a defeated rabbit, she coiled up and retreated to her den.

With nowhere to build their home now and the endless threats from Rajkapur and Lola, Ram-Ram could take no more. So one day, during an argument with Rajkapur, he lost his temper, punched Rajkapur in the face and threatened to kill him.

That, for Pah, was the last straw…'A son-in-law beatin' up mi first-born son, de apple of mi eye, de thread of mi inheritance?' He went mad.

"You go kill mi son. You son-of-a-bitch! You estate jackass! You coolie!" he screamed at Ram-Ram. "You no stay in dis 'ouse one more day. Leeve dis 'ouse an' go now! Now!" he commanded, raging like a mad bull.

Trembling like a coy rabbit at the sight of Pah's raging face, Eve stood there defenceless. There was no mistaking Pah's mood. She knew it was the end – they would not be able to stay there any longer.

They would have to leave now and once again be homeless, only this time they had a three-month-old baby to keep.

In desperation, she and Ram-Ram sought solace in one another. Then after much thinking, they realised that they still had one option left…

'Ram-Ram moder had a spare piece of lan' to de back of she house. If only he could swallow his pride and go and see she – plead forgiveness – den maybe she would let him 'ave de lan', on which dey could buil' dere house,' Eve thought.

And so, out of sheer desperation, she knew they had to utilise that option.

They had to give it their best shot, come what may.

What else could they do?

Chapter Twenty-Three

It was 5 o'clock that evening when Ram-Ram got on his bicycle and cycled down to Esperanza Estate to see his mother. She greeted him icily.

Determined to make it up to her, he wasted no time. "Forgive mi Mah, forgive mi if ah hurt you," he pleaded. "But mi wife, she 'ave a baby now, three mont old an' we 'ave no way to live Mah. Pah don' wan' we dere no more an' we carn' go on de street Mah, wat wit de baby an' dat." He went down on his knees.

He looked at her sheepishly, she staring at him sternly, then she shook her head in consternation. Shocked, she could hardly believe what she was hearing.

"Go on son, go on! Ah listenin' son! Ah listenin'!" She was baffled.

He swallowed hard then continued, "We already have de material to buil' we house Mah, but Pah won' give we de lan'. So were we go go, Mah? Were we go go? We have no way to go now..." His throat went dry.

"If you give mi de lan' Mah, we go buil' we 'ouse dere an' Eve go be good to you Mah. Good to you. You go see." He swallowed and waited.

Unable to see her son in such a pitiful state, his mother didn't have the heart to turn him away. 'She hated Eve for takin' her son away from her, sure, but if she allow him to buil' his 'ouse next to hers, he would not run away dis time. Den, she could exert power over him, rule his life, as she did before he was married,' she was thinking, her mind working overtime.

"OK! OK son! You go 'ave de lan', but you wife be good to mi...do as ah say...you hear mi son?" She was adamant.

Stuttering, he couldn't believe it...didn't think his mother would forgive him and now...?

"Ye-s Mah, Y-es...God bless-s you M-ah, God ble-ss you. She go be go-od to yo-uu Mah. Go-od to yo-uu. Yo-u-go se-e."

Overwhelmed with gratitude, he raised himself up from the ground upon which he was kneeling and was just about to kiss her, when she interrupted his actions. "Bhagwan be good to mi son. He brin' mi son bac' to mi," she said, looking up and pointing to the heavens, as if talking to God, rather than to him.

So overcome – barely able to believe his luck – he just looked at her, didn't utter a single word more, quickly jumped on his bike and cycled back to Carli-Bay Road at breakneck speed, to break the news to Eve. 'Just wait till she hear dis,' he thought. 'His moder who hated Eve was letting dem buil' dere 'ouse next to her?'

He was beside himself, thinking...

Then, as soon as he reached home, he broke the news to Eve and she was over the moon. 'At long las dey woud have a home of dere own,' she thought. 'If only Pah woud let dem stay put until dey buil' de structure of dere house, then they would leave for good.' She felt relieved at the thought.

And so, the following evening, she approached Pah. "Pah," she appealed, "Ram-Ram go only take a few week to buil' we house in Esperanza, Pah, den we go go for good. We go make no trouble Pah. Ah promise. We go only stay for a few week more Pah, den we go go for good."

Pah looked at Eve hard, a stony silence in his look...then..."OK Eve, OK! But dat man mus' buil' de house quick. You hear mi girl?" he warned, "If ah don' see dat man builin' his house quick, you go have to go. You hear mi girl? You hear mi?"

Breathing a sigh of relief, Eve replied, "Oh yes Pah. Oh yes! We go buil' we house quick." Then she made for her room as fast as her legs could carry her and relayed the news to Ram-Ram.

From then on he wasted no time.

Every evening, after sweating his guts out in the sugar cane fields, he would jump on his bike and cycle down to Esperanza to build his house – building, building till the moonlight dimmed. Then, as darkness approached, he would pack up and cycle back to Carli-Bay Road, the dogs barking wildly at his heels.

First, he levelled the earth with great speed; next, he buried the post and concreted it firmly; then, he nailed the rough-cut wooden boards to form walls, leaving square gaps for windows, finally nailing on the silver coloured galvanised roof to the top – to form a roof – to stop the rains from beating in.

Daily he slaved his guts out, often returning home late at night, Eve meanwhile, struggling with baby Sam. With no spare money to buy powdered (kilm) milk, baby Sam had to rely on Eve's breast for survival. He pulled and sucked and guzzled until they were bare of milk, each time drawing in wind. Then, he started to suffer bouts of diarrhoea.

Depleted of energy caring for the baby and surviving on malnourished food, Eve began to have fainting attacks, Lola showing no mercy at all. Instead, she accused her of making tricks to gain attention.

The house building went on however and after three weeks, the bulk of the house was completed. It didn't have windows – only holes – but that didn't matter, for at least they now had a home in which to live. So, unable to stand the strain anymore, they packed their few belongings plus some old rags for nappies, in the worn out trunk which Auntie Nell had given them. Then after saying 'goodbye' to Mah and Pah, they headed once more for Esperanza Estate, to the first home they ever owned – a wooden shack built of rough-cut wood and mud.

It was May 1956. How could she ever forget?

They fixed it up with an old iron bed; a worn out mattress; an iron pot which the Negro neighbour from Couva had given them; some tin cups, enamel plates, an old saucepan and broom, given to them by Shara and Ram-Ram bought an old kerosene stove from the hardware store at Couva, on which they would cook their food.

They nailed and fixed and after a few days of dusting and cleaning, the place began to look like home. And so, Eve decided to prepare a treat for them. She cooked some nice hot darhl and rice and aloo and they ate their fill. They felt good, for it was the first hot meal they'd had for months and they really enjoyed it.

But being so happy now, Ram-Ram didn't waste any time satisfying himself sexually. For, regular as clockwork, he performed, Eve hating every minute of it, but having to endure it as she was duty-bound to.

Not surprisingly, when baby Sam was only six months old she became pregnant again. But the hard work however continued.

Every morning she would wash the old rags (baby napkins) on a big stone in the back yard and spread them on the grass to dry, the insects crawling onto them like dust. Then, she would shake them thoroughly – just in case – before bringing them inside again. Regularly, she hung the urine-soaked flour bag bed sheets to dry out, then she would bring them in and remake the bed, because she didn't have any spare ones to change.

She hustled about the place, bare-footed and bare-bottomed, the tropical wind blowing right up her skirt to her naked parts – she didn't wear any panties because Ram-Ram couldn't afford to buy her any.

Every week she would wash her dress and flour bag petticoat and hang them out to dry, for they stank of stale urine – urine which seeped from the baby's nappies – since they all slept in one bed. But, true to form, she didn't dare complain. She just soldiered on...

Chapter Twenty-Four

Time passed and they continued to make their home, homely. For after a few weeks, Ram-Ram had built a wooden table, two hard-back chairs and a hammock for baby Sam to sleep in. And so before long, the place was beginning to look like home. But with the new baby on the way, they needed extra cash, so Ram-Ram built a shed to the far side of their home and decided to house two young goats within. 'Dey go bring in some extra income when dey grow up and was sole,' he hoped. Looking after the two goats however was Eve's job.

Suffering from morning sickness and getting tired and worn out, she was finding it hard to cope and she was getting desperate.

Three months pregnant now and baby Sam still crying most of the night, she used to have to get up and try and rock him to sleep. And so, groping about half asleep in the dark, she would feed and try to comfort him, Ram-Ram snoring his head off, never making a single move to help with the baby. For according to Hindu customs, men were not childminders – that was a woman's job – so, even though Eve was as sick as a dog, she had to get on with the business of childminding and the other chores too – no questions asked.

Twice a day, she had to cart heavy buckets of water from the standpipe out in the street. She would feed the goats, the hot sun blazing down on her pregnant body. And so, by the time she was six months pregnant, she was getting so tired that she could hardly move her body.

On and on she struggled, until by the time she was eight months pregnant, she had reached a point where she could cope no more. So she pleaded with Ram-Ram, begged him to help her out.

Luckily for her, he took pity on her and bought her a water barrel which he would refill himself every evening. Now, she would not have to cart water from the street anymore. And once a week he did the shopping too – it was a great help to her.

But someone was watching. It was his mother. She was seething...

Jealous of her son toading to his wife, she put the spokes in. She began to complain. She refused to accept that Eve being eight months pregnant and having to do housework, care for the baby and the two goats as well, was all too much for her. So, when her son paid no heed to her protests, she started to swear and curse the hell out of Eve.

Every time she saw her, she would curse. "You nasty f...in moder suk-er. You lazy bich! Su-ckin' mi son blood...You dope mi son, you nogro bich!" she raged. "Ah go make mi son sen you bac to Couva," she howled, shaking her fists at Eve, Eve's stomach retching at the sound of those words.

She used to stand on the back steps of her house and wait for Eve to pass, sometimes putting her hand to her nose and making 'signs' as if to say, 'Eve stunk'.

So jealous and possessive of her son she was. She hated Eve with a venom which was hard to match. She was convinced that Eve was a bad woman – a bad, lazy wife, whom, she decided had to go! And so determined to drive her away, she cursed and cursed the hell out of her.

Chapter Twenty-Five

Barely eight hours of labour pain, it was a quick birth when, on April 28 1957, Eve gave birth to her second son. They called him Ranjit.

With two babies to care for, all the housework to do and two goats to look after as well, it was too much for any child of 16. But stoic as she was, Eve put on a brave front and struggled on.

As May approached, the cane-cropping season was coming to a close so Ram-Ram was at home most of the time. Eve however, continued to struggle – cooking, feeding and changing two babies' nappies – Sam still wearing nappies, wetting himself regularly. But Ram-Ram simply looked on and never lifted a finger once, to help her.

He was having a ball, passing the time with his male friends, weight-lifting, running, gossiping, horsing around and having fun, leaving Eve to struggle with the household chores.

Like a worn out horse she soldiered on till she almost reached breaking point. She became so tired that she fainted a few times, but Ram-Ram was not in the least bothered. As far as he was concerned, housework was women's work and there was no way he was going to join in. What he, Ram-Ram. Never!

As was customary in Trinidad, employed or not, Indian men were known to spend their time with their male friends enjoying sports or going to the cinema – not staying at home helping with housework. That was the culture – an unwritten code amongst Hindu men and more so at Esperanza. Ram-Ram therefore, wasn't going to break that custom.

As time passed, he was more out of work than in it and not having enough money to buy food for his family or powdered milk for the babies, Eve resorted to eating dry roti and salt-fish and mixing the condensed milk with water with which she fed the babies.

And so, undernourished, within a month or so, baby Ranjit started to suffer from diarrhoea and dehydration. A sick child, he cried so much that Eve's patience began to wear and Ram-Ram began to lose his temper.

"Pic dat chile up an' feed it, you lazy ting! Carn' you see de chile is hungry? Feed it! Feed it!" he hollered, not once thinking of feeding baby Ranjit or changing his nappy. He wouldn't be caught dead changing a baby's nappy. 'An Indian man changin' nappies? Never!'

Tempers flared, they started to get on each other's nerves and before long they began to argue. Then one day, he lost his temper, took his belt from around his waist and beat the hell out of her. She grabbed his legs and begged for mercy. "Don' beat mi Ram-Ram. Don' beat mi," she begged as she lay on the floor. But he kept on beating and kicking... then, he gave her one last kick and walked away, she lying on the cold floor sobbing her heart out.

The next day, there was belt marks and bruises all over her body – black and blue all over – but she didn't dare tell anyone, for fear of what he might do to her, if he found out.

With him not working and very little money coming in, he couldn't afford to pay for the Diaphragm sheet (the birth control method widely used in Trinidad at the time) and so, when baby Ranjit was four months old, Eve got pregnant again.

She began to despair...

With two babies to keep, a third one on the way, Ram-Ram not working and hardly any money left to feed and cloth them, she could see no way out. So one day, she lost her bearing and decided to kill herself. She drank a full bottle of kerosene, lay on the floor and hoped she would die.

But it was not to be.

Ram-Ram came home late that evening and found her rolling all over the floor, bawling out with stomach pain. He instantly knew something was amiss, but showed no mercy. Instead, he started bullying her.

"Wat you do? Wat you do? You fuc...n..." he shouted, bullying and bullying until she relented and admitted what she'd done. By then she was vomiting so profusely that he became scared.

He was sure she was going to die, so he panicked and started screaming. "Look wat you go do? You fuc...n fool. Drinkin' pichoil eh!"

Like a madman, he wailed, "Ah go get de police fo' you. Dey go loc you up! You f...in crazy girl...loc you up fo' de res of you life! Crazy! Crazy!" he went balmy.

Lying there, trembling like a dying chicken and scared out of her wits, she thought he was going to kill her. She knew that in Trinidad suicide was a criminal offence and if he did go to the police they would surely put her in jail. She was terrified.

Ram-Ram however, did not carry out his threats. Maybe he didn't want to be lumbered with two babies or maybe, he felt partly to blame... for some reason, he did not tell the police, nor anyone else for that matter. But he was furious. He wasn't going to let her off lightly.

She lay on the floor shivering; a thin flour bag sheet covering her sparsely clad body. She was so sick that it took several hours for her to recover he, never offering any sympathy at all. Instead, later than night, at 7pm sharp, he left her and went to the movies as usual.

Every Saturday night regular as clockwork, he used to cycle down to the cinema at California to watch the Indian movies, but never once did he ever take her. For as far as he was concerned, it was her duty as a Hindu wife to stay at home and look after the babies – not go to watch some God-forsaken movie.

He had great fun going to the movies, but as time went by, he began to return home later and later, sometimes getting back at 4 o'clock in the morning, Eve worrying her guts out, in case something had happened to him.

Knowing full well that the movies finished at 12 midnight, she couldn't understand. Then one night he returned home stinking of perfume and she suspected he was having an affair. So she hatched a plan to try and put a stop to it.

And so, the following Saturday night she locked the door – 'only for a few minutes,' she thought, 'jus' to teach him a lesson.' Then she lay in bed and waited for him.

She waited and waited till she heard the dogs barking, then she peeped through the window and saw him cycling back just a short distance from home. It was 4.30am.

She shot out of bed, bolted the door, put the light out and sat in the dark waiting. All she wanted to do was scare him a little; make him believe that she had left him and gone away. But she didn't know that he had seen the light on, previously. And she didn't bargain for what was to follow...

From the distance, he'd seen the lights on and knew she was at home. So when the lights went out, he suspected she was up to something. 'She, his Hindu wife, puttin' on a show; standin' her ground, showin' him up. Never! Her role was to be a obedient wife, meek and humble, do what she was tole at all time. And now...dis show?'

He went bananas!

"Open de fuc...in door, you arsehole!" he bellowed, banging at the door. But scared as she was, she was determined to hang on – at least for a while – teach him a lesson. But then...Bang! Bang! He started kicking the door down, she, standing inside trembling her guts out.

Terrified, she unbolted the door as quickly as her legs could carry her, he kicking and kicking, in a fit of madness. He just kept on going...

Like a raging bull, he marched straight up to her, punched her in the face and starting beating the life out of her. He punched and kicked, kicked and punched, till she fell to the floor, she pleading... begging for mercy.

"Please don' beat mi Ram-Ram, please..." she begged "Ah won' do it again, please..." but her cry fell on deaf ears. Boiling, he kicked and punched until she began to scream out in pain and gripping her pregnant abdomen, she screamed and screamed and screamed..."Oh God, a'm dyin'. Oh God, a'm dead!" she bawled, as she lay on the floor in agony.

She was just about to abort.

Realising what was happening and scared out of his wits, he called a taxi and they rushed her to Couva Hospital, as fast as they could. But within seconds of arriving there, she aborted – a barely formed baby girl, stone dead!

As she lay on the hospital bed in pain, she looked at her bruised body in despair – the pain of her suffering haunting her – not knowing what was going to happen to her; not knowing what the future held for her...not knowing what to do.

Chapter Twenty-Six

With no future of her own and nowhere to go after recovering from hospital, Eve had no choice but to return to her husband at Esperanza. There, she would try again, do her best to make a go of things.

Grabbing what little work he could find in the sugar cane fields and she struggling with the housework – caring for the two babies and the two goats as well – the little money which they saved to buy food and clothes was soon dwindling away. They could see no end to their life of poverty and misery; no light at the end of the tunnel. Then one day, by chance, Ram-Ram spotted an ad in the Guardian newspaper.

It read:

> 'Improve your prospects for work,
> Learn GCE O Levels (English, Maths, Geography, History) from the comfort of your home.
> The complete course for $10.
> Send for Prospectus now...'

In Trinidad, the authorities were always asking for O levels in their adverts for jobs. Ram-Ram's best friend Ramesh had five O levels and he'd got a job in England and was living there now. He was doing well for himself.

'If only ah could get some O level, den maybe ah could get a job in Englan' and live dere too,' Ram-Ram thought. It was a chance, a gamble – but he had to give it a shot.

When Eve heard about it, her mind began to work overtime...She knew that if he did go to England alone, he would abandon her and the children – leave them back here in Trinidad to a life of poverty and misery. For many a West Indian had deserted their families, once they'd settled in England. She wasn't going to take that chance. So she persuaded him to let her enrol for some courses too.

'She was academically briter,' she reminded him. "Togeder, dey could help each oder out and so stan' a better chance of passin' de exam, den, dey could go to Englan' togeder. An'..." she asserted, "it would be much cheaper too – only $15 for de two course!"

She knew if she pulled that off, he would not be able to desert them. They could leave the children behind and once they settled in England, they could send for them. She could get a good job too; maybe build a life of her own. But she wasn't going to expose her plans! Not now! She had too much to lose.

The once naïve little girl from Carli-Bay Road was growing up fast, getting smarter, learning the art of survival...the game of living.

That evening, they sent off for the prospectus and enrolled for five GCE O level subjects each. It was September 6 1958.

Every evening, after putting the children to bed, they studied until late at night, battling on under the burning kerosene lamp, its glass shade turning black as it smoked away.

Eve was doing well. Each time her corrected assignments came from England, she generally scored between 70 and 90, her favourite subjects being English, Geography and History. But Ram-Ram was doing badly. He struggled with his Maths and so decided to enrol for help – attend evening classes twice weekly at California Government school.

Twice a week he went and was learning much from his teacher Mr Praimchand. He was becoming less short-tempered too – he seemed to be a changed man – his mother, on the other hand, kept up the pressure.

"Bad girl. Bad! College girl? Ha! All dat book an' study stuff, ha! Is fo' de Negro only. Bad girl! Bad! Bad!" she cursed and swore, sometimes putting her finger over her nose, as if Eve smelt. For, according to Hindu customs, academic studying was not considered a good thing for Indian women to do – only Negro women did that and as such, were seen as bad people.

Being a dedicated teacher, a Christian and a Presbyterian, Mr Praimchand sometimes turned up at their home to help Ram-Ram with his studies. Smartly dressed in his starched white shirt and black trousers, he always looked so happy. They used to feed him with rice and darhl and lots of onions, because they knew he liked onions. Then, he would talk for hours about Christianity.

"True Christians," he maintained, "believe in a God dat is forgivin' and so, when husban's get angry, dey did not beat dere wife, but forgave dem." He would look at Ram-Ram then continue, "True Christians believe in a life after deat'. If you live a good life now, you would have a better life next time," he asserted, Eve listening in earnest.

The idea of Christianity appealed to her – it struck a chord in her heart. For, she'd noticed that…the Christians she knew, lived in nicer houses, had better jobs, ate proper food and seemed much happier.

Christian women were allowed more freedom. They would dress their hair in style, cut it short if they wished; wear fashionable clothes, even jeans if they wanted to; unlike the Hindu women who were so dowdily dressed, so serious and so sad.

As girls, Christian women were allowed to mix with boys, even kiss them if they wanted to, in contrast to the

Hindu girls whose lives were so suppressed, especially after puberty. The thought made her sad.

As a Hindu girl, she was battered in her childhood; crushed in her adolescence and now as a young woman, trampled on and stifled in a life of poverty and misery. She could see no hope.

As she thought of her situation, a mood of depression swept over her, like a wet blanket over the troubled waters of a raging sea, it, tumbling in her mind, as she thought and thought...

One day, she hoped she would become a Christian and who knows...?

She was nearly 19 now and becoming a Christian would help her get a job in England – start a new life out there – leave all this suffering and misery behind – but the shadows of the past were haunting her – the orthodox religious life of her father-in-law, played on her soul.

Ram-Ram's father was a Sadhoo, a very religious Hindu man, who lived by the code of its book. He had built an earth altar under his house and every morning before sunrise, he would chant and pray for hours and hours in front of this altar. Decorated with fresh flowers, he would sprinkle it with water from the brass (lotar) jug, chanting, tinkling his little brass bell, repeating the same procedure at sunset.

He used to scare the living daylight out of her and she knew very well that if they did become Christians, it would be seen as an act of betrayal. Ram-Ram's family would never forgive them – they would become outcasts – abandoned by the family for good.

Her confused mind was working overtime, for she also knew that 'as Hindus, there was no hope for her and the children in Trinidad. The very core of Hinduism had crushed her growth; destroyed her development; stifled her soul, her future and the prosperity of her whole being.'

She thought and thought and knew from the bottom of her heart that, 'not only for herself, but for the sake of her children too, she had to become a Christian.' But she wanted to learn more about Christianity, before committing herself.

A week later, she spoke to Mr Praimchand about her feelings and he promised to arrange for Mr Harry Gopual, the Presbyterian Minister from Couva to pay them a visit at their home.

Chapter Twenty-Seven

It was nearly 3 o'clock the following Sunday afternoon when the Reverend Harry Gopaul got off his bicycle and laid it on the grass to the front of Eve's home; the back of the house so overgrown with sugar canes – some growing so tall, lean and bending forwards, others leaning so far backwards that they seemed to bury Eve's shack in the middle.

Her two boys were playing at the front, the fading afternoon sun showering its fluorescent light on their shabbily clothed bodies, they scampering about, unaware of the situation.

Immaculately dressed in his well-pressed white shirt, the seams of his black trousers protruding in a straight line down the front of his well-developed legs, the Reverend stood there for a few minutes, staring at the boys, then...

"Hello! Good afternoon," he greeted, walking towards them. But bewildered by this stranger, the boys just stood there. As if stuck to the ground, they didn't move – nor uttered a single word.

Moving a step closer, "Hello!" The Reverend greeted again. "I am de Reverend Harry Gopaul and I have come to visit your parents," he assured, then it dawned on them who he was.

"Mummy! Mummy! Is de Reverent!" little Ranjit called, excitedly.

"Yes Mummy, is de Reverent. He come to see you!" Sam butted in.

They'd heard so much about this special Reverend who preached wonderful news about a God they called Jesus – a God who brought lovely presents for children on Christmas

Day and now, here he was, standing right here in front of them. Their young hearts were pumping away with excitement.

Little Ranjit led the Reverend Gopaul to Eve, who by now, was standing at the doorway, watching. Ram-Ram was busy digging cassava in the back garden. But when he heard the commotion, he dropped the fork and rushed to the front, wiping the sweat from his forehead onto his dirty sleeve, as he made his way towards them.

"Good day! Mr Ram-Ram," the Reverend greeted, stretching out his hand to shake Ram-Ram's then, turning abruptly to Eve, "Good afternoon Mrs Ram-Ram and how are you today?" he enquired, a hint of humility in his voice.

"Wel' sir, wel'!" she answered, staring in shocked amazement at this handsome young man wearing a dog collar, barely a year or so older than her husband, yet so refined, so mature.

"Come inside an' sit down sir," she invited, shaking a little as she offered him a hard wooden chair. "Would you like a cole drink sir?"

"Sure Mrs Ram-Ram! Sure! Been a long hot ride up here you kno', a long hot journey and …" he smiled, "please call me Reverend Harry. Sir is so stiff, don' you tink?"

Eve nodded and went into the kitchen.

She returned quickly with a glass and a tin of Coke, which was stored in a wooden box in the kitchen. But, instead of drinking form the glass, he wiped the top of the can with one swipe and started drinking straight from it.

"Wel'… did you fine de house ok?" Ram-Ram enquired.

"Not too hard. Not too hard," he assured. "Apart from a few dogs barkin' at me heel an' de sun burnin' me scalp, de ride down here was quite revealin'… Mr Praimchand describe de house well."

He took a few more gulps of Coke and looking around him, he was shocked – shocked at the poverty in which he'd found Eve and her family living. He stared in silence for a few seconds, but then the boys homed in on him.

He bent over, "An' you are master Ranjit?" he enquired.

"Ah like trane engine," little Ranjit said.

"You do? An' why do you like train engine?"

"'Cause dey go traah… taah… taah… like dis," making the noise of an engine with his mouth.

But then Sam couldn't stand the attention Ranjit was getting, so he butted in. "Ah like moto-car," he went.

"You do and why?"

"…'cause dey race down de road like Zoom! An' dey take you anyway…an dey make you win big, big prize! Like dis…" he went, making the sign of a cup with his hands.

As Reverend Harry played with the children, he was shocked to the core of his soul, thinking…thinking of the abject poverty in which he'd found this family – they trying so desperately to survive. The children were dressed in rags; they had no toys to play with and were clearly malnourished. He could see that.

He sat there, shell-shocked

He'd heard a lot about this sugar cane farming estate in Esperanza; how most of the people there lived in mud huts with no running water and no indoor toilets. They used to have to walk a few hundred yards to the back of their homes to defecate or urinate in a hole dug in the ground, with make shift covers carefully disguising them. Now, he'd come face to face with it and it hit him like a bolt of lightning.

He couldn't go away without doing something – he knew that. But he'd only just set up his church in Couva and it was bare of funds. He would pray – pray with the family and hope that God would answer their prayer – that maybe, when they became Christians, his congregation might make a collection or do something to help this family out of their wretched plight. His mind was working overtime…

So he said to the children, "Wel' now, wel'! How about me tellin' you a story?"

"A story. Oh yes. We wan' to hear dat story," the boys replied together, as if in tune with one another.

An articulate man, a charismatic preacher, the Reverend Harry began... the children not making a single sound, Ram-Ram sitting on a chair next to him, Eve plonked on the floor as they listened.

He told them a story from the New Testament about a God they called Jesus Christ. 'How dis God perform a miracle – feed thousands of people from one loaf of bread; how he walk for miles and miles, thousands followin', as he preach about love, compassion and forgiveness towards people – no matter dere race, colour or creed; no matter where dey came from.'

As the Reverend preached, his words held Eve and her family spellbound. They listened in earnest to what he was saying – not a stir from them – then, when he had finished he led them on with the Lord's Prayer, they repeating after him...'Our farder who are in heaven... give us dis day our daily bread... for dine is de kingdom, de power an' de glory. Amen!'

The prayer meeting lasted nearly two hours and they were so moved by the honesty, the compassion with which he told the story, that it touched their very souls. For a few minutes, they went quiet – even the boys did not stir, then the priest broke the silence. "It was time to go," he said, but promised to return the following Sunday for more prayers.

As he waved goodbye that day, a surge of pity ran through this godly man. 'He could not abandon this family – not now, not ever!' he thought to himself.

Ram-Ram thought a lot that day... of Christianity and what it meant to him. But, as far as Eve was concerned, she had long since made up her mind, that one day, she would become a Christian.

And true to his word, the Reverend Harry Gopaul returned that Sunday and every Sunday thereafter, saying prayers and reading from his Bible. Then, after a few weeks of prayers, Ram-Ram decided to attend Couva Presbyterian Church, Eve and the children unable to attend these services because they did not have decent clothes to wear.

They had learnt a lot about Christianity and what they heard they liked and so, after a few months, they decided to get baptised, become Christians. As far as clothes were concerned, Auntie Nell would provide the white outfits for Eve and the children, thereby settling matters.

That morning they were up bright and early. Anxiously, they got dressed in their clean white outfits. Ram-Ram wearing the brown tie which Mr Praimchand had loaned him and they looked smart.

Wading through the crazy traffic, by 9am they reached Couva Presbyterian Church where preparations were already in motion. And so by 10am Eve, her husband and their two sons were about to be baptized.

Auntie Nell was as excited as they were, so she positioned herself firmly in the front row to watch the action.

There were a lot of pre-ceremonial speeches, then it went HUSH. Then she saw the Reverend Harry making the sign of the cross on each of their foreheads and then, she heard him chanting... 'In de name of de farder and of de son and of de holy spirit I, Harry Gopaul now baptise dee,' then, she heard him end with the words, 'God bless you all.'

He gave Ram-Ram a present – a Bible of the New Testament and wished them luck.

It was Sunday April 10 1960 – a day which Eve would never forget; a day which would change their lives forever...

As the ceremony ended she felt as if a great big shadow was enveloping her whole body. She was sure she heard a voice saying, 'And I will protect you, comfort and guide you and take care of you...'

She shook a little then a warm glow seemed to spread over her whole being and she felt good. It was as though she was now removed from the dark dungeon in which she'd lived for so long. Now at long last she'd become a Christian...

She felt happy. She felt elated!

But Ram-Ram's parents had plans of their own.

Angry at their son's betrayal of their Hindu religion, they showed their disgust by staying away from him. Now they would abandon him and his family from their lives for good – now they would become outcasts.

It was she, Eve, who had desecrated their Hindu religion – they were sure of that. And so now Ram-Ram's mother was bent on seeking revenge...

Chapter Twenty-Eight

Ram-Ram seemed to be a changed man. The Christian experience appears to have done that. For one thing, he was listening a little more and he wasn't beating Eve quite so much. But as far as his mother was concerned, she continued to persecute Eve.

"You fuc...in Creole. You bitch! You make mi son tur'n he bac on mi God. Bhagwan go fix you. Go burn you alive! You Negro!" she cursed, each time she saw her.

The Hindu women also, didn't like Eve's lifestyle and so they too had their say. "Only Creole woman do all dat studyin' O level stuff," they gossiped. "Hindu wife mus' cook, clean, look afer she chilren, not do all dem bookwork an' goin' after some God-damn Cristan church. Creole stuff! Creole stuff!" they taunted, whenever they saw her passing by.

Eve used to get so upset when she heard their nasty gossip, but she was defenceless to do anything about it. She had become a Christian, but still her troubles did not go away, it seemed. Now, she did not know where to turn.

They were lapsing with their studies too – in spite of Ramesh's encouragement from England. What, with the housework, the children and the two goats to look after, Eve could not complete her assignments in time and so, she knew that she would never be able to take her exams the following year and therefore not make any progress in her life.

She began to despair.

They were nearing the end of their tether, when they remembered Mr Jaggernath. He was Eve's uncle who always maintained that he would help any relatives in trouble. 'Dey would go to him for help to get de piece of lan' in California to build dere new house,' they thought.

A Head Bookkeeper at the sugar plantation in Esperanza, Mr Jaggernath wielded a lot of influence. And now that the plantation owners were selling land in California to their workers at $1,000 a plot, Eve decided to seek his help. 'If only dey could get a piece of lan' dere, dey could build dere house on it wit de $3,000 dey had save. Den bein' near de main road, dey would be in a much better position for Ram-Ram to fine work and dey would be wel' away from de cursin' of his demented moder,' Eve thought.

But when Ram-Ram went to see him, Mr Jaggernath refused to help. "De lan'? Oh dat! My boy! All gone me boy! All gone!" he asserted firmly, then…"an' tell Eve, Uncle Jag been askin' after she an' de chilren, eh, me boy!" he concluded, swiftly showing Ram-Ram the door.

"Finish…! We all finish…!" Ram-Ram sobbed when he returned home that day, the distressed Eve standing there powerless, a feeling of hopelessness enveloping her whole body, as she listened.

She shook with fear.

Once again, she was refused help; robbed of a piece of land, this time by her own uncle. She was devastated.

Drowning in her sorrows, shortly after that episode an unexpected visitor turned up. It was Mah. Mah hardly ever gave Eve presents, but this time she brought some fruit, "Bananas and oranges for the chilren," she insisted.

She was always nagging about how Eve and the children were shabbily dressed but she never bought them any clothes. "Smarten youself up girl! Smarten youself! Oh you husban' go leave you for anoder woman you kno'," she warned Eve.

As far as she was concerned, the poverty stricken Eve was an embarrassment to her and so she limited her visits. On the few occasions however when she did visit, she always made a swift departure, complaining that the journey there was too long and too tiring.

Abandoned by her rich relatives, Eve tried her hardest to survive. But the more she tried, the more she failed. Or so it seemed.

She just couldn't see a way out. Then, she remembered the letter which Ramesh had written from England. In it, he'd said that many girls from Trinidad were going to England to train and work as nurses. 'De English hospitals were cryin' out for dese girls to mann dem,' he wrote. 'But you mus' hurry. Write to de British Consulate in Trinidad and get dese hospital address girl, because de immigration law is about to change and dey are recuitin' fast.'

This news offered her a glimmer of hope so she wasted no time. Speedily, she sent off a letter of enquiry to the Consulate's office and within a few days, she received 50 hospital addresses.

Mustering as much speed as she could, she posted applications to 30 hospitals in England – from London to the north-east, then she went and saw her headmaster to seek a reference.

'Eve is kind, honest, reliable and trustworthy,'

he wrote.

'She has struggled hard against abject poverty, embarking on further education to try and improve her life and I am convinced that she will work hard to achieve whatever goals she set her mind to. I recommend her.'

'What a reference!' she thought, as she read it out to Ram-Ram. 'So kind. So compassionate, a man.' She was sure in her heart that if any, this reference would get her somewhere. But just in case, she and Ram-Ram registered to take five GCE O level exams, come the following year. So determined she was, to better herself, she had to pull out every stop.

The next job was to get their passports organised, so Ram-Ram got cracking with the task.

Every week, he spent all day down at the Red House at Port of Spain, pushing and shoving through the throng of people, all seeking passports; rushing in their hundreds to get it fixed, before that deadline – before the immigration laws in England changed.

They were desperate people.

Down at Red House in Port of Spain, they filled out the forms which would then be sent off to some named official – a headmaster or chief-of-police – to be signed and returned. Then an official from the Red House would check and check…every minute detail, before giving it the all clear.

Daily the people waited outside, pushing and shoving, some jumping the haphazard queues, sometimes cursing, sometimes swearing, in order to get to the official first. So chaotic it was. It was like a mad house!

With such a disorganised system of administration, it was not surprising that it took months and months to get a passport ready, so Ram-Ram did his utmost to get things moving early.

Meanwhile, the replies from England were coming in hard and fast. 'Dear Miss R…' each read. 'We regret to inform you that you have not been successful in your application for the post of student nurse…Unfortunately, you have not met the educational requirements for entry…'

Heartbroken, Eve disposed of the rejects one by one – all 29 of them. She could see no light at the end of the tunnel. Her world was collapsing around her…

But, one person never gave up on his friends.

Back in England Ramesh kept on writing, urging, encouraging, reminding them that…'de Immigration Laws was about to change next year. So, if dey want to get to Englan', dey better hurry.' He'd found a job for Ram-Ram at a shoe factory in Northampton. 'He will sen' him de letter from de employer offering him de job. He would also sen' him a letter from his bank, stating that he would put up de $1,000 security and a letter offerin' him accommodation too' – such a loyal friend, he was.

On hearing the news, Ram-Ram was ready to grab at the chance and go, but Eve had other plans. She knew that if he did go to England alone, he would abandon her and the children back here in Trinidad – to a life of poverty and misery – for the rest of their lives. So she used every trick in the book to try and persuade him to change his mind.

She'd heard about a politician in Port of Spain – Mr Gossh, the Minister for Overseas in Trinidad – how he'd helped many Trinidadians get to England. She would go and see him.

She had to give it a try.

"Wat if you don' get de job in Englan' Ram-Ram, an' you carn' fine a place to live? Wat go happen to you den? Carn' you see? If we go an' see Mr Gossh," she appealed, "he go help mi get a job in de 'ospitol, den we go go to Englan' togeder. Den, if we 'ave trouble, we go help each oder out. Carn' you see dat?"

Eve was learning the game of chess; the art of survival and her plea hit a core in his bone.

He didn't want to go and leave his children behind, but he couldn't stay in this hellhole either. 'Eve was rite,' he thought. 'If she did go to Englan' wit him – as much as he didn' want her around – at lease she could help him out, should dey encounter any trouble.' He never liked being alone, so he decided that they would go to Port of Spain and seek Mr Gossh's help.

Poor Eve. She thought she was learning the game. But what she didn't understand was the name of the game – the intricacies of High Politics. She really didn't understand what she might encounter when she met Mr Gossh.

She just wasn't equipped.

She and Ram-Ram certainly could not read the mind of a corrupt politician. They were too simple. All they knew was that they had to go and see the 'Big Man' – give it their best shot.

They simply did not understand...

Chapter Twenty-Nine

It was nearly 12 noon when they arrived at Mr Gossh's office and what a day it was; the sun beating down on the rickety jerky bus, the passengers fanning themselves frantically to try and keep cool. It was March 2 1961 and as it transpired, it was a day Eve was unlikely to forget.

Outside Mr Gossh's office, throngs of people waited anxiously to see him; some arriving as early as 7am armed with packed food and bottles of drinking water; some sitting on benches; others standing, cursing and swearing as the hot sun blazed down on their lightly clothed bodies. The Indian women were clutching their rotis; the Negroes, their bread in baskets; all waiting, hoping and praying that Mr Gossh would be their saviour – help them to get to the only place they wanted to go – and that was England.

They waited and waited... and by the time Eve and Ram-Ram were summoned to see him, it was nearly 3pm.

He got up from his chair reluctantly, held out his right hand and shook each of theirs in turn, then sat back again, abruptly. He barely looked at Eve.

"Wel' is Mr Ram-Ram, ah see," he said, glancing at the letter which they'd sent him, now lying purposely placed under his nose. "Sit down. Sit! Sit!" he commanded, pointing at the two chairs strategically placed directly in front of him.

He hardly gave them time to sit, when... "an' now Mr Ram-Ram, what can I do for you?" he growled, not taking a slight bit of notice of the jittery state they were in.

He already knew why they were there – it was all in the letter – but he was playing the game and playing it well, just to make sure that they understood that he was in command.

"Wel' you see Mr Gossh, Si-i-r," Ram-Ram stuttered, "Mi wife Eve, she apply to many of dem hospital in Englan'," he was sweating... "to get de job to study nursin' S-i-r, but she carn' get in."

"So? Mr Ram-Ram... So?"

"So, we come to see if you go help we sir...We hear you help plenty of people." Ram-Ram swallowed, nervously.

"Help plenty of people eh! To study nursin' eh!" He looked at Ram-Ram hard, an angry look on his cold stern face, then barked, "You know wat dis nursin' job is? Hard work, mi boy! Dog work! Dog!" His angry eyes trailed to Eve then quickly back to Ram-Ram again.

"You wan' you wife to look after dem English lunatics boy? Dose mad-hat people in de mental hospital? Scrubbin' bedpan, cleanin' shit! An' dey wan' five GCE O level to rake dat shit! Is dat wat you wan' boy? No boy! No...You wouldn' wan' you dog to clean dem luny shit!"

He stared at Eve hard, then delivered the final blow. "Mark my word, boy. Mark my word! If you an' Eve ever get to Englan', you woud be back on de first ship boun' back here. Take my advice Son! Take my advice...Forget all dat hog-wash stuff. Be a good man Son an' take you wife back home where she belong." And with that he stood up briskly, like a piece of stiff wood and showed them the door.

They crawled out of his office like two dead ducks – defeated; only in their case, they didn't have the power to fight back.

Unable to believe what she just heard, Eve felt powerless to launch an attack. She just didn't have the muscle to defend herself. She was too poor and weak to contemplate it.

He knew from their letter that they were as poor as beggars, almost starving, yet he showed them no mercy, no pity; treated them with such disdain.

What a contrast to the kindly headmaster who gave her such a wonderful testimonial; wrote nice things about her; treated her with such respect. She couldn't understand...that 'whereas, he was a teacher and a Christian, Mr Gossh was a Hindu and a politician' – therein lies the difference.

Even though she was 20 now, her simple mind failed to grasp the workings of a high-brow corrupt politician; a man who sought power for his own ends; a man who would do nothing to risk his own position. She simply didn't understand...All she knew was that her world was caving in on her and she didn't know where to run.

As they headed back home that day, a feeling of despair overcame her. She was choked!

She sat quietly thinking... then suddenly it dawned on her...'Mother Mary! The Irish Catholic nun who ran St Luke Convent! She will help.' She didn't give her the job scrubbing floors, but she'd promised to help her, if she needed help. 'Come back and see me if you need help,' she'd assured her. 'She will go and see her.'

'Such a kindly face she had; such a godly woman. Jus tink,' she was thinking... 'If ah coud get a reference from dat convent, it go carry so much weight. It go boun' to help mi get into one of dem English hospital. Dats it! Nex' week ah go go an' see Moder Mary...' She felt sure Mother Mary would help.

There was no time to waste. So the following Tuesday, she got on a bus and went to see Mother Mary at St Luke Convent in Couva.

Mother Mary greeted her warmly. She was happy to see her. But when Eve told her that she was applying to the hospital in England to study nursing and asked if she would give her a reference, Mother Mary swiftly made the 'sign of the cross' and enquired about the children.

"And your children Eve? I hear you have two now. Are you taking them with you?"

"No Moder," Eve replied, naïve as she was. "Ah go leve dem wit mi Mah and Pah an' when ah go qualify ah go sen' for dem."

Poor Eve!...

Mother Mary's face dropped instantly; then she put on a smile – an angelic one, a curious one. Curious but disappointed: disappointed but angelic.

Hastily, she pulled out a pen from her side pocket and scribbled a note, folded it, sealed it in an envelope and handed it to Eve. Then as quick as a flash, she made the 'sign of the cross', whispered, "God bless you my child," and politely showed Eve the door.

Glad to get that envelope and anxious to open it – the naïve Eve just wanted to have a peep. Naïve as she was, she felt sure it was good news. And so, as soon as she returned home, she opened the envelope.

It read:

'TO WHOM IT MAY CONCERN.
Mrs Ram-Ram has been a visitor here. She once applied for a job as a cleaning lady, but was unsuccessful. I believe she is now applying for a post as a student nurse in England, leaving her two children behind with her parents. May God go with her.'

Eve nearly fell off the hard chair on which she was sitting. 'How could she, Mother Mary, such a godly person, always looking so serene in her black robe and white hood; such a holy person, be so unkind, write such uncaring words about mi? Not a word about mi character, ability, kindness, nothing! Nothing!'

Eve was devastated. In her naivety, she failed to realise that although Mother Mary was a Christian, she was a Catholic nun: a priestly woman who held strong views about procreation and the role of a mother in society. 'A mother's role,' the Catholic priests believe, 'is to look after her siblings – that was the will of God; not abandoning them for some self-gratifying goal.'

Even though Eve was as poor as a beggar and never had sufficient food to feed her children, that did not matter to this priestly woman – her role was to follow the teachings of God and Catholicism. And so in that respect, there was no difference between what were Catholic values and that of Hindu teachings.

Sitting there with the letter in her hand, Eve felt betrayed... broken... 'Three people in whom she'd placed her trust in, betrayed her. Even dis God-fearing woman give her a testimonial dat was not fit to throw in de bin?' She was shattered! She felt she had nothing to live for – but she knew she couldn't give up – she had to keep going, if only for the sake of her two children.

So, she kept on sending the applications and praying. 'Maybe one day, luck would strike,' she hoped... She was hoping for a miracle!

Every week when Ram-Ram came home with the letters in his pockets, she would rush to the door with excitement. But all she ever got was 'Rejections'.

Losing her grip on life, she was just about to give up all hope of ever going to England; of ever getting her O levels; of ever getting out of the misery in which she'd lived, when, surprise, surprise... one day, as if by miracle... a letter came.

It read:

'Dear Mrs R... I am delighted to offer you the post of Student Nurse at Springvale Hospital...'

Shocked to her bones, she couldn't believe what she had just read. She went numb. She fell to her knees and prayed... surprised... delighted... elated... happy...
She was praying...

Just when she was about to give up all hope, God had answered her prayer, it seemed.

She couldn't believe it.

She read the lines over and over again, her heart pounding, thumping, beating ten to the dozen, her eyes wet with tears. The letter went on to say 'that she must get vaccinated against smallpox, tuberculosis, poliomyelitis and she must bring these plus her Birth, Marriage and Baptismal certificates with her. She would be able to start her Nurses Training,' it confirmed, on May 30 1962.

Overcome with emotions, she couldn't remember what date it was. All she knew was, that it was a Thursday; it was December 1961 and she was 21 years old.

Over and over she read the letter, a lump forming in her throat, she, trembling, sweating, unable to comprehend that finally, at long last, her luck was changing. 'She wasn't sure she would ever be able to take de exams; she didn't have any GCE O levels, yet dey had accepted her at Springvale Hospital? God had answered her prayer – it was a miracle!'

She'd heard of London and Birmingham and Liverpool but never Castleton. It was a small place really, hidden up there in the north. They couldn't recruit local nurses to man their expanding hospitals, so they'd sent off publicity brochures to the Commonwealth countries – places such as Ireland and the West Indies to try and recruit English speaking nurses.

It was by chance really, that she'd applied to Castleton. She'd sent off the remarkable references which the Reverend Gopaul and her headmaster had given her. In it, they had said wonderful things: 'about her character; about how she was studying hard, had reached the O level standard and was waiting to take her exams; about how she'd struggled against poverty to try and better herself and her family. They felt sure she would achieve anything she'd set her mind to.' Such inspiring words they had written.

She was overcome.

She'd sent off the application like all the others and waited. She prayed, but never believed that God would answer her prayer, but still, she kept on trying and praying.

Every night, she would get down on her knees and pray… beg God to help her out of the mess she was in. And now, out of the blue it seemed God had answered her prayer?

Now, here she was on bended knees clutching the letter firmly in her hand – so overwhelmed she was, that all of a sudden she burst into tears and started crying her heart out.

'At last! At last! She had got into a hospital in England!'

She only had five months left in which to make the necessary preparations. The passports were already in motion, but there was something else she had to do…

She must hurry – there was not much time left… She must visit her parents urgently – tomorrow if she can; try and persuade them to look after her two children, whilst she was away in England, training to be a nurse.

She hoped they would agree…

Chapter Thirty

The following Sunday evening, Eve went to see Mah and Pah and read the letter out to them.

Mah never believed that Eve would ever get into a hospital in England and now that she was confronted with the truth she went pale. As for Pah, well, he simply went cold, stone cold; blown! They certainly did not want to look after Eve's two children whilst she was so far away in England, so they put on a front – cold, icy, frosty. But that did not deter Eve. Determined as ever, she mustered every trick in the book to try and get them to agree.

It was the only chance she had and she wasn't going to give it up. So she quietly resorted to blackmail – almost! For as far as she was concerned, nothing was going to stop her now.

She told them that if they refused to look after her two boys, she would leave them with a friend in Upper Couva and go to England anyway.

And Pah went numb!

The words rang in his ears like a fireball. It struck him where he least wanted to be struck. It hurt his Hindu pride as sure as a ball had hit him in the tenderest part of his groin.

He couldn't allow his grandchildren to be looked after by strangers. What! Never! The local Hindus will sure as hell turn their backs on him, scorn him; squeeze him out. So reluctantly, he agreed to look after the boys, Eve promising faithfully to send them money for the boys' keep.

She was growing up, slowly but surely. She didn't realise it, but she was learning the art of survival – 'tactical persuasion' – the name of the game; a game which she herself didn't even recognise.

She only had a few months left in which to make the necessary preparations. Not much time really. So, the following Monday, she and Ram-Ram were up early, ready to make the journey to Sanfernando to buy some new clothes.

The journey there was hot: the passengers sweating like mad on the bus; their anxious bodies clinging to their hot seats; the rains which tended to fall in January did not materialise.

On it ploughed – the rickety old bus, struggling up the steep hills, screeching on its big wheels each time it stopped to pick up some passenger or the other. On it trundled, struggling for breath, so that by the time it reached the terminus at Sanfernando, it was almost on its last legs. And Sanfernando was crowded with shoppers; the place was buzzing with action.

They got off and made their way down Coffee Street, the town awash with shoppers, some pushing and shoving through the thrusting crowd, each trying to get into the shops first, to pick up the best bargains.

They scrambled their way through the narrow hilly streets and headed straight for the big stores, the red/white striped canvas canopies overhanging, almost touching the streets; street vendors sitting underneath these, trying desperately to flog their wares.

A couple of Negro ladies sat on wooden benches selling roast corn (roasted on a coal-pot right there on the spot). Two Indian ladies sat discreetly in corners, meticulously dressed in pink and white saris, their borders shimmering gold; each wearing heavy gold necklaces and large earrings; earrings which hung neatly from their ears, gold studs shimmering on their noses.

There they sat in discreet corners, selling beautifully designed Indian jewellery, shimmering gold, eye-catching diamonds and ruby-stoned jewellery, stunningly displayed in glass cabinets. There were others selling homemade rotis and curried channa; shrimp and darhl pouri too, at 50 cents each; the odd vendor flogging anything from scrubbing brushes to spoons, in order to try and scrape a living.

And of course – the ice cream man. He kept shouting, "Come and get you ice cream! Come an' get you ice cream! 30 cent a come! Freshly make from a pale rite under you nose."

All the popular flavours were on offer – from coconut to soursup. Mouth watering they were, as he scooped them up in piles, each on a nice large crispy cone.

They went like hot cakes!

In and out of shops Eve and Ram-Ram belted, trying their hardest to barter – to pick up the best bargains – pushing their way here; thrusting forward there; Ram-Ram's shirt clinging to his sweaty body, like fungus on a damp day.

Eve spotted a piece of pink floral slipper satin material – an odd piece really but cheaply priced – enough to make a 'going away outfit' so she bought it. Then she bought a piece of white satin for her petticoat; some other pieces of cast off materials; two ready-made cotton panties, a brown pull string handbag and a pair of brown high heeled shoes; all for $100. She felt good.

Ram-Ram was busy too, scooping up the bargains for his 'going away outfit' and other necessities and he felt relieved when it was all over.

When they had finished, they treated themselves to some ice cream and toulum (coconut cakes made with molasses) and found that in all, they'd spent $300. They had picked up some excellent bargains and Eve was over the moon. All she had to do now was get her outfits made. And so a few days later, she visited Auntie Phyllis to get that arranged.

Auntie Phyllis was a seamstress in Upper Couva who'd promised to make Eve's outfit, free of charge. She was delighted to see Eve and when she saw the materials, she decided to make a dress with a 'keyhole' neck and one with a 'sweetheart' neck with the cast off materials.

A 'two piece suit' will be made with the pink floral slipper satin as her 'going away outfit' and Eve was delighted with the news.

After greeting Eve, Auntie Phyllis took the measurements – with precision. Then she fed Eve with nice hot darhl and rice and fried salmon, which she had prepared before hand and offered her some nice cold lime punch to wash it all down. Eve thoroughly enjoyed it.

But as she sat at the large well-polished table eating her meal, she was overcome by the luxury in which Auntie Phyllis lived. She never thought such a lifestyle ever existed and now she was seeing it with her own eyes. She was dumb struck!

She ate her meal quickly, then had a long chat with Auntie Phyllis about England and the possibilities out there. They talked and talked for a while and before they realised it, it was time for her to return home to the mud hut and squalid poverty which almost drowned her. Only this time she didn't mind going back there – because this time she had something far more constructive to pit herself against.

She was going to England to start a new life and there was no time to wallow in pity. She must hurry; get her visa organised.

Chapter Thirty-One

Springvale Hospital had sent her all the relevant details and now that she was accepted in a nursing school, the British Consulate is more likely to give her a visa without much hassle, she hoped. So, the following Wednesday, she and Ram-Ram were up bright and early. Armed with their passports and other documents, they boarded a bus and made for the British Consulate's office at Port of Spain.

It was wet that day – February 5 1962, and although it was the end of the rainy season, the rains came pelting down. It was as though the heavens in all its glory, decided to drain its last drop of water down upon them. But they soldiered on.

Having arrived early, Eve decided to sit on a long wooden bench under a makeshift shelter outside the Consulate's office; the rain dripping like snakes along its windowpanes, the little Negro receptionist busy typing away. 'Click! Click! Click! Click!' she went, her fingers racing away at great speed.

Every now and then, a smartly dressed woman (the Consulate's Assistant) kept calling out a name. And in they rushed; hundreds of them stalking the place; some sitting, others standing, umbrellas over their heads; all waiting, waiting anxiously to get their visas – break the deadline – get to England before the new Immigration Laws came into force.

Daily, they turned up (no appointments necessary) giving their details at the desk and waiting... waiting. Sometimes they waited for hours, drenched under the frequent downpours, only to be told they had to return another day. But still they kept on coming.

Eve too waited and as the afternoon wore on, she began to panic, fearing that she also may have to return another day. But then, suddenly, someone from the office called their names. It was exactly 4pm.

As they made their way into the Consulate's Office, fear gripped her soul and she began to panic.

'Wat if he don' give mi de visa? Wat will happen to mi den?' she thought, her heart heaving, her body trembling, then…'silly to tink like dis…?'

She dismissed the thought and strode forward, her heart in her hand, trying her best to put on a brave face.

She faced the Consulate, nervous as a weather beaten dog.

A short fat man in his fifties or so, Mr Wittington had a chubby red face. He didn't shake her hand, just smiled quietly at her.

He looked at her steadfastly from above the rim of his spectacles which hung precariously on the tip of his nose, his bald head shining under the lamp, a few grey hairs sticking out at the sides of his temple – it showed his age. He glanced at Ram-Ram, his eyes moving quickly back to her.

"Sit! Please. Sit!" he commanded, ushering her and Ram-Ram to their seats. He looked at the papers on his desk then peered at Eve again.

"Springvale Hospital I see? And the vaccination, inoculation certificates, all here I see? Tuberculosis, smallpox, polio…all here I see. And where did you have these done Mrs Ram-Ram?" He was searching – searching Eve's eyes for clues – very much aware that the papers under his nose could well have been produced by deception. Bribery was rife in Trinidad and in desperation, many a folk had turned to bribery for a chance to escape to England. And so, Mr Wittington wasted no time, but set about probing.

Shaking like a leaf, Eve put on a brave face and answered, "At Dr Dil in Couva, sir."

"Oh yes. Yes, yes it's all here," he asserted, pulling himself short, yet taking command of the interview. "And the two children, Mrs Ram-Ram? Who will take care of them?" he continued, a look of concern on his face.

"Mi parence sir. Ah go sen' money from mi nursin' job to pay for dem food and clodes, sir."

"I see, I see," he replied, screwing his face up as if he'd just heard some bad news. "I see. I see." He affirmed, more or less to himself, shaking his head, thinking...

He didn't utter a further word. He simply looked at Eve from above the rim of his glasses and 'Bang!' he stamped the visa.

Mr Wittington was a kindly man, who having lived in Trinidad for many a year, knew all too well, the meaning of poverty – the misery in which Eve, her husband and her children existed. He'd seen it all with his bare and naked eyes. And now it was right here, right under his nose, staring him in the face –'evidence' revealed in the papers sitting in front of him; revealed in the kindly testimonials, staring at him from his desk.

He didn't have to dig any deeper.

He knew that as a nurse, Eve would have a secure job, earn a regular salary; enough to send home to Trinidad for her children's keep. And he had no doubts that she was sincere in her undertakings, for when he'd read the reference from the Reverend Gopaul, his heart sank.

He knew he had to help her. He saw no reason for delaying her suffering anymore and so he stamped her visas without further ado.

He looked at Ram-Ram enquiringly and asked similar questions. He checked the evidence of the security which his friend had provided from England; where he was going to live; his employer; how long he intended to stay.

On and on, he probed... the answers right there in the papers in front of him, but still he kept checking; probing, questioning, scribbling here, scribbling there... over and over, he went, digging. He had to make sure that immigrants leaving under his jurisdiction were legal and above board.

He looked at Ram-Ram seriously, then 'Bang!' he stamped his visa too.

'After years of suffering and now...?' They couldn't believe their luck.

They had barely three months left before they could depart for England. Now, all they had to do was book their travel tickets and soon they will be on that boat to start a new life, in a land they called, 'Mother England'.

Eve didn't know whether she should jump or dance! Sing or cry! All she could do was bury her head in her hands and cry for joy.

'How their luck was changing?'

Chapter Thirty-Two

They were supposed to book their tickets three months in advance, but now they only had a short while in which to do so – they must hurry! So that very evening Eve got all the papers together, ready for Ram-Ram to take with him to the Travel Agent at Port of Spain, early the following Monday morning.

That Saturday afternoon, Ram-Ram went as usual down to the sugar plantation's office in Esperanza to collect his wages. Happy as a lark, he was cycling back home at great speed, thinking 'how his luck was changing' when suddenly... B-A-N-G! A big truck ran straight into him. He didn't stand a chance! His skull crushed to pieces, blood gushing all over the place, his bicycle spread across the road in splinters. He died instantly.

When his mother heard the news, she howled and howled like a demented creature. Maybe she had a guilty conscience at the way she'd treated both he and Eve, or maybe she just couldn't get over the shock. Who knows? But she just went berserk!

She wasn't happy about them goin' to Englan', 'but at least she would be able to see dem when dey return to Trinidad on holiday' she thought. 'And now he was dead! Stone dead! Gone! His life rung out of him in such a bad way?'

Her heart pained at the thought of never being able to see him again and her body just crumbled to pieces.

Tortured as if put on the rack, she screamed and screamed, so much, that no one was able to console her. She just went to pieces.

She was not the only one grieving her heart out though, for broken on the inside, Eve too was in pain, grieving, shocked. She went numb! Stoned! Almost dead!

She was crying, not loud, but deep down from within her belly, but somehow, the tears just wouldn't flow.

Only moments ago her luck was turning. Since she'd become a Christian so many good things were happening to her. God made them possible, it seemed. And now? Her husband, dead! She just couldn't take it.

She stood at the scene of the crash shocked, pained, trembling like a half-dead butterfly, unable to comprehend what was happening to her, unable to pull herself together. Now she must bury him and she just couldn't take that.

She simply lost her bearings.

It was decided that it would be a quick funeral and during the ceremony Ram-Ram's mother howled like a wild animal; Eve and the children remaining in a permanent state of shock. She was beside herself – unable to comprehend what was happening to her, the pain in her heart almost unbearable.

But she had her two boys to think of. She had to muster her strength: try and pull herself together, if only for their sake. Her mind was in turmoil...

That night, the tears finally came. It rained down her cheeks like an over-flowing fountain as she cried and cried...her thoughts wheeling...leaping in bounds...as she thought and thought...until eventually, she fell asleep.

The next morning she woke up determined to continue with her life. It was as if she went through some kind of metamorphosis – a transformation – bringing her the answers she so sorely sought.

Now, she was ready to give it a go...

'She was offered de chance to go to Englan' to start a new life; remove herself from de dungeon of misery and cripplin' poverty in which she almost drowned. When she finish her nursin' trainin', she would take her two boys back to Englan' with her, never to return to Trinidad again – she knew that. She mus' take that chance now. Go to Englan' on her own, come what may.

'She must book that ticket now.'

The following Monday morning, February 24 1962, she got up bright and early and boarded a bus to take her to the bank at Couva. Their savings were in joint names and so all the money was now hers by law, so she drew $2000 from Barclays Bank out of which she would buy her ticket.

She had to pay the full fare in advance and return for the ticket two weeks before departure – no questions asked – for that was how they did things in Trinidad.

And so, armed with the money, her passport, the necessary documents and certificates, she jumped on another bus and headed for the Travel Agent's office in Port of Spain.

She felt good.

The journey there was rough and bumpy, the little breeze blowing through the bus's window barely cooled the passengers; most wearing hats to shade themselves from the heat. Eve didn't have one.

At Port of Spain's only Travel Agent's office, several people were waiting anxiously to book their tickets; some pacing up and down the street outside, moaning impatiently at the hoards of people who'd turned up (many a folk had previously crowed the British Consulate's office but did not get their visas, returning again and again, ever waiting…ever hoping). Still they came… But for the lucky few who'd got their visas they thronged the streets outside the Travel Agent's office anxiously waiting to book their tickets and be on their way.

Eve too, joined the crowd, but she didn't have to wait long. She was there barely an hour when, without much fuss, she booked her ticket to take her to England on board a Spanish boat they called *'Montserrat'*.

She was to call back two weeks before departure for her ticket.

Clutching the receipt in her hands as she walked out, she could hardly believe it had finally happened. Here it was, right in front of her eyes – Confirmation – 'in black and white' of the ticket which would take her to England.

She buried her head in her hands and sobbed and sobbed...

In a few months' time she would be on board the *Montserrat*, bound for a new life in England and somehow she knew that nothing in this world could ever stop that from happening...

She was almost in a state of stupor.

Chapter Thirty-Three

Time soon passed and now, here they were, on their way to Port of Spain harbour, Eve and her two boys in one car, the rest of the family in two others, the cars hooting their horns frantically, trying to get through the throngs of friends and neighbours who had gathered round to see her off; some blocking the streets or standing outside their front doors; others in their front yards, all waiting to wave their last 'goodbye'.

It was like a pantomime. But somehow amidst all the mayhem, the cars managed to pull out and be on its way.

They drove through the mad traffic with as much speed as they could muster, finally arriving at Port of Spain's harbour – just managing to make it in time.

At the harbour, Eve stared in amazement at the vast ship already docked and waiting, its huge belly almost touching the harbour's edge; crowds of people gathered ashore, all waiting eagerly to send some member of their family aboard that ship to make it to England.

Eve felt sad: sad not because she was going away, but because she was leaving her two young children behind. But she knew she had to pull herself together, try and put on a brave face. There was no turning back. She had to move on.

'One day she would take her chilren to Englan' with her,' she knew that; so she mustered all the strength she could summon, straightened herself up and got on with the task in hand.

It didn't take long for her to get through the necessary formalities and so by 1.30pm, May 4 1962, Eve was on board the *Montserrat* bound for a new life in England.

They'd shed their tears; they'd said their 'goodbyes' and now she was here sitting all alone on the bunk of the *Montserrat*, thinking...

Feelings of joy, of sorrow, of hope, of fear, enveloped her whole body. Like a wet blanket across the throbbing sea, it took over her soul and she felt scared. She was leaving her two young children behind to start a new life in a far away place they called England, but she didn't know what she would find there. She didn't know much about the people, their culture, their way of life; nothing! Nothing! And she was scared! She'd planned to return and take her children back to England with her, but now she wasn't sure if that dream would ever materialise.

Her aching heart was pounding, throbbing, as she sat there thinking...'she was takin' a chance, a gamble wit her life and dose of her chilren too, but anyting was better dan de one she was leavin' behind.'

The tears were rolling down her cheeks as she unpacked the few belongings she had, but she knew deep in her heart that she had to move on. There was no turning back now...So she wiped her face and tried to muscle what little strength she had left.

Putting on a brave front, she dried her tears, got changed into her pink floral cotton frock and headed straight for the deck.

Apart from a few people standing here and there, the deck was almost empty; the deep blue-green waters of the Caribbean ocean splashing its mighty waves onto the sides of the big ship; the ship rocking, heaving over the spurious waters. There seemed to be nothing but desolation and emptiness surrounding her now – the little island of Trinidad just a blotch of dark patch fading away in the background.

She never dreamt that a ship could be so well decked out. Fitted wardrobes and mirrors; bunk beds with soft mattresses and adjoining bathrooms with soft toilet paper–

were all part of the scene. Yet, this ship was making its last journey. Her mind was playing havoc...

As she sat there thinking...watching the waves tumble around her, she began to feel dizzy, sick. Everything seemed to be going round and round in circles in her head. She clutched her sickly stomach, it churning and churning, round and round inside her...(she had taken the sickness pills, but even the best of those could not protect her from the wrath of the mighty ocean).

Retching like mad, all of sudden she puked...vomited all over the deck, clutching her aching stomach as she did so, praying in her heart that she would not die. But then...after a few moments she felt relieved. She lay back on the chair to try and get some rest but soon fell asleep. When she woke up about half an hour later, it was nearly lunchtime, so she went down to her cabin, refreshed herself and headed for the dining room.

It was jam-packed with people – the women now wearing colourful dresses; the men in different coloured shirts and trousers; others still in their suits.

Vast quantities of food were laid out on long tables at either end of the dining room; cold salads, pickles, sliced ham and beef, boiled potatoes, thin long sticks of bread, sliced red watermelons and oranges too.

Within a few minutes the passengers were assigned to their tables; the waiters, dressed in white shirts, black trousers and black bow ties, scurrying about the place like wild rabbits; some carrying several plates of food at a time. Eve wondered how they ever managed to balance these.

With so many people to feed, there were two sittings and a choice of meals on offer. Some had hot meals; meat, boiled potatoes, peas, carrots, cabbages and hot gravy; others chose rice or yam with meat and vegetables, whilst some preferred the cold spread. The main course was followed by ice cream or fresh fruit or rice pudding. And hot black or white coffee sweetened with plenty of sugar, rounded off the meal.

The evening meals were just as enticing with a selection of cakes, sandwiches and tea at teatime – the kitchen staff doing their best to keep the passengers posted, by displaying the menus daily on a card outside the dining room, so that passengers knew in advance what they were getting.

What a scene it was! And as an extra treat, the sometimes-comical waiters did their best to keep the passengers entertained.

But Eve was feeling too sick on the first day to manage the spread, so she had some soup, a little bread, some sweet coffee and made her way back to her cabin to rest.

Chapter Thirty-Four

She rested for a while then later that afternoon went back on deck to get some air. It was packed with people, some lying on long deck chairs, huge sun umbrellas towering high above their heads, shading them from the sweltering heat as they relaxed.

Not wanting to make a fuss, Eve seated herself quietly next to a Negro lady, who at first hardly noticed her.

Dressed in black with short black curly hair straightened back with a hot comb and clipped in place with grips, she looked about fifty or so. She was plump and had a friendly air about her.

Silence prevailed, then after a few moments she looked at Eve in a curious way.

"Well girl, wat you goin' to Englan' for?" she asked, winking one eye in a friendly manner.

"Mi?...Am goin' to do nursin', man," Eve replied, surprised that this lady spoke to her.

"You don' say! Nursin' eh? You not goin' to look after dem lunatics out dere, eh girl?" she probed. "Deres lot of them madhouse hospital in dere, wit mad people in dem girl, an' dem pickin' dem pretty West Indian girl to go clean up dem shit! You not one ov dem? Eh, babyface?" she howled, breaking out into such fits of laughter, she almost rocked the boat.

"No Miss...?"

"Joy!" she interrupted. "Joy!"

"Ah get in a General Hospitol in Castleton," Eve assured her.

"Castleton eh? You don' say." (Joy had been to England many times before and she knew the country fairly well.) "Ah hope so girl. Ah sure do hope so! Ah sure do hope is not one ov dem lunatic one girl. Ah sure do hope…!" she added, shaking her head as if to reassure herself.

Eve paused…then… "An' you Miss Joy, wats you move den?"

"Mi, girl? Am a singer man! A singer! London full ah dem nightclub man! So ah go hit de road man! Hit de road!" and with that she burst into song, 'Hit de road Jack, don't you come back no more, no more, no more, no more! Hit de road Jack, don't you come back no more…!' Her voice so deep, husky and inviting that before long a huge crowd gathered around her, miming, clapping and joining in the song.

On she bellowed, fancying herself as an Ella Fitzgerald, the passengers egging her on, boosting her ego onwards.

But as she sang the song, it bore a special meaning to Eve, for whether that hospital was going to be a Mental Asylum or not, somehow she felt that she was hitting the road, never to return to Trinidad again.

The seasickness however continued to plague her. She became so sick that she couldn't go to the dining room for her meals. And Miss Joy didn't waste any time. As soon as she heard Eve was ill, she went down to her cabin to visit her.

For three days she fed her with hot soup and bread. Then she gave her a pink rose which she'd made herself from crepe paper. For, back in Jamaica, she made crepe paper flowers and sold them for her living – but no one knew that. Now, here she was, tending Eve as no one had done for a long, long time, hoping that one day she would become a famous singer.

For three whole days Eve was sick, the old ship tossing and tumbling, the ferocious waves turning her non-seafaring stomach inside out. Then, miraculously, on the third day, the sickness passed and she felt much better. She was back to her normal self again and back trailing around in Miss Joy's company, having fun.

The passengers, having realised that Miss Joy was a singer, eagerly invited her to the bar, where they would shout, "Come on Joy! Let's hav' it girl, let's hav' it!" She however, needed no encouragement. She was always ready to let rip...ever hoping, ever dreaming...

She would go... "Oooh! Ahhh! And ...if I rule de worl'!" and the waiters would get hysterical, shouting in their pigeon English, "Morre! Morre! Miss Ella," (for them, she was the great Ella Fitzgerald herself). "Morre! Morre!" they shouted and she would let rip... the crowd going wild as she sang different songs, from 'Mac the Knife' to Pat Boone's 'ballads'. But 'Hit the road' was her favourite song – and when she sang it, the passengers used to shout, "Yeah man! Never to come back again..."

In fact, rumour had it that she was going to England to clean the toilets – but, who cared? Miss Joy was making people happy and they loved her – every minute of it – they thrived on it.

And so at night-time, the ship's bar teamed with life – the ship's captain and some of his officers always joining in.

He used to sit at a special table with the woman he had chosen from amongst the passengers. According to rumours, he would wine her, dine her and bed her and she would be known as the 'Captain's woman' and so accorded the best of everything the ship had to offer. It was an unwritten code which no one dared to question.

Occasionally, this spirit of bacchanal would be interrupted by a deafening noise – the loud blowing of the ship's horn – a blasting noise, which indicated that the ship was making good progress, or that it had spotted some form of human existence in the distance.

Unbelievable moments they were as time passed. Twenty days of blissful happiness! Moments which Eve would treasure for the rest of her life! Moments which she would never forget.

She didn't have to cook. She didn't have to clean. She didn't have to care for the children and she didn't have to slave either. For once in her life, everything was laid out in front of her and she felt good.

Twenty days of heavenly bliss... cruising from Venezuela to the Canary Islands... finally docking at Southampton, England. England! The country they called 'Mother England'. England, the land where Eve hoped to start a new life...a new beginning.

Chapter Thirty-Five

Eve woke up that morning to the most deafening sound. It was the *Montserrat* blowing its horn madly, flashing its lights, giving it signal that it was about to approach Southampton's harbour.

She looked through her cabin's window and from the distance, all she could see was what seemed like red spikes (chimney pots) on blobs (houses) scattered here and there on flat lands, seemingly floating on the sea. It was Southampton.

She'd packed her trunk the day before and it was now with the rest of the passengers' luggage, ready for transportation to the docks. So, after a quick breakfast, she returned to her cabin to get changed, in readiness for 'disembarkation'.

She changed her underwear then put on her satin petticoat followed by her pink floral two-piece suit. Then, she fixed her hair, powdered her face, applied the red lipstick on her lips and pinned the black half-moon shaped hat firmly onto the crown of her head, its white netting hanging just a little over her face, faintly disguising her beauty. Finally, she sprinkled some perfume onto herself, tossed a few basic toiletries into a bag (a present from Marla), slipped into her brown shoes, pulled on the long white gloves which Auntie Nell had given her and with the brown pull-string handbag in her hand, she was ready for what lay ahead.

She was leaving the ship on which she'd spent 20 glorious days. And as she looked around her cabin, she felt sad: proud of herself – but sad that she was leaving it. She wanted to cry, but the tears just wouldn't flow. 'Englan' was waiting,' she thought. 'She must pull herself togeder.' So she took one last look at the cabin, braced herself and headed straight for deck.

The deck was jam-packed with passengers, such a huddle of noise, excitement, some of them shouting, "Southampton! Southampton! Here we come!" Then all of a sudden, Miss Joy got down on her knees and began to pray, 'Oh Moder Englan'! We here! We Here!' she was praying, mumbling, more or less to herself.

It was May 24 1962 and although it was late spring, it was cold in comparison to the warmth of the Caribbean, which they had not long left behind. Now here they were, West Indians aboard a ship, each dressed to the hilt; each trying to make an impression on the host country – the men wearing brown or cream suits, brown or black ties and hats to match; the women in different coloured two-piece suits or dresses – some floral, some plain, with white or coloured gloves and hats finishing off the costumes.

Hats it seemed were the natural accessories of West Indians at the time – different shades, different designs. It was the fashion and they looked a picture in them.

Now, here they were, immigrants on deck, dressed in their best outfits, ready to set foot for the first time on a land they called England; a shimmer of sunlight beaming down on their bodies, forming stripes and patterns over the different coloured costumes, Eve standing amongst them like a shy princess.

It was a sight to behold!

She stood there anxiously, combing the passengers, when all of a sudden Miss Joy called, "Hey Eve! Wat you all dress up in gloves for girl? You goin' to meet de queen?" and they all laughed, so loud that Eve felt embarrassed. She blushed and went a little quirky.

As the big ship reached nearer the harbour, Eve could see a lot of commotion going on.

A huge ship lay silently by, workmen scurrying about, racing here, racing there, busy easing crates of cargoes from its deserted carcass; a few steamers jetting about the place; one, it seemed, carrying Port Officials. It hovered around the *Montserrat* then, all of a sudden, it drove ahead, leading the *Montserrat* on to Southampton's harbour.

As the *Montserrat* eased its huge belly closer to the harbour, Eve noticed several people standing at Dock No 6. They were wearing dark coats and some were in woollen hats, all relatives of some passenger or the other.

Packed liked sardine on deck, the passengers seemed happy, chatting, laughing, anxiously waving to their relatives. Then, all of a sudden, Miss Joy hugged Eve and they started to cry; each promising to write to the other; each promising to keep in touch – Promises! Promises!

After a few moments of hugging and sobbing, they calmed themselves down, wiped their tears and began to laugh...

Eve's eyes was combing the shore again, looking for her friends, when she spotted someone. It was Ramesh with his wife standing next to him – she'd recognised them from the photos they'd sent her.

They were smiling and waving and Eve's heart accelerated at the sight of them. She felt queer.

For a split second, she closed her eyes and prayed...'Please God. Please help mi fine a new life in Englan'. Oh Moder Englan'! Please...' she pleaded. 'Ah hear so much about you an' de chances you give to people all over de worl'. Please Moder Englan', please give mi dat chance too.'

She had had so many phases of bad luck and now here she was at last, about to embark on English soil for the first time in her life and she couldn't believe it was happening.

Bracing herself, she straightened up, walked gingerly down the gangplank, about to make her first step on British soil, excited yet nervous, Ramesh and his wife, Myrna stepping forward to greet her.

She was cold, for she wasn't wearing a coat and so she shivered a little. But that didn't matter, because at last she was on British soil and she felt good. She had landed – at last!

As she stood there looking around her, she was overwhelmed by the warm reception friends and relatives were giving to their West Indian guests, but there was no mistaking who were the hosts.

They were wearing dark coats, black or coffee-coloured and some of the women wore woollen scarves tied round their necks; all carrying spare coats for their guests – but none of them wore hats.

They were hugging and kissing each other, "Oh my Joycelyn! You lookin' good girl," or "Oh my Wilfred, you lookin' great man," they kept greeting each other, Eve hardly believing what her eyes were seeing.

Myrna too had a coat for Eve, but in the heat of the excitement she forgot to give it to her.

Taken aback by Eve's beauty, so slim and petite, looking 15 at 21 and the mother of two children too, Myrna stood there for a moment, mesmerised. Then suddenly, she remembered the coat.

Pulling herself short, she placed the coat around Eve's shoulders, declaring, "Oh my Eve! You look so good girl!" and kissing her on both cheeks, they started to cry. They sniffed and cried for a few moments, then quickly pulled themselves together and all three headed for the Immigration Department.

The Immigration Officer did not waste any time. He looked at Eve's passport and papers. "You are going to be a student nurse I see?"

"Yes, sir," she replied, shaking with nerves.

"At which hospital?"

"Springvale Hospital, sir."

"Your vaccination papers please, Madam?"

She pulled out the folded papers from her pull-string handbag and handed them to him, nervously. With precision he scrutinised them, searching every detail, Eve standing there trembling like a withered leaf. Then, he looked at her and without saying a further word, stamped her passport and handed it to her.

She held the passport in her hands, her fingers trembling like mad, then she noticed the stamp: 'Indefinite Entry,' it read.

"Indefinite Entry! Indefinite Entry! Oh! Myrna," she cried, her heart jumping for joy.

It was all over in a jiff and Eve breathed a sigh of relief. 'How her luck was changin'. But she must tank de hospital for dat, for it was she, de Matron, who had sent her de necessary instructions to help her get through de "Immigration formalities".' Now, her heart was dancing with happiness.

She wanted to hug the man, kiss him, squeeze him, but she knew she had to restrain herself. Now, all she had to do was get her baggage checked, then she will be on her way to meet the man from the British Nursing Council.

Her heart was thumping like mad...

Chapter Thirty-Six

It was nearly 3pm that afternoon when Eve walked out of the Customs Department to meet the man from the British Nursing Council. The Matron had informed her that he'd be waiting at Southampton's harbour to meet her, but she didn't expect to see him wearing a placard on his back. There he was, this tall Englishman, 50 or so, standing all alone, the cold spring wind blowing through his mousy-coloured hair, as he waited.

Having just spoken to and sent off a student nurse to her destination, he turned around swiftly and it was only then that Eve noticed the words, 'British Nursing Council for England and Wales' printed on a placard on his back.

She was aghast with surprise.

Recognising her from the photos she'd sent to the Nursing Council, he walked straight up to her, a warm smile on his face.

"Are you Mrs Ram-Ram?" he enquired, courteously and shook her hands.

"Yes sir," she replied. She was nervous.

"I am George Archibald from the British Nursing Council. Nice to meet you Mrs Ram-Ram. I hope the journey here was not too tiresome."

"It was fine sir," she replied, swallowing the lump which had just formed in her throat.

Cutting in swiftly, he continued, "No doubt you'll be hungry Mrs Ram-Ram. Over there... (pointing to the end of the harbour) is a café where you will find refreshments. I have made the necessary enquiries for your travel. Here are the train times for your journey to Castleton. You will need to change stations before you get to Castleton, Mrs Ram-Ram, as you will see from the papers here."

He pulled out 'the train directions' explaining it all to her: where to board; at what time; where to change; what it would cost. Everything! But he was sounding very tired. He had spent all day helping prospective nurses to get to their destinations; ushering them here, ushering them there and now he was getting quite worn out. But he was their host, a representative of the 'Nursing Profession' and he wanted to do his job well – just like a true professional would.

Still smiling a little, he looked at Eve and with warmth in his voice enquired, "I understand you will be staying with friends in Northampton over the weekend Mrs Ram-Ram and travelling up to Castleton on Monday morning?"

"Yes sir," her heart was beating wildly.

"And what time do you plan to leave Northampton?"

"Nine o'clock in de mornin' sir."

"Good! Now, let's see... that will take you...you will change...and you will arrive at Castleton at 2.30 in the afternoon. I will telephone Matron about this and inform her that you will be staying with friends over the weekend."

He pulled out a card from his pocket. "Here is my telephone number Mrs Ram-Ram. Should you encounter any difficulties, please do not hesitate to phone me. And here is Matron's number too. If you do happen to suffer any delays or problems on your journey there to Castleton, do phone Matron."

He handed her both cards then, after a slight pause, he added, "And please telephone Matron's office when you arrive at Castleton's station, Mrs Ram-Ram."

He stood still for a moment looking at the ill-dressed Eve with concern in his eyes, then..."And what about money, Mrs Ram-Ram? Do you have enough for your journey up there to Castleton?" he enquired.

Taken aback by the generosity of this man, "Oh yes, sir," she replied, sheepishly. "Mi frien' go look after mi," she assured him.

He looked at her, the concern in his eyes showing, then he said, "Matron will be expecting you at 2.30 on Monday afternoon. Have a good weekend Mrs Ram-Ram," and with that, he turned to Ramesh and Myrna and ..."Nice to meet you too," he greeted, shaking their hands, each in turn.

Mr Archibald was a tired man.

He turned to Eve again, paused, then said, "Well Mrs Ram-Ram, I hope your stay in England will be a happy one. I look forward to meeting you again as a Registered Nurse in three years' time. Opposite the café you will find taxis which will take you to Southampton's railway station, from where you will be able to board a train for Northampton. Good day to you all," he concluded and with that he walked away briskly.

For a moment, Eve stood there motionless. 'Dis man from de Nursin' Council had it all work out, yet he was so hospitable, so friendly, so warm, so accommodatin'?'

'All mi life ah was treated cruelly by men and now such kind-ness dish out to mi by a foreigner – an' Englishman too. Ah'd come to dis strange land not knowin' what ah would fine and now de first man ah encounter...Is dis wat Englan's about? Is dat wy so many West Indian write home sayin' nice tings about Englan'?'

She couldn't believe it! She was choked.

For a moment she stood there speechless, watching Mr Archibald as he disappeared in the distance, thinking...finding it all so incomprehensible – so hard to understand.

She couldn't speak. She couldn't move. She just stood there tongue-tied.

"We got to make a move girl," Ramesh asserted, interrupting her thoughts. She jumped!

They didn't waste any time. Hurriedly, they flagged down a taxi to Southampton's railway station, then they boarded a train to take them to Northampton.

It was 5pm when they finally arrived at 27 Gower Road and Myrna fed them with a nice hot curry meal, which she'd prepared before departing. Then, when they'd finished eating, she suggested that Eve freshened up.

She gave her a clean towel to wash and indicated that she changed into something more casual – like the pair of trousers which she'd just loaned her. But Eve was shocked, taken aback. For back in Esperanza Indian women were not allowed to wear trousers and now Myrna was telling her to do just that? She was beside herself and even more surprised when Myrna told her to get washed.

She'd never heard of people getting washed and changed after their evening meal, so she was baffled. But in true spirit, she did as she was told.

After that, they all went into Myrna's bedroom and started to gossip.

They talked and talked till nearly midnight; about life back in Trinidad; about the possibilities in England; about anything and everything... then Myrna dished out hot chocolate drinks and suggested they retired to bed.

Eve got changed into the grey flannelette nightie which Myrna had lent her and settled down to sleep at the bottom of Myrna's bed – cramped and cold, she was – even though Myrna had given her an extra blanket.

She shivered all night.

The next morning they had cornflakes and boiled eggs for breakfast, then Myrna gave her a present: a lime-green furry three-quarter-length jumper and Eve's face beamed with joy.

After breakfast, they went for a walk in the park where they talked and talked for ages, it seemed, and Eve felt good in the first jumper she'd ever owned – Myrna, not being able to afford a coat as a present – but that didn't bother Eve in the least.

Though Eve was enjoying herself in the company of her friends, Monday morning soon came and Eve had to leave for Castleton and her destiny.

She was ready.

They were up early that morning and now here they were at Northampton's train station, Eve hugging and kissing Myrna as they said farewell, she promising faithfully to write to Myrna. Then she boarded the train that would take her onwards to Castleton and her destiny, carrying all her worldly belongings in a little trunk which Mah had given her.

It was 9am.

Chapter Thirty-Seven

She sat back on the train bewildered...not knowing if she could ever survive on her own, especially in a strange land; not knowing how she would cope with the people, their different cultures and customs. 'But anyting was better dan de life she left behind,' she thought.

Now, here she was, age 21, sitting on a train on a cold Monday morning, May 26 1962, bound for a destiny in a place they called Castleton – a place where she would train as a nurse; a place where she hoped she would start a new life...

She sat back on the train thinking. She was determined to make a go of it – make a success of her life. One day, she would return to Trinidad and bring her two children back with her, never to return there again...

Her mind was working overtime... as the train trundled on. It was a harrowing experience changing trains. And now, before she knew it, the train to Castleton had almost reached its destination.

She noticed that some of the passengers were already putting on their jackets and coats, others removing their belongings from the compartments above; a few women looking at their hand mirrors, doing their faces, trying to smarten themselves up.

She too, tried to smarten herself up, did her best to look good, make an impression, but she didn't have a mirror. Besides, there were other things on her mind, and so as the train neared its destination, her heart began to beat faster.

Here she was at last, in this amazing land of splendid architect and beautiful sceneries; a land which many West

Indians said had so much to offer. Here she was at long last about to arrive in Castleton: to a destiny not yet known.

Her heart was thumping; her mind wheeling, tumbling, gripping her with fear as she tried to figure out what lay behind that unknown territory; the signboard in the distance, barely visible now.

From beneath the mist that surrounded her thoughts, she could just about see the masses of red brick houses on either side of the railway track. Then, the signboard became clearer as it read: 'Castleton'.

Her heart was jumping for joy, the fear disappearing in the excitement as the train hissed, screeched and came to a sudden halt: its puff of smoke melting away in the misty background. Then like birds, the passengers flew off the train, swiftly heading for their different destinations, quietly disappearing, she following their trail.

First she went to the ticket collector and nervously handed him the ticket. Then she followed them – but the passengers familiar in their own surroundings briskly disappeared, leaving her all alone. Lost! Abandoned! By her own destiny.

For a moment she stood there numb, not knowing what to do. Then she remembered: 'She must phone Matron.' But she didn't know how to use the telephone. She'd never used one before. She must think fast...

She saw the cars parked in a row with signs on their bonnets which read 'Taxis for Hire' and she remembered what Myrna had told her, 'al de driver wear black uniforms,' she'd said. And Matron had given her firm instructions too – 'she must take a taxi to the hospital,' she'd written. So bracing herself, she walked towards the first driver.

"Are you de taxi?" she enquired.

Puzzled by her question, the driver smiled and replied, "Yes Miss!"

"Could you take mi to Springvale General Hospitol please?"

"Certainly Miss. Certainly!" he replied, waving his cap in the air and jumping out of the taxi.

He put her trunk in the boot of the car and she got into the back seat. And as he sped through the busy town centre, she could see intrepid shoppers racing in and out of shops, chasing up bargains, it seemed. Some of the familiar names like Woolworth, Marks & Spencer and Barclays Bank were evident and she felt relieved.

Whizzing his way through the curves and bends of the town, he assured her that Springvale General was a nice hospital (it was such a relief to see a smile on his face after the seriousness of the passengers on board the train). Then all of a sudden he blurted, "Here she comes Miss!"

"Ah beg you pardon?" Eve replied, taken aback by his expression.

"Here she is Miss! The General Miss. The General!" he repeated, as if he was referring to some powerful being from the 'Armed Forces'.

Eve looked at the direction in which he was pointing and her heart began to beat with excitement. She read the words 'Springvale General Hospital' over and over again – her heart almost stopped beating. She stared in amazement at the hospital, its red brick buildings sprawling out in front of her, occupying acres of land, it seemed; but confined within the four walls of that territory.

There seemed to be a hush, the taxi driver gone quiet, as Eve stared at the hospital buildings. Then, within minutes the taxi rolled inside the gates and the driver got out at the Enquiries Department. He rang the bell and without much fuss, quickly shifted Eve's trunk from the boot of his car.

She got out of the car as quickly as she could, paid him 1sh 6d for the fare and barely had time to thank him when – as quick as a jiff – he jumped into his car, shouting, "Good luck!" and drove off at great speed, leaving Eve standing there all alone, waiting…waiting…

Chapter Thirty-Eight

She stood there, trunk in hand, trying hard to compose herself, when suddenly, as if from nowhere, a tall graceful-looking lady appeared. She was about 50 or so, dressed in a long black uniform and wearing a white fan-like cap on her head. She was the Matron.

Having been informed that Eve had arrived, she rushed out quickly through the swing doors and into the entrance where Eve was standing, waiting to greet her.

Like an angel, Matron appeared, a warm smile on her face, her baby blue eyes alight as she greeted Eve.

"Good afternoon," she said, stretching out her hand to Eve, the smile on her face kindling with surprise, as she looked at the simple girl, so unsuitably dressed, standing in front of her.

Remembering what Myrna had told her: 'You mus' take you gloves off and curtsey, wen you meet de Matron,' she'd warned. And so, Eve curtsied, too nervous to reply.

"I hope you had a good journey here Eve?" Matron enquired. "Please don't strain yourself with that trunk. Mr Hopper will take it in for you." She rang a bell and within seconds Mr Hopper, the porter, arrived.

"Mr Hopper," she said, authority in her voice, "This is Eve. She has just arrived from Trinidad to start her nurse's training here. Would you please take her trunk to Room 6, in the nurses' quarters, where she will be staying. Miss Perth cleaned it up this morning and it should be ready for occupation."

Matron Shaunessy was a busy lady who had to get on with the business of making Eve feel at home. She whisked her off briskly down the corridor, Eve shaking almost visibly at the knees.

"So tell me Eve," Matron enquired, "How do you find our cold country in comparison to the sunny Caribbean, eh?" she laughed (trying to put Eve at ease) but Myrna had warned her that she must be 'careful' and 'courteous' at all times. 'Matrons are such superior people,' she assured her.

Eve was just about to reply when Matron, sensing her nerves intercepted, "Never mind young lady. We'll soon get you warmed up – as warm as a baked potato!" She chuckled so loudly that Eve, dropping her guard for a moment, couldn't help but laugh too.

She led Eve through a long stone corridor, down some steps onto a concrete pathway then into the nurses' dining room. "This is Eve," she said to Mary, the kitchen maid. "Would you please prepare a pot of tea and cakes and take it to Room 6 where Eve will be staying." And with that, she hurried away so quickly, hardly giving Mary time to reply, Eve struggling behind her trying to keep pace.

She climbed up a few stairs, then sped like lightning along a further corridor straight into the nurses' quarters and Room 6, Eve trotting nervously behind her.

"This is your room Eve," she said. "I hope you like it. Miss Perth cleaned it up this morning, so you should feel comfortable. I hope your stay here will be a happy one," she added. "I will see you at 9am tomorrow morning, in my office. Don't worry…just a few formalities…a few papers to sign," she assured her. "I have instructed one of the nurses to take you there. Meanwhile, I shall leave you in the capable hands of Mary. Our Mary will take good care of you." And with that she was gone – off like a rocket, as quickly as she came.

She hardly had time to leave the doorway when Mary entered with the tray of tea. On it there was: a silver pot of tea covered with a woollen tea cosy; a silver jug with milk; a silver bowl with sugar; two white china tea cups and saucers;

two silver teaspoons; china plates and an assortment of cakes and biscuits.

"Here ya are," Mary said, putting the tray down on a locker beside Eve's bed. "Ya mus' be a tire after dat lorn jornie fro' Northamton, so ya need ya strenth back," she asserted, chuckling as she said so. She poured out a cup of tea for Eve and stood back, struck by Eve's beauty: her simplicity. She took an instant liking to her.

Overcome by such generosity and kindness, Eve swallowed the tea quickly, then Mary poured out another cup for her and said, "Ah hear ya like curries. We ga tell de Chef to fix up sum nice curi an' rice fo' suppa fo' ya." (Eve didn't like curry really, but they were so kind to her, she didn't want to make a fuss.)

"Wel'..." the friendly kitchen maid said, "Ah mus' leav ya now. Ah hav' lots ta do. Cher up! We ga look after ya!" she assured her. "Suppa is at 6pm an' Matron ask Cynthia to tak ya to dining room," and patting Eve on the shoulder, she smiled and scuttled away like a wild rabbit.

Taken aback by the hospitality of these two women, Eve forgot to say 'thank you' as Myrna had taught her to. So gobsmacked she was, she sat there in a state of shock, staring in amazement at the lovely room in which she'd found herself.

Decorated in pink floral wallpaper, its windows painted white; an enamel wash hand basin underneath, with two clean white towels hanging at its sides; a polished wardrobe and dressing table with mirrors to the front; a large single bed with a thick mattress and white linen cover over it; a square-shaped apparatus under the windows (radiators to keep the room warm, as she was later to find out) and an adjoining bathroom next door. She sat there, looking around her, almost mesmerised... as she thought...

'Here she was, in a lovely, comfortable, warm room; an English maid bringin' her tea on a silver tray; an English porter fetchin' her trunk to her room; fresh clean towels an a warm bathroom in which to bathe; nurses uniforms bein' provided shortly – washed, starched and sprucely ironed; hot meals on hand served to taste an a monthly salary on top of it all?' She was overcome!

'Back in Trinidad, she slept on a cold hard bed in a mud hut; wit no proper food to eat; no clean clodes or shoes to wear and she rarely had knickers to cover her bare bottom. Coloured people used to run around like slaves behin' dere white bosses, servin' them – bein' ushered here; ushered dere. An' above all, her own husban' and family treated her wit such distain, such abysmal cruelty?'

'And now, all of a sudden, de table had turn. How her luck had changed in dis strange land amongst strange people – so kind, so caring – dey were.'

Lost in her own thoughts, she hardly heard the knock on the door. It was Cynthia, the Jamaican nurse, whom Matron had sent off duty, to keep her company.

Chapter Thirty-Nine

Tall, muscular and skinny as a rake, Cynthia stood at the door, a broad grin on her face, her hair neatly pressed back from her dark elongated face.

"Hey man! I am Cynthia," she greeted. "Matron sen' me to see you OK. How is tings man?"

For a split second the bewildered Eve stared at the 20-year-old lanky Jamaican nurse, standing there grinning, so happy, so full of confidence. It was hard to believe.

"Ah see dey gave you plenty ah cake man!" Cynthia declared, as she walked through the opened door. "Let's have anoder cup ah tea eh!" she insisted.

She sat on Eve's bed, poured two more cups of tea, handed one to Eve and kept one for herself, then continued talking. They talked about her journey to Castleton, then Cynthia told her a little about nursing; her shifts, starting time, finishing time and what she hoped to learn on her first course – the teapot now empty. Cynthia then went down to the kitchen and brought back a fresh pot of tea.

They talked and talked and laughed a lot having eaten all the cakes and drank the second pot of tea; then they went into the living room and played some of Cynthia's records. Jamaican reggae and some calypsos too, she jigging away, Eve laughing her head off.

It went on and on for a while – this bacchanal – then before they knew it, it was supper time. And so Eve got changed quickly into something more casual and together they went down to the dining room for supper.

As the nurses came in they wanted to sit on Eve's table to hear all about Trinidad and her journey to Castleton. They gossiped and chatted together and enjoyed the hearty meals of curried chicken and rice. But Eve noticed that the Nursing Sisters sat on separate tables – tables reserved specially for them.

Dressed in navy blue uniforms with long sleeves; black belts held together with silver buckles; white well-pressed aprons and white wing-shaped caps spread out like eagles and pinned firmly onto their heads, they looked so prim and proper. They appeared so neat, it was as if they'd never done a day's work in their lives.

They were given silver salver service – each with her own linen serviette neatly rolled in silver rings. And they were served before the nurses too. Eve noticed, that as each nurse entered she curtsied and had to ask the Sister's permission to enter and leave the dining room.

It was her first experience of 'deference to rank and file' – an implicit authority in force and she felt daunted by the whole scene.

She soon learnt that her first shift was to start at 8am and finish at 1pm. Matron had arranged that Cynthia be given the same shift too, so that she could keep an eye on Eve – help her to get settled. And in line with their keeping, the Chef too had visited Eve during his coffee break that day to ensure that she was given the meals she liked. What hospitality!

Next on the agenda was getting her uniforms prepared, so at 2pm the following day Cynthia took her down to the sewing room to get fitted. But when the seamstress saw her, she joked and laughed so much saying, 'how skinny Eve was – how she could wrap her tape measure ten times over around her waist,' and she had Eve in stitches. She was so friendly – this seamstress, that Eve couldn't stop laughing.

With that task over, they went into the sitting room and played some more music, a few nurses joining in. "Let's have it Cynthia!" they shouted, she, getting on the floor and jigging away; they clapping like mad, the music blaring away in the background...'some BG plantain, does full up de pot!' On and on it went...and they had so much fun.

Then two days later, Eve's uniforms were ready – half a dozen pale blue cotton dresses, white aprons and white caps and Cynthia showed her how to make them into butterfly shapes, ready for wearing. Eve felt really proud when she tried them on.

She enjoyed her first few days on shift and on her day off she was able to stay in bed for as long as she wished, Mary bringing her breakfast in bed: a tray of bacon, eggs, fried tomatoes, bread and a hot pot of tea.

What a treat! What a difference to the slaving and suffering in abject poverty which she'd endured back home in Trinidad? It was like living in a different world now. No worries, no stress, her body being so well nourished that she was getting stronger and healthier by the day.

She felt so privileged.

Sometimes Cynthia would take her to the town centre and teach her how to shop. For she'd never shopped on her own before, especially in a big town and so she lacked confidence, especially with the self-service shopping. But Cynthia soon taught her a lot on that score.

When she received her first month's salary, she was so excited that she and Cynthia went on a shopping spree. She bought powder and lipstick, stockings and perfume, then she and Cynthia went into a café and enjoyed a treat of tea and cakes. After that, she went to the Post Office and bought a Postal Order for £5 and posted it to Trinidad for her children's maintenance (for, being a good mother, she was determined that they should have a good life too).

They had a nice time and after all the spending and spreeing, she still had £2 left so Cynthia took her to Barclays Bank and showed her how to open her first bank account in England.

It was the first bank account she'd ever opened and she felt as rich as the queen herself.

At her first assignment during induction training they taught her how to make beds: how to fold the corners neatly ('Matron would inspect these,' she was warned). How to roll patients from side to side; how to bathe them; the certain ways of lifting them and particular care in serving them their meals. It was an eye-opening experience for her, but she enjoyed every minute of it.

She had learnt a lot during that time and it wasn't long before her four weeks induction training came to an end. Soon, she would have to start her three months' preliminary training course and she was looking forward to it.

It wasn't long before it was all arranged. The nurses' van was to pick her up from the nurses' quarters at 9am every day and bring her back at 5.30pm each day, Monday to Friday. She was so excited.

Finally the big day came. It was Monday 1 July 1962 and the nurses' van picked her up for the first time to take her to the nurses' training school.

Anxious and a little jittery of the fact that she was about to start a new experience, she worried herself sick. But little did she realise what she was about to experience.

Little did she perceive what awaited her...

Chapter Forty

At the nursing college the three tutors were busy preparing the agenda. Like commanders in the army, these academics of the nursing profession stood out – ready to look after their student nurses like fowls about to brood over their young chicks.

First, there was Miss Dove. Slim and petite, about 40 or so and always looking so immaculate and clean in her green uniform, you got the impression that Miss Dove never touched a bed-pan in her life. She used to zip around the place as quiet as a mouse, so quickly, so light on her feet she was, that you never heard her coming. She taught 'Hygiene and Nursing Practice'.

Next was Mr Baldwin. A thin lanky man with a mouth full of rotten teeth. Mr Baldwin taught 'Anatomy and Physiology'. He used to reel those off like the alphabet – such a genius, he was. He also ran the Venereal Disease Clinic and taught VD too.

A funny comical man, he was always cracking jokes about his patients with VD and you got the feeling that he never took anything seriously, but anyone under his charge knew better.

In order to illustrate a point he would say that his aunt had syphilis or his uncle had gonorrhoea, then he would shout, "Eve! You come from the West Indies. Tell me, how many people you knew from your home town who suffered VD? Your brother? Your sister? Your aunt or uncle?" and the nurses would go into hysterics, laughing their heads off. Then immediately he would fix his eyes on Sandra and shout, "Sandra! What is the treatment for gonorrhoea?" And God help Sandra if she didn't know the answer, for that was the type of teacher he was.

Proud of his profession, he taught his subjects with a ferocity unknown and 'make no mistake' the nurses respected him for it.

Plump and red-faced, about 45 or so meet Miss McDermott. She walked with an air of authority about her, her green long-sleeved uniform showing the bulge of her fat belly. And with the sign 'Principal Tutor' fixed firmly on the door of her office, no one had any doubts as to who she was.

Apart from teaching 'Signs and Symptoms' and 'Diagnosis and Treatment of Diseases' she took charge of everything in that teaching establishment.

It was rumoured that she was the highest paid nurse in the business and so the nurses feared her. They used to try and take her off – crack 'funny jokes' about her and though they were scared of her, she was on the whole, highly respected.

Miss McDermott elicited a kind of commandeering air which made everyone know their place.

One day, Eve had no choice but to see Miss McDermott about reclaiming her bus fares and she trembled at the thought of seeing her – the nurses having warned her that Miss McDermott would wipe the floor with her. So, bracing herself she knocked on Miss McDermott's door.

"Enter!" Miss McDermott commanded.

Shaking like a scared rabbit Eve entered.

"Good morning Miss McDermott," Eve said, curtseying a little, her knees wobbling as she did so.

"Good morning Eve," Miss McDermott replied, looking at her sternly from above the rim of her glasses. "And what can I do for you?"

"Is Friday today, Miss McDermott an' ah com' fo' mi refun' fo' de bus fare."

"Oh indeed! It's Friday Eve... Friday and I've forgotten all about it. Let's see...Your tickets Eve?" she requested, combing Eve with her eyes.

Eve opened her handbag, searching for the tickets. "Wel' e-mm-h!" she coughed, fiddling about nervously in her handbag as she tried to fish them out. There were only two.

"Ah only got two, Miss McDermott," she protested pitifully, handing them to her. "Ah los' de res' some wey. Ah don' kno wey. But ah need de money bad! Miss McDermontt! So bad...to buy a radio for mi room." She was crying.

"Ah does feel lonely sometime, Miss McDermott! So lonely..." she appealed, the tears just about to flow, Miss McDermott listening.

She knew too well that Eve had only recently arrived from a far away land to this strange town of Castleton. 'She's sure to feel lonely...a radio would be good company for her,' she thought.

She paused, looked at Eve from above the rim of her spectacles and declared, "Well Eve, let's see... 10 days at 1sh per day equals 10sh. There you are Eve... 10sh for your radio... sign here please."

Eve nearly fell to the floor. Taken aback for a moment, her heart quickened. '10sh would certainly be enough to pay a deposit for mi radio,' she thought to herself. Flabbergasted, she looked at Miss McDermott, not knowing how to react.

'What a surprise. Everyone say she was such a bitch. Yet here she is, so kine, so assurin', so carin',' Eve thought, her stomach doubling up in knots. So overwhelmed she was that she raced out of the door as fast as her legs could carry her, forgetting to say the two important words Myrna had taught her, which was... 'thank you!'

She was enjoying her training and every morning she would get up early and have a nice breakfast of cereals, bacon, egg and tea, then she would be taken on the nurses' van to the Nursing College. There, she would be served with good old English mouth watering lunches like: steamed steak and kidney pudding, carrots, peas or runner beans and potatoes, followed by treacle pudding and custard or mixed fruit and ice cream. And hot percolated, milky coffee always completed the treat.

"Come on ma darlins," Jeanie the cook used to say to the nurses. "'Ave some more!" and she would pile dollops onto their plates. Then, she would turn to Eve and say, "Look at ya! Al skin an' bone. Ah go fatten ya up, ya little peaky!" and she would pile Eve's plate sky high; no matter how much she protested.

Eve was her special pet and she spoilt her shamelessly.

The nurses were so friendly towards Eve, each insisting that she sat next to them. And sometimes, during lunch break – intrigued by her long black hair, which almost touched her waist – they would take it in turns to comb it.

Sometimes, they showed each other photos of their families – so friendly they were. And sometimes, they played netball to wile the time away.

They never treated her as a person of a different race or colour. Instead, they showed her love and respect; a kind of love which even her own family had failed to give her.

She could hardly believe it. She was overwhelmed.

Chapter Forty-One

Every evening, when Eve returned to the nurses' quarters she would have a quick supper then retreat to the study where she would meticulously write and re-write her notes in a fresh notebook, as was advised by her tutors. Then when she'd finished, she would revise and revise until she'd memorised them well. Finally, at midnight, tired and worn out, she would have a quick hot bath and retire to bed with a nice cup of hot chocolate, only to get up at 7am the next morning to repeat the same regime all over again – so determined she was to make a success of her nursing career.

No one realised how simple a background she came from, for she was doing so well academically, but not so technically though – she didn't know how to use the telephone.

One evening, she answered the telephone and put it straight back on the hook, then went to fetch the person whom the call was for. She had in fact cut off the call but did not realise it.

The nurse concerned went mad and from that day on she treated Eve like an idiot and word soon got around that she was backward: stupid!

It was the first unpleasant experience she was to encounter but she wasn't going to let it spoil her happiness. As far as most of the nurses were concerned, they still liked her and sometimes on a Saturday night, they would invite her to go dancing with them. But being brought up the way she was – she at first refused then, after much cajoling, she eventually relented and went out with them.

They had so much fun together that she hoped it would never end.

Back in the classroom however she continued to shine. At the end of the Preliminary term, she came 'second' – the first foreign student to gain such a position and so, to reward her, the hospital gave her a prize – a book token – and she felt so proud.

She was so happy, she couldn't wait to write home and tell Mah and Pah.

With the Prelim course successfully completed, she was sent to work on the wards to gain practical experience in nursing techniques. And every three months, she would be shifted to a different ward to try and gain a broad spectrum of practical experience – practical knowledge in the general nursing field. Then at the end of each 'ward experience', the nursing sister concerned would make an assessment of the work she'd done – file her progress or failures in a special book called 'The Book of Schedule'.

She was doing well and she felt happy. And being the person she was, she never failed to keep up her obligations and responsibilities towards her children.

Every month she used to send money and clothes to her two boys back in Trinidad and what little was left over she saved religiously...for that was the type of person she was.

She was happy! She was blissful! She was getting on well and before she knew it Christmas came.

It was her first Christmas at Springvale Hospital and what an eye opener it was. The nurses gave a big party at the nurses' quarters and it was quite an experience – what, with male guests hovering all over the place, Eve kept her eyes wide open.

Choc-a-bloc – the spread which was laid out was quite enticing. There were: cheese on sticks; sausages on sticks; mixed sandwiches; an assortment of cakes and drinks – such as gin, rum, whisky, cans of beer, coke, lemonade, tonic water, some fizzy drinks and a big bowl of rum punch to finish it off – glasses and paper plates stacked high on the tables conveniently positioned in one end of the room. But what caught Eve's eye most, was the tall Christmas tree standing in the far corner of the room.

Different coloured tinsels, coloured bulbs, an assortment of hanging ornaments, little light bulbs – almost setting the tree alight – adorned the tree; a little white fairy with silver-coloured wings, stuck at the top of the tree, completing the décor.

She had never seen a Christmas tree before and she gazed in amazement at it; its lights flickering on and off; the whole tree shimmering with life, as Judy tried to explain its significance.

"The Christmas tree was a token of the celebration of Christianity – the birth of Jesus Christ," Judy tried to explain, the ear-thumping noise in the background deafening, the nurses and guests dancing, jigging away to the music of The Beatles, Elvis Presley and other famous names of the time – blasting away on the record player which they had borrowed.

Some of the nurses were wearing different coloured paper hats; some pulling crackers; some sitting at the sides of the room; others lying on the floor; men drinking beer from large cans; most of them dancing and frolicking the night away.

They danced and danced and some got drunk. They laid on the floor, men kissing women, each clinging to the other: some rolling on top of one another. It was bacchanian!

Eve stood in the corner staring…lost in her thoughts…as she watched the nurses kissing and cuddling, then disappearing with these strange men to have a good 'you know what'. Bewildered by what she was seeing, she wondered if this was how Christ meant Christmas to be. For back in Trinidad she had lived a sheltered life; brought up in the strict Hindu tradition, where sex outside marriage was prohibited. 'Couples must know each oder and dere family's background and certainly must be marry to each oder, before dey could go off and have sex,' she was taught.

She should have been happy, but she was sad!

Lost in an experience in which she was trying to participate, drowning in a world of which she knew nothing of, she sat there dumbstruck; not knowing how to react; how to respond; then all of a sudden, she felt sick, dizzy and ...like a dead rat. Bang! She fell to the ground, stoned out of her mind...

The rum punch had taken its toll with a vengeance, it seemed.

Two nurses rushed over quickly, picked her up, took her to her room in the nurses' quarters and put her to bed. They stuck a rubbish bin under her bed and told her to vomit in it if she felt sick. "Under no circumstance must you get out of bed, should you feel sick," they warned her sharply, then left.

That night, she retched and retched...her stomach churning inside her like a grater. She vomited and vomited...until there was nothing left. The next morning she woke up with a stinking headache but she had to go to work and so reluctantly, she dragged herself out of bed, got washed and dressed quickly and reported for duties as usual.

She was 15 minutes late...

Chapter Forty-Two

Time moved on and she had reached the end of her second year's training. She'd passed her exams with flying colours, coming 'second' in both her first and second year's training and she felt really good. She was enjoying her nursing career.

In the Geriatric Ward where she was seconded, she made friends with Maisie who took her under her wing. Plump and jolly and 40 or so, Maisie had four daughters and she frequently brought in photos of them to show Eve, so proud of the girls she was.

She liked Eve so much that sometimes she would invite her to her home for supper and sometimes for Sunday lunch too. She used to cook roast beef and Yorkshire puddings and they would all sit in front of the burning coal fire and enjoy their meals.

Eve had never seen a coal fire before and she watched with excitement as the burnt out coals spat out of the fire and darted forwards, occasionally landing on the grate. And sometimes, whilst the beef was roasting in the oven, Maisie and her husband Frank, used to take Eve for a drink in the local pub. There, they would enjoy the camaraderie, the buzzing warmth, the friendliness of the local people. She was having such a good time.

Her assignment in the Geriatric Ward was soon completed and she was sent to the Medical Ward E3 where Cissie, now in her third year, took her under her wing. She used to take Eve to the bathroom with her to help bathe the patients. Once there, she would sneak in some cigarettes and a few cups of tea. Then, she would have a good old puff, always ready with an excuse, if ever she should get caught.

A great escape, it was. For whilst in there, Cissie used to tell Eve lots of stories about her boyfriend Freddie.

"Every weekend," she declared, "Mi and Freddie would go pub crawling. And sometimes he would get so pissed," she continued, "Ah used to have to cart him home bodily," she giggled. "He'd lost many a job because he was so pissed and couldn't get up for work the next morning," she chuckled so loud that she and Eve went into hysterics – they had so much fun together, in that bathroom.

Prefabricated tales they may have been, but she had Eve almost buckling up in stitches.

Habitually, Cissie would spend hours in that bathroom, skiving from other chores, only to come out when most of these other jobs were done.

Sometimes, when she put talc and cologne on the patients to freshen them up, she would spray some on herself too – under her arms and beneath her breasts –'to keep mi old man happy!' she would say and the patients used to laugh out so loud, it sent Eve into hysterics.

Happy times they were indeed – times Eve hoped would never end…But her final year soon came and she was seconded to the Surgical Ward – July 1964. And her camaraderie with Cissie came to an abrupt end.

One of her tasks in the Surgical Ward was to remove stitches from a patient's wound and nervous as she was, she tried hard to give it her best shot.

She clipped and pulled…clipped and pulled…her heart thumping inside of her, the senior nurse standing beside her watching as she clipped…and pulled…slowly…slowly…with care, removing all five stitches.

"Well dan! Ah gaye you 99 owt ah 100," the patient said, laughing his head off. "Ya don' it wit so mach expurt, who wad ah taught ya a navice, gal?"

He guessed from her nervousness that it was the first time she had ever removed stitches from a patient's wound and he didn't feel any pain at all. He winked at her wickedly and patted her on the shoulder.

Now she'd gained one more set of experiences to log in her Schedule and she felt good.

She soldiered on and before long, February 1965 came. It was nearing the end of her final year so the pace was hotting up. For having attended many lectures earlier that month, she took her hospital finals (a kind of mock exam in preparation for the real thing) – the State Finals. But when the results came she was in for a surprise…She scored top marks in three subjects: First in Anaesthesia; First in Nursing Practice and First in the Hospital Final itself.

She was over the moon, her heart beating ten to the dozen when she read the results.

She read it over and over again…just to make sure she was reading it right. She was so happy, she wanted to write home and tell Mah and Pah straight away, but she had to do some swift thinking… The State Final was a much tougher exam, she knew that, so she decided to wait until she took that exam and wait for the result before she would write home and break any news to Mah and Pah.

She didn't have to wait long. June 1965 soon came and she took her State Final exam and waited…

She'd passed the Hospital Finals with flying colours, but 'the State Finals were a different kettle of fish,' so the nurses had warned her. 'The State Finals was a tough exam and if she didn't pass it, she could never practise as a qualified nurse in England,' they'd asserted.

But being a nurse was her life now. It had given her hope, security, happiness, a future without which she might well be dead! So she waited in awe for that letter to arrive…
She waited and waited… and when on July 24 1965 'that letter' – 'that notice' finally came, she was scared…

With trembling fingers and shaking like a leaf she broke the seal and opened it. So scared she was; scared in case she might see the word 'FAIL' but then…suddenly…she read the words, 'I have pleasure in informing you...' Her heart missed a beat; she was sure she'd read it wrong.

She took a deep breath then continued reading...'that you have successfully passed the State Final exam.' Her heart almost stopped. She burst into tears. She couldn't read anymore.

She had waited so long for this day; worked so hard for it and now it had finally arrived. Now, at long last she was a qualified nurse? She was choked.

In a few weeks' time she would receive her registration then she would be able to practise as a professional nurse, hold down a professional job, have security for the rest of her life. She, Eve, the girl from the back streets of Carli-Bay Road will never have to starve again.

Clutching the letter in her hand, she cried so loud, she could hardly control herself.

The hospital was proud of their nurses' achievements too, especially that of Eve. For she was a stranger in a foreign land, so unobtrusive, so lacking in confidence, yet able to gain such distinctions – they felt duty-bound to recognise her achievements. So the Management Committee decided to give her a special treat. They arranged a 'Special prize-giving Day' and invited the Mayoress to present her with her prize. And a reporter from the Northern Echo came to record the scene.

Chapter Forty-Three

What a day it was – August 6 1965, a day Eve was never to forget. How could she... ever?

There she stood. Proud on this warm August day as the Mayoress shook her hand and handed her the prize. There was a speech and 'congratulations' but she couldn't remember what was said. So excited she was, so mesmerised with the whole scene.

All she could remember was her thinking to herself... 'If only Mah and Pah were here...if only.'

The next day, Cissie brought in a clipping from the Northern Echo for her to see. It read:

> TRINIDAD GIRL SCOOPS TOP PRIZE
> Trinidad born Miss Eve Ram-Ram was voted 'Nurse of the Year' by Springvale Hospital Group today. She won First prize in Anaesthesia, First prize in Nursing Practice and First prize in the Hospital Final too – the first foreign-born nurse to achieve such distinction in the North East of England...'Three Tops in One Go!' ... and the first, ever to be voted 'Nurse of the Year' by that Hospital Group. She was presented with her Badge of Honour today, by the Mayoress Mrs Mabel Osgood and this shy but unassuming nurse took it all in her stride as the crowd erupted in rapture...

As Cissie read the clippings, the tears began to flow down Eve's cheeks. 'How her luck had changed.'

She must break the news to Mah and Pah straight away! There was no time to waste! So she took the cuttings from Cissie and that very evening, wrote:

Dear Mah and Pah,

How are you an' de children? Ah hope all is well an' you receive de money which ah sen' you las' mont. Hope de weader is not too hot over dere. Aldough Augus' has jus started here, de weader is still cole out here. Sometime de sun does shine, but de cole win' does blow straight through you. Ah hope dat one day you go come over an' see for youself.

But oh Mah and Pah, ah have such good new' fo' you! A couple ah weeks ago, ah pass mi Hospital Finals an' would you bileve it, ah got 3 prizes. First prize in Anaesthesia, First prize in Nursing Practice and First in Hospital Finals. Den las' week, the State Final result came. An' ah pass dat too. Dere was a big celebration Mah and Pah as de Mayoress presented mi wit mi badge and prize – 'a Book Token' so ah go buy more book to study wit.

De man from de newspaper was dere too, Mah an' Pah an' he write a big story about it. Ah save de cuttin' for you an' you go see de Mayoress presentin' mi wit mi prize. Oh Mah an' Pah!

Well dats all fo' now Mah an' Pah. Give de children some kisses fo' mi an' tell dem ah go sen' some mor' money next mont.

Look after youself, Mah an' Pah. Until ah hear from you.

   Love and kisses,
    From you daugter,
      Eve

When Raja read the letter to Mah an' Pah, Mah started to bawl. As for Pah. Well, he was so shell-shocked, he just didn't know how to react.

'She, his Hindu daughter Eve, who once live like a beggar, abandon by him. She, de girl who couldn' achieve anyting on her own was makin' a name for sheself in Englan'; gainin' top awards; bein' write about in de newspapers; takin' her place in society?'

He couldn't believe it. But it was right here – the cuttings from the newspaper – dangling under his nose!

He felt guilty. He felt sick. 'Guilty' of the cruelty he had dished out on her, 'sick' because he had abandoned her when she was so poor, penniless and needed him so badly.

He knew he should be proud, but he felt sad. He felt bad. He felt sad. He just stood there, numb!

'He'd treated her bad, sure! But dat was all in de past now, forgotten. She had forgive him, hadn' she?'

He must share the good news – news of her achievements – to all, even though he knew deep down in his heart that he didn't do much to help her get there.

And so before the week was over, he and Mah told everyone in Carli-Bay Road about Eve's achievements – 'how dere daughter Eve was makin' a name for sheself in Englan'.' And he showed them the cuttings from the newspaper – the photo of Eve and the Lady Mayoress – to prove it.

Funny, isn't it, how all of a sudden, Mah and Pah were proud of their daughter Eve and her achievements? And how, all of a sudden they wanted the world to know about it too?

Their pride had somehow got the better of them, it seemed...

Chapter Forty-Four

Michael Flackerty was an astute businessman who never let an opportunity pass him by. Having arrived in England from Ireland in the '60s, with just £1 in his pocket – within a few years, he had built up his estate agency business into a million pound empire and aptly called it 'Flackerty Estates'.

He had his own way of doing business. If a buyer came to him, he would compromise on his commission and if necessary share it with other estate agents just to get the deal.

Shrewd as he was – he never let a buyer slip through his slippery fingers. He always found some way of clinching 'the deal' – such a cunning entrepreneur he was.

But one smart buyer was about to enter his domain and his life would never be the same again.

Having passed her exams and got her registration, Eve was doing well working on the Medical Ward. Every month, after sending money home for her children's keep, she would put some aside and so before long, she had built up quite a sum and felt ready to return to Trinidad to bring her two children back with her.

But first, however, she had to find somewhere for them to live since, she was living in the nurses' quarters where children were not allowed. So, she went to Flackerty Estate Agent to see if they could help her find a place to live.

It didn't take long – Michael Flackerty soon got the ball rolling and within a week, he'd found her one.

A one bedroomed flat – there was a bed, a table, two chairs, a cooker and a shared bathroom – 'not a lot really, but it had to do, at least for de time being,' she thought. There was much to sort out. There was no time to waste. So she paid the £500 deposit and bought the flat: 5A Mustard Place, Castleton. It was the first flat she was to own and she was ready to move…

Skeletal though it was – scantily decorated and sparsely furnished – little did she know, that this flat would be the first step to her becoming well…guess what?

She didn't have time to think and in any case, her self-esteem was too low…She had too much on her plate to even contemplate such nonsense…She was far too busy to think the unthinkable!

And so having sent off the necessary papers and got the children's passports and paperwork sorted out, she booked her flight with British Airways, ready for her journey to Trinidad.

It was to be a short trip.

No fuss, no ceremony, she was soon on the plane and arrived in Trinidad in no time. But when she got there she quickly realised that things had not changed much at all. For apart from the advent of electric lighting in Couva and a few more concrete built houses, things seemed to be at a stand still – much the same as it was before she left.

This did not surprise her though for the pace of life in Trinidad was always very slow.

She had much to accomplish so she spent two short weeks visiting a few relatives here and there, then she was back on board flight 210, with her two children, bound for England.

It was December 5 1965, a cold winter's day, when they returned to Gatwick, England. The snow pelting down in buckets, white flakes covering their coats as she and her two boys made their way for the train journeys which would eventually take them to Castleton.

With the snow blustering down, Sam nine and Ranjit eight, were shivering like mad; bewildered by the strange faces they were seeing; unhappy about the coldness of the place, but they didn't make a fuss – Eve making a special effort to comfort them. She wrapped them well with their woollen hats and scarves and snuggled them close to her to try and keep warm, then they quickly boarded the train onward bound towards Castleton.

It was a long journey back, having to change trains as usual and it was nearly 6pm when they finally arrived at 5A Mustard Place, cold, tired and hungry. But what a surprise they had, for Michael had spruced the place up. He'd purchased another bed and settee; bought some more food, set the coal fire alight and the place felt warm and homely.

And to top it up, six fresh red roses lay on the table with a card stuck on it which read:

"To Eve, I miss you Queenie…Michael!"

Overcome with emotion, Eve read the card over and over again, just to make sure she was reading it right. She never thought she would find love again and now…?

She tried to dismiss the thought. Pulling herself together she got the boys settled and she was just about to start preparing the supper when the doorbell rang. It was Michael.

When they'd first met he'd shown some interest in her, but she never thought…?

He'd even taken her out for an Indian meal and the waiters cracked a lot of jokes about them, but she didn't think anything would come of it – her spirit was too crushed to think about such fairy tales. And now, here he was, standing in her doorway…?

Her heart was beating 'a thousand to the dozen'.

She introduced him to her two boys and somehow he took an instant liking to them. He liked their shyness, their simplicity, their somewhat good behaviour and he was madly in love with their mother, Eve. He wanted a readymade family and he'd found one and now, there was no time to waste – no stopping him.

They talked and talked a lot that evening, he stoking the fire in between to keep it alight; the boys hovering curiously around him, so well behaved, he couldn't help but like them. Then he ordered an Indian takeaway and all four sat down to a hearty meal.

They enjoyed a meal of chicken curry, rice, darhl and pratha, followed by hot milky coffee. They all joked and laughed and had so much fun, but before they realised it, it was time for him to go.

He stood outside the door that evening, kissing Eve goodbye, his heart pounding, he, knowing deep down within him that he had found his soul mate. For, from the conversations they'd had, he knew that they had much in common – their feelings when they touched each other; their understanding of life; their desire to better themselves; almost everything they shared that evening rang a bell.

And so, as he stood outside the door that evening, his heart thumping away, he knew he shouldn't waste a moment more. So he broke the silence, headfirst – for that was the kind of man he was.

"Will you marry me Queenie?" he said woefully, love in his tender blue eyes.

She didn't have to think much for she too had fallen madly in love with him.

"Oh yes! Yes! Yes!" she replied, her heart pounding, just about to melt as they clung to each other, kissing and kissing...she, madly in love with him and he with her...

It was a quick wedding, January 6 1966, Michael Flackerty married Eve at Castleton Registry Office and cold as it was, no snow fell. Instead, a shimmer of sunshine rained down outside on them; he in his dark suit, she in her cream two piece and they glowed with happiness.

It was as if the heavens in all its glory were showering its blessings upon them; they beaming with joy; her two boys not missing a trick; the guests enjoying the spread laid out tastefully in the hall they'd hired. They were so happy! It showed on their faces.

A simple wedding really, no fuss, no big ceremony and no immediate honeymoon either – both had to report for work the following morning. They'd planned to have a honeymoon later – that was a certainty. But right now...

The camera clicked... the photos taken... they laughed and laughed so much, both so secretly proud of the other... their eyes dancing with joy.

Only this time Eve knew that she was going to spend the night with a man she was madly in love with; a man who hopelessly adored her.

Chapter Forty-Five

Eve and the children were settling in well. Now working in the General Wards at Castleton Hospital she continued religiously to save her surplus money – just in case.

Michael too was doing well. His estate agency business thrived as never before. But since their individual flats were too small for them to live together, they continued living separately in their own flats, spending as much time as they could together. But that was not to be for long.

Not liking such an arrangement, on January 6 1967 he sold his flat, bought 'Mirabell', a five bedroomed mansion at 15 Lovell Close, in the suburbs of Dumbay and moved Eve and her two children in with him.

Eve's flat being empty now; she decided to rent it out – not so much as a business venture, but more as a means of bringing in some spare cash. And so with the extra money coming in, her savings soon grew and before long she had enough money to buy another flat. So she bought 'Cheetas' a two bedroomed flat at 7 Huntington Road and rented that one out too.

Eve Flackerty was fast becoming a shrewd entrepreneur and she didn't even realise it.

Not long after however, on realising that her rental business was thriving, she decided to cut down on her nursing hours and pursue her long-held passion for 'charity work'. For being an underprivileged child herself, she'd always taken an interest in disadvantaged children.

Noting how 'mentally retarded' children suffered prejudice and bad treatment by society, she decided – that with time on her hands now – she must do something about it.

It was something which had long been close to her heart and now that she had the funds and time, she could pursue it. So she set up her first holiday home for mentally retarded children – a project which would give families respite from caring for their loved ones whilst they had a break – at the same time, giving the children a little holiday too.

It was July 7 1968 when she opened that first home, aptly calling it '7 Days' and as she set about organising and putting motions into practice, little did she know that it was the start of a dream she never thought was possible.

As the project got on its feet, she had so much fun watching the children playing simple games like bowls and doing basic tasks such as laying the dining tables and cooking and she felt proud – not least of all from the 'Thank You' letters which came pouring in from parents, when they returned from their holidays.

These achievements lifted her spirits so much that she decided to open up another holiday home.

The gap in her ventures however and the demands for her Homes were growing so fast, that she felt that she had to try and fill that gap – meet the needs of these families. And so, by 1975, she had opened six '7 Days' homes.

In fact, the budding entrepreneur was slowly turning into a Patron as well – only things were moving so fast that she hardly had time to notice it.

Much to her surprise, the property letting side of her business was thriving too. The demand for rental accommodation was escalating at such a pace that she decided to tap in. She used the rental income from her existing properties, borrowed some more money from the banks, bought some more properties, gave them a face-lift and rented them out too.

The once fledgling hopeful – now a fully-fledged entrepreneur, kept investing and investing...that by mid 1977 she had ten rented out properties and six Holiday Homes. She was indeed a multi-millionairess but that didn't change her. She just carried on as before with an air of simplicity that spelt out the woman she truly was.

Working so hard, spending countless hours raising funds for her 'charity homes', she didn't fail to get noticed – much was written about her in the newspapers. She was indeed making a name for herself, but she was getting tired, exhausted at times.

The doctor had warned her. "Lay off, Eve! You're working too hard!" he'd said. But she didn't take heed of his warnings. Ignoring it, she just carried on until one day she collapsed with pneumonia and nearly died.

But for the nurses, she would have been 'well and truly under'.

They put her on a saline drip and pumped antibiotics into her until she sweated and sweated...having nightmares, waking up, then lapsing into a coma – Michael, Sam and Ranjit watching hopelessly over her, fearing she may never recover. But then, 'as luck would have it' after a few days of treatment, her condition improved miraculously. And within a week or so, she was better.

It wasn't long before she was back on tracks again. Eve, the girl from the back streets of nowhere wasn't going to give up the chance to make money – lose opportunities when they were more or less dangling in front of her. She continued on her opportunist journey.

Her ten rental property businesses were at their peak. And the five bedroomed mansion which she shared with Michael, complete with fitted wardrobes and cooker, Sun Logia and garage, tennis court and swimming pool, was quite something.

She felt really good.

Her charity business was making its name too and Sam, now 20, was put in charge of managing its affairs. Ranjit at 19 decided to go to India to do charity work over there.

The days just flew by. She had much time on her hands now and she knew she had to expand her empire. 'Dere were opportunities ahead. She must not let dem slip through her fingers,' she assured herself. So she kept going.

She was on the lookout for these when, would you believe it...her uncle from Rio Claro in Trinidad died suddenly and left her his whole estate – a plantation of several acres of cocoa and coffee.

'She had stretched her resources to its capacity in Englan' and now dis opportunity had arisen, so suddenly in Trinidad? She had de skills and de money and now dis land too?' She must move fast...move as quickly as she could...give it her best bite.

Though she loved England she hated the cold and always hoped, deep down in her heart, that one day she would return to Trinidad and settle down there – in that warm and sunny climate. And now that the opportunity had arisen and she was rich, it was time for her to take up the challenge.

'She would buil' her exotic villa dere, complete with ten bedrooms, sunny verandas, tennis courts, swimming pools; flowerbeds and palm trees to the front. Mangoes and other tropical fruit trees in the back.'... Her mind was working overtime.

The dream that she once dreamt was about to come true. And so, after discussing her plans with Michael and having spent sleepless nights, she booked a flight with British Airways on a Boeing 707 to take her to Trinidad.

Only this time, she was a multi-millionairess.

The girl who was once homeless, penniless and survived in a mud hut with no knickers to cover her bare bottom and no shoes to wear, was now going to build one of the biggest mansions Trinidad was ever to see – with millions and millions to spend.

How the tables had turned.

Chapter Forty-Six

Things were moving fast. Here she was at 40, sitting on a Boeing 707 bound for Trinidad, busy rustling up plans to build her new villa in Rio Claro. It was April 6 1980.

Raja was busy too, helping to find a local builder, drawing up plans and liaising with the Trinidad government to build her villa out there. But unknown to her, somehow he managed to spare a moment or two to talk to the Trinidadian reporters. And now at Trinidad's only airport, he and other members of the family waited... and waited for her to show, then all of a sudden, as if by magic... she appeared.

She walked down the aeroplane's steps feeling proud but then... Click... Click... Click... Click! Lights flashing everywhere! Newspaper men scuttling all over the place, pushing and shoving, each trying to get the best shot of her; to make headline news; to break the news first.

It was like pantomime.

Disturbed by this sudden unexpected surge of media attention, she dived for cover, frightened, bedazzled in her cream two-piece suit. But Raja quickly raced to her rescue. He grabbed her hand and together they belted down the tarmac as fast as their legs could carry them, jumping into the first taxi they could find, the media hot on their heels.

With speed, other members of her family grabbed her belongings and followed suit too.

Feeling guilty at what he'd done...which resulted in this hot pursuit of her by the media, he, Raja – her beloved brother, was unable to greet her as he should have done. And now he felt guilty.

Proud of his sister, he'd told the media all about 'how she'd become a multi-millionairess in Englan' but naïve as he was, he didn't expect them to pounce on her, descend on her like a set of vultures. And now – he'd paid the price for it – as he watched her in a state of shock. She was so distressed.

He felt guilty! He felt bad! All he could do now was try and protect her.

As the taxi bolted its way towards Couva, she noticed that a lot of changes had taken place.

Like a concrete jungle, concrete buildings had sprung up all over the place. There were people diving in and out of shops in Upper Couva, bumping into each other, each trying to pick up the best bargains, it seemed.

'She must explore her homeland, note de changes,' she thought. 'But right now she had so much to do...' She would do the exploring some other time.

'She was going to buil' her mansion in Rio Claro and she only has a few weeks in which to make de necessary arrangements. She must hurry! Get tings moving! Only den would she have time on her hands to sample de changes of her birthplace...and have some fun.'

Hastily they drove through the hustling, bustling traffic in Upper Couva and when they finally arrived at Raja's house, it was 6pm.

They made such a fuss of her, trying to make her feel welcome, that she was overcome.

They served her with a meal of nice hot darhl and rice and fried salmon followed by ice cream sundae and hot milky coffee to wash it all down. And they talked and talked and laughed and gossiped about her trip over there and her escapades in England, but she was so tired that she retired early. She lay on a bed of silk sheets over a soft thick mattress thinking... The bed being so comfortable, that within a few minutes she fell asleep.

When she woke up the next morning, Raja was waiting for her. He had the newspaper, the Trinidad Guardian in his hand.

It read:

QUEEN EVE RETURNS IN TRIUMPH!
The once poverty-stricken Eve who lived in a mud hut, returns to Trinidad a multi-millionairess.
She made her fortune in England as a Property Developer and now plans to build a multimillion-dollar villa in Rio Claro.
This shy, unassuming lady took it all in her stride, but no doubt, as the camera clicked today when she landed at the airport, Queen Eve was secretly wallowing in pride. There seems to be no end to the quest of this bedazzled lady who once walked the streets of Trinidad, homeless, penniless and barefooted.
Bravo Queen Evita!

Eve could listen no more. She put the hairbrush down and started to cry. She couldn't believe what she was hearing.

She sniffed and cried, then took a deep breath and quickly tried to pull herself together, knowing that, though shocked at what Raja had just read, secretly her heart was bubbling with joy. She felt a deep glow rising inside her. A kind of elation! Elated, because at long last the country of her birth was recognising her. Recognising her achievements – the media giving vent to it – writing about it.

She took the papers from Raja and sat there holding it in her hand, numb! She couldn't speak – not a single word...no movement, nothing!

But there was work to do, ambitions to realise. She had to make a move, fast.

She tucked into her breakfast of eggs on toast followed by sweet milky coffee which Raja's wife had prepared, then after freshening herself up, she and Raja set off for Rio Claro.

They drove through the bustling traffic with some trepidation, but it wasn't long before they arrived at Rio Claro Junction. From there they drove on through a road leading to a narrow winding dirt track. On and on they drove – through this track – miles and miles of coffee vines laden with red coffee beans; vines growing haphazardly on either side of this track, wrapping themselves like snakes around tall poui and cedar trees; trees standing like sentinels around both sides of this unkempt dirty mud track; their branches so overgrown they hung like umbrellas about to touch passers-by as they walked beneath them; trees with yellow oblong shaped cocoas, ripe and almost ready to split open and drop on the heads of any invaders who dared to invade their territory.

As they drove through this forestry of plantation, Eve noticed a few wooden houses dotted here and there; some leaning so far to one side – as if they would tumble in the strong wind; their galvanised roof tops shimmering under the sunlight; their small windows shining like torches through the wavering breeze.

'What a sight it was. Almost like heaven – untouched; unkempt; unspoilt! Idyllic paradise!' she thought.

Hot and sweaty, she and Raja forged through that tapestry of forest, then she spotted Uncle Baj's old house.

There it was, standing on tall wooden posts buried in the middle of the plantation, it seemed – its unpainted jalousies creaking in the wind as they drove closer. It was leaning so badly to one side, it gave the impression that if a strong wind blew, it would surely tumble over.

Raja had employed people to reap some of the cocoa and coffee beans, but no one bothered to care for the house. There it stood, battered with the tropical winds, surrounded by this forestry of cocoa and coffee beans – a tropical unkempt paradise, it seemed!

They got out of the car and for a moment Eve stood there staring… She stared at this huge plantation; its atmosphere so peaceful, so tranquil – a little piece of paradise which was all hers.

She could hardly believe what her eyes were seeing.

'She would pull down dis old house and buil' her multimillion dollar villa dere. A little piece of heaven in de middle of Paradise Island.' Her mind was buzzing…

She stood there mesmerised by the beauty of the place, unable to move; unable for a split second to think clearly. But she knew she had to make a move. There wasn't much time left. She must get going…

Chapter Forty-Seven

Over the next few days Eve and the builder went up to Rio Claro and worked and worked. They finalised the plans; worked on the estimates; worked on the costs; worked on everything till they got it down to a fine art. Then she paid him the deposit and left him to get on with the task of building her multimillion-dollar villa.

With the building project well in hand, she decided to go shopping. She went down to Port-of-Spain's shopping centre and bought herself some summer clothes – red, green, orange, yellow, blue – all bright coloured clothing, and shoes to match too. Then she treated herself to some nice hot roti sandwiches from the street vendors who were selling outside the shops. She felt really good that day – an inner sense of happiness!

It wasn't long though before word got around about her...Like wildfire it spread. Rumours – that she had returned from England a multi-millionairess; that she was wearing such nice clothes and jewellery and talking so posh, when in fact she didn't speak or dress any differently at all.

But still the rumours flourished.

And so daily they flocked in – relatives, friends, they all came to see her – how she looked; how she dressed; how she talked. Everything!

On they came – some out of curiosity; some out of jealousy; most treating her as though she was some kind of celebrity, showering her with gifts, cash, anything they could lay their hands on. Even Sumin, Ram-Ram's sister came to see her.

"You looking good, sis," Eve greeted her, putting her arms around her shoulders, embracing and kissing her on both cheeks, Eve's gold identity bracelet dangling from her wrist.

"Oh Eve! Eve! Yu-u look great sis," Sumin replied, stuttering, shocked at the transformation of this once bedraggled girl. So beautifully dressed she was, in her mini-skirt, showing off her slim brown legs, jewels dangling from her lovely body. Sumim was finding it hard to believe what her eyes were seeing. 'She Eve, de girl who once came to her barefoot and beggin' for lodgins was now a multi-millionairess. So rich – yet so down to eart', ordinary! She hadn' change a bit,' she thought.

They talked and talked and drank lots of Coca-cola, Sumin unable to comprehend the 'guts' of this girl, Eve; unable to fathom out what made her tick. She wanted to spend a lot more time with Eve but her lover was sick at home and she had to leave. So she gave her $20 and departed quickly.

Eve spent the next few days visiting most of her relatives; spending a day here; a day there – each treating her as if she was royalty itself. They fed her with the best food, and pampered her with presents – from perfumes to toiletries; clothes to cash. But Mah's gift was the best of all – a gold thick-set diamond cut bracelet – beautifully crafted, specially designed for her.

Overwhelmed, Eve did not know what to make of it all.

They'd treated her as it she was the Queen herself because they had high hopes of her – hopes that one day their sons and daughters will go to England and 'make it big' too. The immigration laws had tightened up since Eve's time, but that didn't dent their dreams for their offspring. They hoped deep down within their souls, that Eve would be the executioner of those dreams – help their offspring get to England. So they crept and crawled, begged and pampered and showered her with gifts – she, being so embarrassed about it all – she did not know what to do.

She didn't need these gifts, but she couldn't hurt their feelings by refusing to take them. So she took them and did what she did best – gave it to the poor.

Pah's behaviour however, bothered her most – it was putting her on edge.

He worried himself sick, if she sat in the sun. He used to rush over with an umbrella and coax her to shelter under it. And if the sun was too hot when she went in to town, he would race behind with an umbrella for her to take with her. He seemed to want to protect her, even from the sun.

Now, whenever he went into town, he would bring back barah (Indian pastry) and chana and sometimes he brought back sugar cakes too. Then at mealtimes, he insisted that she was served first and given as many helpings as she needed.

What a fuss he was making of her?

What a change in him? It was as though he had gone through some kind of metamorphosis – showing remorse for the way he'd treated her when she was poor. It seemed he was now regretting every moment of that time and was trying so hard to make it up to her.

Before, she was the 'black sheep' of the family. Now it seemed, she was their great 'white hope'.

Secretly however, she was enjoying the fuss they were making of her. But she had other matters on her mind…She had important business to attend to and she must not forget that. So, every few days, religiously, she travelled up to Rio Claro to oversee the building of her multimillion-dollar villa.

The builder was making good progress. The foundation was laid; the bricks and mortar was taking shape and Eve was indeed a very happy woman. So she spent a little time having fun; sunning herself down at Mayaro beach; whiling the evenings listening to the steel bands at the Flamingo and Hilton hotels; spoiling herself with the mouth watering West Indian gourmet food on offer.

She was enjoying herself so much, when one day she was taken by surprise...

It was during her final week's stay that Michael suddenly announced that he was flying over from England to join her. It was a surprise visit, but he wouldn't say why.

She worried herself sick, tossing and turning all that night wondering. But come next morning she was glad to see him.

The frequent trips overseeing the building of her villa continued, but in between, they both had a great time wiling the evenings away at different venues.

They watched and listened to the steel bands as they pounded away, making beautiful calypso-type music from the notes the musicians knocked into those antiquated oil drums. And they went to the calypso tents and heard the Calypso Kings – The Mighty Power, The Mighty Shaker and others singing many of the famous calypsos of the time – folk-type music, which spelt the mood of the period – calypsos such as '...Australia you lost, the West Indies is boss...' and ...'bottles and stones falling an' no place to shelter' (songs about cricket). And they whistled and hooted, clapped and roared and laughed themselves silly.

But amidst all the fun, Eve knew that Michael had something on his mind. It was a secret which he could no longer keep. And so, within a few days of his arrival, he booked a table for two at the Hilton Hotel and broke the news to her.

It transpired that shortly after Eve had left for Trinidad she was awarded a Damehood for her charity work with the mentally retarded and their families – 'A ground-breaking venture,' they said, 'pursued with all the courage and dedication she could muster.' And so, the committee concerned decided to award her 'a Damehood' – an honour befitting her dedication and actions.

That evening as she and Michael sat at the Hilton Hotel he handed her something. It was the letter from Rockingham Palace.

Shocked, she could hold back the tears no more. She broke down and started to cry. She just couldn't believe it.

'A dream beyond her wildest imagination!' It was as if she had come full circle. Everything happening all at once...'her wealth; her dream home; recognition by her own country and now...dis too!' She was crying so much that Michael had to comfort her. But she had good news to celebrate and so after a lot of hugging and kissing and drying of tears, Michael finally ordered the meal.

They had a typical West Indian meal. Caribbean style soup for starters, dressed crab in salad, yam, sweet potatoes and callaloo (Caribbean style vegetable) for their main course; two whopping banana boats for sweet, followed by hot sweet milky coffee to wash it down and a full bottle of Champagne completed the meal.

They ate and laughed and chatted about what she would wear for the ceremony at Rockingham Palace, she breaking into fits of laughter.

They were so happy that she hoped the day would never end. But her days of fun in Trinidad were soon coming to an end. They had one more day left, then they would be back on a plane to England where one of the highest honours awaited her.

It was a citadel she never hoped she would climb! A dream she hardly believed would ever materialise! And now...?

She could hardly bear to wait.

Chapter Forty-Eight

"Fasten your safety belts," she heard the voice saying as she and Michael sat back in their seats on the jumbo jet, ready to depart for England. Her heart was thumping – feelings of excitement, exhilaration, funny feelings deep within her soul stirred as she thought of the glory which awaited her.

'She, Eve, de girl from nowhere was about to get a Damehood in Englan'. Honoured by de Queen herself?' She couldn't believe it. But it was true alright – right there in the letter which Michael had given her to read.

Her nerves began to get the better of her. She felt queasy...She felt sick...Her head spinning. Like a big wheel, it spun, then all of a sudden...SP-LA-SH! She vomited – vomit spurting from her mouth; like an angry river, it spurted – as if about to burst its banks – it gushed out...all in one go. But fortunately for her, Michael held the vomit bag under her mouth, just in time to save her from embarrassment.

"Are you alright?... alright?" She heard the voice saying; she couldn't discern who it was... the Hostess maybe? Or someone else?... voices... voices... calling out, then... "It's alright! It's... alright!" she heard Michael saying as he tried to calm her down.

She could feel him holding her hand and stroking her shoulders gently as she wiped her mouth with the wet flannel the Air Hostess had given her. Then after a few moments, she felt better, relieved...She rested her head back on the headrest and tried to relax for the rest of the journey.

It was June 2 1980, 2.15pm, when they arrived at Heathrow Airport. Tired and anxious, they were in a hurry to catch the train onward bound to Dumbay. There was no time to waste. They must hurry, get there quickly – so much to do and so little time left.

She had to arrange for a 'special outfit' to be made for her to wear at the ceremony; travel arrangements to be made; hotel bookings to arrange for them to stay a night or two in London. Such a lot to do really and such a short time in which to do it?

But Eve was not phased. As soon as she got home, she got cracking.

First she arranged the costume-making with her designer, Alice Potterton. Alice was one of the most famous dress designers in England at the time and it was agreed that Eve would visit her studio regularly for ongoing fittings. Sam too was busy making travel arrangements and hotel bookings for the 'big day'.

Before long, matters were well in hand and Eve continued to pursue her charity business with vengeance. Such a lot to do, so much to keep up with, it seemed. What, with the reporters following her every move – reporting bits here; bits there in their newspapers – almost daily – articles about her seemed to appear. She was working overtime.

'7 Days' was making headline news now. And with the clients' relatives sending countless letters of 'Thank you' and 'Congratulations' about her forthcoming Damehood and the clients themselves lapping up their holidays at '7 Days', Eve could do no wrong, it seemed.

She was riding on a crest wave... that seemed even bigger than the stars...

But time passed quickly and before she knew it the 'big day' came. It was November 12 1980, the day she was to receive her Damehood. They had spent the night before at the Belview Hotel, Eve having tossed and turned all night long...She hardly slept a wink.

She was up at 5am that morning, so excited she was.

After a quick breakfast, she had a shower and got dressed in her pink two-piece designer made suit and coat; a white hat bordered with gold and decorated with a few black flowers; a pair of black shoes; white gloves and handbag; plus a small diamond necklace with diamond ear studs completing the outfit – Alice Potterton having the honour of dressing her.

They were ready. Alice Potterton had done her proud and she looked stunning.

Cruising down The Mall in the black limousine they'd hired, they arrived at Rockingham Palace at 10.30am. The red and black suited Guards saluting them with precision as they drove through the golden gates, Eve sitting back proudly in the limousine, taking it all in.

After parking, they made their way by foot – discreetly guided – until they reached the Picture Gallery where they were greeted by the Queen's right hand man himself, Eve looking around in awe at the environment in which she'd found herself.

Thick red carpet on which to walk; big oil paintings hanging on the walls – paintings by Rembrandt, Picasso, Van Gogh, Baptiste; portraits of the Queen's family and of herself – all painted by artists of the day – hung in semblance, as if ready to spring out and talk to the onlookers.

Eve kept on staring…lost in that world of 'make belief'…when very quickly they were ushered in groups of ten, to the threshold of the ballroom, where the ceremony was to take place.

It was exactly 11am when Eve's name was called…

Gingerly, she walked along the red carpet into the Queen's Ballroom, the Queen – dressed in a blue suit and wearing just three strands of pearls around her neck – stood there patiently, taking it all in her stride.

As Eve walked towards her, a man handed the Queen the 'Badge of Honour'. Eve bowed, curtsied (almost on bended knees) her body trembling on the inside. Then, she straightened herself up quickly and the Queen shook her hand and hung the 'Honoured Pendant' around her neck.

She could see how nervous Eve was so she wasted no time in making her feel at ease.

"It's a pleasure to meet you Mrs Flackerty and it is of great consolation to me, on hearing of the wonderful work you have done with disadvantaged children," she said.

"Thank you Mam," Eve replied, bowing again, courteously, the Queen standing there, warmth in her gaze.

"And I heard you started life as a poor barefooted girl in the back streets of the Caribbean. Such courage! Such dedication! What an inspiration to us all!"

Eve hardly had time to answer when she was ushered out quickly, without further ado.

It was all over in a jiff and she walked backwards as she was told to do.

As she walked out of that ballroom and headed towards her family, words could hardly describe the feelings which stirred within her...feelings that were hard for her to convey.

They went to the state Guest Room where the celebrations had already started. Michael and Sam looking so smart in their Savile Row dinner jackets, white shirts and black bow ties; Eve, having to muster all the strength she could, to hold back the tears.

They dank Champagne and enjoyed the spread and they talked and talked and they laughed... Eve hardly believing her luck. The pomp, the ceremony, the glorious moments, the biggest day of her life!

She, the girl from Carli-Bay Road who was once so poor, had now climbed a citadel where few had dared to reach.

Excitement! Exhilaration! Her mind leaping in bounds... when... the Footman suddenly opened the door to the forecourt and... Click! Click! The cameras went into action – lights flashing around her, almost blinding her, cameramen trying to get the best shot, each hoping to make their fortune with that little piece of 'snap shot!'

It was like all hell let loose.

The next morning, her photos appeared on every front page of every newspaper in the land… almost all angles… all guises… But for her, the Telegraph seemed to carry to best story. It read:

> MULTI-MILLIONAIRESS TAKES THE HONOUR
> Multi-millionairess Eve became a Dame at Rockingham Palace today. 'Queen Eve', who was once a penniless girl living in a mud hut in the back streets of Trinidad, was honoured with a Damehood by the Queen at Rockingham Palace today and the unassuming 'Dame' took it all in her stride…

As she read the words, tears began to well in her eyes; tears, not of sadness, but of joy; tears, not of sorrow, but of glory; tears – a mixture of surprise and happiness; tears, reminding her of the biggest day of her life – the day when she received her Damehood; a day for the history books; a day, she could never, ever, forget!

She had to pinch herself to make sure all this was real. But it was real alright – she was holding the Honorary Badge – it was right there, dangling from her neck.

She squeezed it over and over again, just to reassure herself that it was real.

'She must phone Raja,' she thought, 'Break de news to him; send him de cuttings from de newspaper.' There was no time to waste.

But oh how she wished Mah and Pah were here to enjoy these glorious moments with her. Alas! – they had departed from this world a short while ago. She'd made a quick journey there – attended the formalities and their funerals, but had to make a speedy return back to England as there was so much going on in her life over here.

'And now? ... never mind! Mah and Pah. Never mind! Your daughter Eve, de once poor penniless girl from de back streets of Couva had received her Damehood yesterday, Mah and Pah, from de Queen of England herself and Queen Eve, as de press now dubbed her, is in her element, her crowning moment of glory.'

'If only you were here to see...'

Chapter Forty-Nine

For the next ten years, life for Eve was hectic as she continued to build her empire. She bought ten more properties – five houses and five flats and rented them out. She sold five of her previous properties at a profit, banked some of it and ploughed some into buying accessories for her multimillion dollar villa in Trinidad. Now, in 1990 she was the proud owner of 15 properties, six Holiday Homes plus her villa in the Caribbean.

Though her business empire was managed by her appointed manager – her son Sam – there was still a considerable amount of work which she had to do herself. Work such as, vetoing the bills, visiting clients (which she always preferred to do herself) updating her charity work, as well as keeping up with movements regarding her villa.

She was working so hard that she was getting exhausted, worn out, so she decided to take a break and spend a week or two at her villa in Trinidad. But before going away, she spent that Christmas of 1990 with Michael, Sam and his family at her home in Lovell Close.

They had a lovely time together, enjoying the beautiful warm atmosphere of the crackling coal fire; tinsel and Christmas trees; ribbons and crackers and they had a lot of fun opening their Christmas present too.

They ate turkey and roast potatoes, sprouts and peas; Christmas pudding topped with cranberry sauce and drank lots and lots of wine. But something wasn't quite right...Michael was unusually quiet and Eve put it down to his feeling 'under the weather'.

He'd planned to take a break and go to France, when she returned from her holiday in the Caribbean and she knew that would lift his spirits. So she wasn't too concerned about his apparent 'quietness'. It didn't dawn on her that something else might be amiss; something else might be bothering him. And so, two weeks after Christmas she left as planned for her holiday in Trinidad.

It was January 7 1991 when she boarded 'Virgin Atlantic' and headed for Trinidad, her multimillion-dollar villa having been completed and furnished; Raja racing about to add the finishing touches, in time for her arrival.

It was cold that day at Heathrow Airport. Sprinkles of snowflakes like white mist covered the ground here and there. So she boarded the plane with great speed.

But when she sat back on the aeroplane, waiting for the flight to take off, she remembered the funny feelings – that queasy feeling deep down inside of her...when she kissed Michael goodbye.

Putting it down to jittery nerves, she quickly dismissed the thought and set her mind on the task ahead.

She knew that back in Trinidad, Raja was waiting for her; waiting anxiously to fill her in with the good news; news about her villa and its possibilities; about everything. So she felt relieved and lay back in anticipation of what was to come.

And true to form, Raja left nothing to chance. He had the place spruced up, almost shining and hired two servants to cater for her every needs – get her meals ready; prepare her bath. Everything.

In short, he catered for her every whim!

And now, here she was, several hours after leaving England – landed in Trinidad – walking down the gangplank, proud as a princess, noting the excitement in Raja's face as he greeted her.

As they drove through Rio Claro she noticed that there was much progress being made – progress beyond her wildest imagination.

The once narrow muddy street which led to her villa in Rio Claro was now a wide pitch road; many of the old wooden houses nearby, now replaced with concrete ones. Palm trees lined the road on either side, small tropical gardens to the front of these houses, flower pots boasting tropical plants adorning their front steps.

Driving through her land – acres and acres of coffee and cocoa plantation – her villa appeared in view. Large pruned gardens – circles and squares of tropical flower plants peeping out behind hibiscus hedges – to the front; pots of geraniums and Anthurium lilies adorning the front steps, its tiny buds signalling its readiness to burst into plumage. And like sentinels, tall white painted balustrades and glass louvered windows about to salute her.

Aghast, amidst such spectacle, she could hardly wait to get in to her villa. Excitedly, as she neared it, she jumped out of the car and made a dash for it, Raja racing to open the front door.

She stared at the spectacle which unfolded in front of her: ten bedrooms and two reception rooms each with brass door handles; two bathrooms with showers and sinks with brass taps; a games room; a tennis court plus a swimming pool, its blue waters rippling away under the dazzling sunlight. It was sheer magic.

She stared and stared, as white lace over pink, yellow and blue bed covers emerged before her eyes. White lace hoods drooping above the beds; shimmering glass tables, each with a glass vase filled with fresh tropical flowers and placed in its centre. White two and three piece soft cushioned suites and polished cabinets filled with crystal-cut glasses adorned the reception rooms; basket chairs strung along the plush verandas; servants scurrying about the place trying to make a good impression.

Bewildered! Eve sat down with Raja to take a breath or two, but she hardly had time to take in the splendour, the decadence of the place, when one of the servants breezed in with a bottle of ice cold Champagne plus two cut-glass flutes on a tray.

Mesmerised by the magnificence of the place, her heart bubbled with joy, as she and Raja sat on the veranda sipping Champagne; the cool breeze blowing gently through her jet black hair. She was overcome.

She couldn't believe her luck? 'Here she was, de girl from nowhere, sitting in her multimillion-dollar villa mansion in de Caribbean, sipping Champagne, watching de blue waters of de pool ripple by, servants scurryin' around her?' It was almost beyond belief.

Her thoughts were playing mayhem when suddenly, "Dinner is serve Madam!" the little Negro servant, Joyce, announced, curtseying and smiling as she did so, her white teeth sparkling, her dark skin shining under her spruced blue and white uniform, her well-pressed black hair tied back from her forehead.

"Thank you Miss…"

"Joyce," she replied shyly, bowing a little then scuttled away, without saying a further word.

Eve and Raja seated themselves at the long polished dinner table; well-lit candelabras meticulously placed along its smooth surface; spotless china crockery, cutlery and shining glasses specially imported from England, all laid out before her, with precision.

"Thank you for this meal, my Lord," Eve prayed, before they started to eat. For, ever since she'd become a Christian, she always offered thanks to God before eating a meal.

They had eddoes and echroe soup for starters; sweet potatoes, yam and rice (cooked Caribbean style) and roast pork for their main course; salad, bread and cold meat, laid out as a side dish; iced snowball in silver cups, topped with sweet red syrup for sweet. White wine galore! And sweet milky coffee to wash it all down.

What a meal! It was a real Caribbean treat!

But as they sipped their French Sauternes and ate their mouth watering West Indian gourmet food, Eve was unusually quiet. Her mind was working overtime...finding it hard to come to terms with her luck. 'De decadence which now surrounded her. Dis huge villa, de swimming pool; acres and acres of plantation land; de servants; de lot!'

She was almost in a state of shock, quietly musing...

It was a long and tiring day for Raja and so, after dinner, he said his goodbyes and went home to his wife, leaving Eve to bask in her newfound splendour.

After dinner, she sat quietly by the swimming pool, surveying her luck, hoping deep in her heart that this 'bubble' would never burst. Then after a quick shower, she phoned Michael and retired to bed early.

The next few days were spent dining with friends and relatives at her villa; sipping Champagne and wine by the side of her swimming pool and dancing the nights away to the sound of the steel bands she'd hired.

She went to the calypso tents with Raja and some friends and she visited 'steel band alley' down at Port of Spain too; then she went and spent a day with Raja and his wife in Couva.

It was a pleasant day at Raja's, enjoying the company of the many relatives who visited her there. She spoilt herself rotten, drinking wine and cola and sampling exotic foods which Raja's wife cooked for her. But the day passed quickly and it was soon time for her to return to her villa in Rio Claro.

On her return that evening, she phoned Michael as usual, before retiring to bed, only to be woken early next morning to a telegram.

It read:

'HURRY HOME – BAD NEWS – NO TIME TO EXPLAIN'
Michael xx

She dropped the telegram, panic-stricken. She was shaking with fear.

'What could it be? What could it be?' she asked herself, distressed, shocked out of her wits; unable to comprehend why Michael did not tell her when she'd spoken to him on the phone, only last night.

She rushed to the telephone and tried to phone him again, but there was no answer.

She tried and tried; again and again, only to find that his telephone line was engaged. So, distressed – almost at breaking point – she phoned the airline and booked an emergency flight back to England, leaving her servants to inform Raja of her sudden departure. Then, she wired a message to Michael, informing him that she was on her way home...

Chapter Fifty

It was 9am that morning when Eve sat on a Virgin Atlantic plane, bound for England.

She had spent just over a week in Trinidad when she was forced, so unceremoniously to return home.

And now here she was once again sitting on a plane making her way home to England; in a state of shock, trying desperately to figure out what the hell was happening...not knowing what awaited her.

Meanwhile at Heathrow Airport in England, Michael waited anxiously; waiting...waiting for her to arrive.

He didn't have to wait long. As soon as the plane landed, Eve rushed towards him.

"What is it? What is it Michael?" she screamed, panicking, "I tried to phone you but I couldn't get any answer."

He grabbed her hand firmly and took her to one side.

"Now Eve calm down. Calm down! I beg you."

"Tell me Michael! Tell me! What...? What...?" she was beside herself, distressed with worry.

"Eve! Oh Eve! Eve, it's Ranjit!" the grief stricken Michael replied, "He's dead! Eve, dead!"

"Dead? Oh God! No...No!" she burst into tears, sobbing her heart out, the disturbed Michael doing his best to calm her down.

"Oh Eve...Eve...Sh-oo-sh! Sh-oo-sh!" he tried to console her, holding her firmly in his arms, pity in his eyes as he tried to comfort her.

"Eve...?" he said, choked. He couldn't finish what he was about to say, she, crying so much, so distraught she was.

She was howling.

He did his best to calm her spirits, then they flagged a taxi and made their way to the side of the waiting train. He hugged her comfortingly for a few seconds, then gingerly they stepped into the train and slowly sat down.

As the train pulled out, he held on to her hands, comforting her, caressing her face, gently wiping the tears from her face, trying hard to soothe her pain.

But nothing it seemed could stop her from crying. She cried and cried, until there were no more tears left, then finally somehow, she managed to pull herself together.

After a while and after he was sure she'd calmed down, he tried to finish what he was about to say. Gently, he broke the rest of the news... of how Ranjit was blown up by a terrorist bomb on his way to a charity event at the border of India and Pakistan...

The news hit her like a bolt of lightning and like a piece of stone, she froze and could cry no more. It was as if all the tears that had sprung from within her had suddenly dried up and there was no more left for her to shed.

She just sat there numb – Michael sitting beside her in a state of turmoil.

He had just broken the worst news in the world, to a woman he was once madly in love with and now she just sat there, broken, in such a poor state of shock...unable to react.

Once he was crazy about her: would do anything for her. Now, that magic was gone, that light was out.

He knew he had more bad news for her...but he couldn't let on. Not now! It must wait.

He sat there quietly beside her lost in his thoughts, as the train sped its way onward bound, towards Dumbay.

Chapter Fifty-One

It was a quick funeral on that cold March day, March 13 1991. For – as requested by Eve – after the usual tests, enquiries and examinations, they had flown Ranjit's body speedily back to England, where it would be cremated. A quiet funeral – just a few mourners – Michael, Eve, Sam, the priest and two friends. No fuss, no ceremony.

Quietly the priest chanted a few prayers, then the splintered body was taken away to be cremated, Eve so broken on the inside, unable to cry. She just stood there numb.

Dressed in his dark suit and standing next to the broken Eve, Michael stood there, a very disturbed man, a forlorn look on his face. He had more bad news to break, but he couldn't do it. Not now! Not during the funeral. 'He would break that news later,' he said to himself.

Out of sympathy, or for reasons best known to themselves, the media did not follow Eve around or chase her about either. But the next morning, the news of Ranjit's death and his funeral was plastered on the front pages of all the major newspapers in England. They certainly did not let her off easily.

That night Eve bawled herself to sleep. It was as if all the tears which had built up inside her had suddenly burst out. Like a fountain, it spurted and she cried and cried and cried...

For the next few weeks, things sobered down a little. Eve desperately trying to pull herself together; Michael most of the time, hovering quietly in the background, carrying a dark secret on his conscience.

She soldiered on until before long, she was more or less back to her normal self.

Her '7 Days' Holiday Homes were doing so well that she decided to open another one. And so, on August 6 1991, amidst full regalia, she opened her 7th '7 Days' Holiday Home – the media and everyone of importance seemed to be present.

Dressed in full ceremonial robes, with the gold Mayoral chain flashing around her neck and shoulders, the Mayoress made the opening speech:

"Friends, ladies and gentlemen,"

she said…

*"It gives me great pleasure to open '7 Heaven' the seventh Holiday Home, a charity enterprise inspired by this brave and inventive lady, Eve.
We all know what the 7 Days Holiday Homes do, so I shall not reiterate any more. But…"*

The crowd burst into applause, her speech receding into the background as they went on and on… clapping, hooting, whistling. Then after moments of hysteria, there was a sudden silence as she broke the Champagne bottle – the audience soon going into a crescendo again, Michael standing by quietly, almost aloof.

He could see the glow of happiness on Eve's face. She was back to her old self again – well almost back to her normal self – and he felt good. Good but sad.

'The time was right for him to break the news,' he thought.

And so that very Friday evening, he took her out to dinner at the local Indian restaurant.

As the Indian music played softly in the background and the handsome waiters immaculately dressed in their black and white uniforms busily scurried about the place, Michael sipped his wine slowly and stared into Eve's dark watery eyes, then whispered, "Eve I have something to tell you."

Unaware of the blast that was just about to be fired, the beautiful Eve, looking radiant in her red evening gown, looked at him and grinned. She thought he was being funny.

"Eve! It's serious Eve! Serious! I...I...it happened so quickly Eve," he blurted.

"Happened? What happened Michael? What? What?" the grin on her face disappearing as she questioned him, her eyes flaring alight.

"I didn't mean to Eve. I didn't mean it."

"Mean what Michael? What?" her eyes on fire now, the expression on her face changing to anger as she sensed disaster looming.

Unable to cope with the impending disaster; unable to hold back any more, "I... I... I've been having an affair!" he blurted, the contours on his face showing pain. Riddled with guilt, he delivered the blow.

"You what?"

She went mad.

She was just about to hit him. Pick up the plate of food and throw it at him when she came to her senses. She had to think fast.

'If she did that, de media would have a field day – her reputation would be ruined; her business career would be finished. Everyting! Everyting that she worked for would be thrown to de wolves in one mad moment...gone!'

'She must try and keep calm, if only for appearance sake,' she thought, but she was livid inside.

Doing his best to calm her down, Michael poured another drink. "Have another drink," he said, guilt showing in his searching eyes.

She looked at him hard, rage showing on the contours of her face, she, trembling, as he poured and she drank and drank...

He paused; waited till she'd calmed herself a little then reeled out what had happened.

Slowly, slowly he told her how he'd met this other woman, his voice barely audible now.

"She'd come to his office looking for work and things just developed from there," he said. He tried to explain 'how they were drifting apart; how she Eve, was too busy with her properties and charity work; how they never had any time to spend together and have fun as they used to before.' "Many a time, I tried to tell you that," he said, "but you were too busy to hear the warnings. Then I met Sharon and we fell in love."

He talked and she listened, drinking herself unconscious... until there was nothing more left.

Not a thing she could do would ever change the situation now. He was in love with someone else and nothing she could do would ever change that. Her marriage was 'on the rocks'.

She must go away and think. She had a lot of thinking to do...

For the next few years they continued living separate lives – he doing his own thing, she doing hers.

They still cared for each other – they never lost that – but that love, that passion, that fire which once burned within them; that spark for each other was gone! Lost forever! And she knew sooner or later they would have to divorce.

'Her marriage was crumbling and there was no turning back. It had broken down and there was not a ting she could do about it.' Then finally the day of reckoning came.

It was May 10 1994, the day when Eve stood at Castleton Assizes listening to the case of her divorce; the day her Decree Nisi was being granted, Michael being absent.

It was all arranged amicably. No fight. No conflict, Michael having given her the mansion at 15 Lovell Close in which to live.

For some reason, the media didn't make a fuss either – barely two lines appeared in the newspaper column, simply stating 'that multi-millionairess Eve was granted a divorce from estate agent Michael Flackerty.'

For once, Eve Flackerty did not make headline news. She stood at the court, feeling so sad, so alone, no Michael beside her.

'Now at de age of 54,' she was thinking, 'she owned over 15 properties, seven Holiday Homes, a mansion in England, a multimillion-dollar villa in de Caribbean. She had climb de ladder of success, of prosperity – from bein' de barefooted girl in de back streets of Couva to becomin' a Dame and a multi-millionairess – but what was de point of it all, when she'd lost de only man she'd ever loved. Now at 54, she was once again alone.'

No one to love. No one to care for her.

That night she cried and cried and howled and howled like she'd never done before.

Chapter Fifty-Two

She woke up the next morning to a loud knock on her door. It was the postman with a parcel for her.

Eyes red and swollen from all the crying she'd done during the night, she opened the parcel with some trepidation. But to her surprise it was a present from Sam: a bottle of Laura Ashley perfume and a card which read:

> 'To a very special Mum
> Just to let you know we care.'
> Sam xxxx

On realising how much her son really loved and cared for her she nearly burst into tears again. But it made her feel good once more and so relieved, she tried to take control of herself – stop herself from crying.

She bathed her pitted eyes and tried to pull herself together.

'She had so much goin' for her. A lovin' son. A warm family. And…she had come such a long way. If she let herself go now, she may never rise up again. She could well sink back down the slippery slopes of misery from which she'd long ago escaped. She must not give up. Not now! Not ever!' she thought.

Bracing herself, she resolved over the next few weeks to do the things which she knew best and that was building her business empire. Eve Flackerty, it seemed, was getting back on tracks and her heart was beginning to glow again.

For the next few years, she kept herself really busy building up her portfolio of properties. She bought ten more properties and sold five, investing £100,000 of it in Shell and BP shares. And so now, instead of just making money from her properties, she was making huge sums from dividends and 'payouts' from these oil companies too.

There seemed to be no end to her appetite for gaining wealth and her ability to make more of it. Indeed, she seemed to have the 'Midas touch'. The genius in her; that business guru – just thrived and thrived...

Racing around in her blue Mercedes, combing her properties, keeping up with her charity work for her homes and having the media write about her work too, was something in which she wallowed.

It gave her a buzz.

The media was showing so much interest in her, that one cocky newspaper reporter even approached her to write a book about her life. But she declined politely.

She had given many a party at the Holiday Homes for the siblings and their families – treats of sandwiches and cakes; ice cream and soft drinks and hundreds of balloons were being released in the gardens to celebrate birthdays and other occasions.

Her eyes used to light up as she watched them enjoying themselves, playing, frolicking around. And her heart used to bubble even more when she read the articles about her parties in the newspapers.

But she was working herself to the ground and so every now and then she was obliged to take a short holiday and spend some time at her villa in Trinidad. There, she would wile the time away either swimming in the pool in the cool of evening, sipping rum and coke, or giving lavish dinner parties. Then, after a week or so, having revitalised herself, she would return to England fresh, ready to face new challenges.

No matter what life threw at her, she always seemed equipped; ready to bounce back, facing whatever challenges lay before her.

Alas! There was another surprise to come and what a surprise it turned out to be. She couldn't believe her luck!

Soldiering on without much thought, one day a letter came hurtling through the letter box.

Opening the letter without giving it much thought, she nearly fell off the chair on which she was sitting when she read its contents. It was an invitation from Rockingham Palace for her to attend the Queen's annual garden party at the palace.

Her heart bubbled with joy.

There was much to do preparing for the occasion; racing about here, rushing about there, getting her outfit ready; as well as keeping other matters in hand. She simply wanted to look good – look her best on the day.

She decided on an ice-blue outfit. An ice-blue summer dress; a white hat bordered with a few off-white roses; white shoes and handbag with white gloves to match and a simple diamond necklace with matching ear studs completing her attire.

She was 61 years old now and very concerned about her age, but when she tried on the outfit a couple of days before the occasion, she was amazed at how lovely she still looked.

Finally, the day of the party came and she was in her element, her favourite reporter having joined her to cover the occasion.

She and Sam drank Champagne and enjoyed the spread: an assortment of cold meat and sandwiches; French bread and butter; salads and coleslaw; a variety of cakes and a good selection of wines to drink.

Food galore it was. All laid out so sprucely on long tables covered with crisp white linen – tables placed almost neck to neck along the freshly trimmed palace lawns.

She mingled with the guests – dignitaries of all sorts – mayors, mayoresses, politicians, writers, scientists, charity workers, business gurus, millionaires and millionairesses – each stalking the other – talking, laughing, exchanging a card or two; all having fun. But beneath the glitz and glamour of the occasion, serious (unwritten) business was taking place – some dignitaries exchanging business cards discreetly.

The cameras clicked, 'Click! Click! Click! Click!' they went – each recording for posterity's sake; for the history books; for their family albums – this very special day in their lives. On and on, it went, this party of a lifetime.

What a day it was! A day Eve was to record in her catalogue of achievements. A day which she was never to forget. How could she...ever, ever forget?

She had achieved what she had never dreamt possible. She was at her zenith once more, almost at the top of her pinnacle and she wallowed in it.

'She had had her spate of bad luck,' she thought. 'First de death of her son, then de divorce. Bad luck comes in threes – so the saying goes. It couldn't happen a third time. Could it?' She didn't want to think of such things.

But then one day...

It was May 31 2002 (how could she ever forget?) when 62-year-old Eve decided to paint the back half-walled fence of her mansion at Lovell Close. The painter had let her down and so frustrated she decided to do it herself. 'The exercise will do her good,' she thought. So she climbed up the short ladder and was busy painting away when a few blobs of paint accidentally dropped onto the neighbour's concrete patio in his back yard.

That evening she apologised deeply to them. She offered to clean up the paint; do anything to appease the situation but they refused all her offers point-blank.

They boiled with anger and fumed with hatred. Hatred not so much because of the spilt paint, but because they envied her: her astounding success; her dynamic personality; her Damehood; her 'write ups' in the newspapers; her everything! And now that she was on her own they seized their chance to knock her off her pedestal; knock her down with vengeance, if they could.

Collaborating with another neighbour, the police were phoned. The police were told that Eve had purposely thrown the paint onto the patio of their back yard – that she was seen doing so and that they had video evidence from the camera they'd installed to prove it.

They hated her with a venom that was hard to describe. And now, at long last, they had their chance to seek revenge.

'They would have her arrested; wipe the smile off her smug face once and for all...'

Chapter Fifty-Three

It was nearly 2pm that fatal day when Katie from Maloney & Co Solicitors led Eve from prison cell number 1 to the Interview Room at Brickwater Police Station. She'd planned to interview her first, take a few notes before Detective Haggie began her interrogation. But they barely had a few minutes together, when Haggie knocked on the door and entered.

Impatient to make a start and not prepared to give an inch, Haggie was ready to deliver her onslaught. She switched the tape-recorder on and began...

"There's been an allegation that on May 31 2002 you caused Criminal Damage to the property of the people that live next door – 13 Lovell Close – that you splattered paint on the concrete path of their rear garden causing damage to the value of £75 to this rear garden belonging to Dan Ballantine, intending to destroy or damage or being reckless as to whether such property would be destroyed or damaged.

"What have you to say about that?"

She delivered her blow... to the point... with vengeance... all the time looking straight into Eve's eyes, searching, searching for... God knows what. Hoping maybe to find some clue which would send Eve straight back into cell number 1. Such high-falluting words she used, as if coming straight from a law book, it seemed – half of which Eve could not comprehend; could barely understand.

As she fired the questions, Eve nearly fell off the chair on which she was sitting, the onslaught ringing... ringing in her ears like an alarm bell.

For a moment she couldn't speak. She just sat there, almost paralysed.

Shocked at the 'charge' and the estimated 'cost' of damage of £75, she went numb.

"Come on! Come on! What have you got to say?" Haggie probed aggressively, not allowing Eve time to think.

Shaking like a leaf, the confused, distressed 62-year-old Eve tried hard to pull herself together – nervously stuttering...

Taking a deep breath she tried to explain that 'she was painting her back fence when some paint accidentally spilt onto the neighbour – Mr Ballentine's – back yard.' But Haggie wouldn't have it.

Eve didn't get to finish what she was saying when Haggie butted in. For sensing Eve's vulnerability and realising that she was at the point of cracking, Haggie laid on the heat.

'If she could pin that charge there would be one more 'point' scored on her target, her Book of Achievements – the ladder of promotion. She had one prime fish in her net and she wasn't going to let it slip through he slippery fingers that easily. Never!'

So she probed and pressed, stating that she had a witness – a Miss Ely, to prove that Eve had purposely splashed the paint...Katie sitting next to Eve, listening.

"This Miss Ely," Haggie went on, "from 6 Horsefield Road, which is to the back of your house; she left her back door open because she's got a cat and she'd like it obviously, to be able to come in and out, regardless of what's going on outside."

"She could see you on the ladder, leaning over Mr Ballentine's fence. You wafted the paintbrush around and there's paint on it which splattered all over the rear of his back garden..."

"I did no such thing! As I said before, some paint from my brush accidentally spilt over onto Mr Ballentine's back yard and..."

Again, she didn't give Eve time to finish what she was saying.

Determined to press charges on this vulnerable fish, Haggie kept up the pressure...

Unabated, she continued, "You wafted the paintbrush around for 30 seconds, causing a considerable amount of damage which has amounted to £75 worth of cleaning materials that have to be used to clean up the mess."

She gave Eve a look, as if she had just pierced a dagger into Eve's heart. Eve sitting there, beat! Almost as if she was dead!

'£75 of cleaning materials – to clean up a few blobs of paint spilt on a concrete back yard? Oh God! Oh God! How pathetic!' Eve was thinking. 'It cannot be...'

She mustered her strength and tried to fight back – defend herself, repeating what she'd just said– that 'it was an accident.' But being an honest, decent minded person, she never thought of challenging Haggie's questions – words, in the Statement now being recorded, which were fired at her.

And so consequently, the interview continued... unabated...

On and on it went... inconsistent – sometimes pathetic – sometimes macabre...Haggie keeping up the pressure; hoping to bring Eve to breaking point...Katie sitting there, not making a single attempt to intervene. But then...

"What I would like to put to you," Haggie proceeded, cocky as a rooster, quite sure that she had the case in the bag, "that I have clear evidence of you carrying out the actual..." (She was referring to some video evidence she had) and Bang! Like a dagger, Katie intervened, thrusting in. She didn't give Haggie time to finish what she was saying.

"You are not going to arrest my Client for this!" Katie asserted, as if thrusting the sword in. "If you wish to, then I want to see the video. I am asking you to stop! I want to see the video! If you want a further interview, we will view the video and put further questions…" Katie erupted.

Like a volcano she sparked, almost knocking Haggie off her pedestal.

About to wet her pants, the self-assured Haggie was now a bag of nerves – her voice becoming throaty, "I…" she couldn't finish what she was saying and the interview was stopped. She paused… took a deep breath then after a minute or so the interrogation continued.

"At this point, the lady from Horsefield Road called the police. Mr Ballentine was not in. He was out…" she said, the broken Eve sweating, listening, when Zoom! Katie cut in again.

"You did not disclose this when you made the Disclosure! This was not in the Disclosure!" Katie attacked, her eyes on fire – game, set and match. She was almost about to hit the roof.

"I need to get it clarified!" Haggie went throaty again. "Mr Ballentine was not in that day. It was a neighbour, Miss Ely, who established that you caused the damage, otherwise I would have got a statement from him as to the incident."

A further pause… Katie staring her in the face as she waffled. The confused Eve not really understanding what was going on… then… Haggie continued.

"Do you recall the police coming around that day?"

"No! No one came."

She looked hard at Eve and continued the onslaught.

On and on it went…about whether Eve had any 'issues' with the neighbours.

'All this anger, frustration, aggression, time, money…wasted – for £75 worth of damage to a neighbour's concrete back yard. How pathetic! How sad,' Eve thought.

For a solid hour, Haggie interrogated. Questions, Questions! The 62-year-old Eve sweating her guts out, exhausted. Then finally, when she could fleece her no more, Haggie switched the tape off, frustrated.

In the subsequent typewritten report of that taped interview, it was stated that Haggie had 'sealed' the tape in the witnesses' presence. But that was not true at all! She also stated that it was an 'accurate record' of the interview. Again, not true!

For the interview was flawed from start to finish. Inaccuracies, inconsistencies, macabre…so many errors. So much expense, costs, for a pathetic £75 worth of spillage of paint onto a concrete back yard. It was laughable beyond belief!

There was also the fact that Eve was only given the Search Warrant when she was about to leave the police station, after being imprisoned there, that day (June 3rd 2002.)

So many of her Human Rights were being violated…it seemed.

It was not until 3.15pm that day, when she was finally granted 'unconditional bail' and relieved, she and Sam jumped into the waiting limousine and headed straight for Sam's house as fast as the limousine could carry them; she, trying hard to erase the stench of that prison from her distressed mind.

The next day, the news was plastered on the front pages of most of the newspapers:

'Empress Eve, the multi-millionairess, was released from Brickwater Police Station's prison today on Unconditional Bail on a charge of Criminal Damage to neighbour's property…'

… it read.

"Oh no! No, no!... I'm finished," she howled, as she read that piece. But there was nothing she could do to stop the rumours spreading.

Once more she felt powerless.

That night she cried herself to sleep howling and howling like a demented animal...

Chapter Fifty-Four

There were so many flaws revealed in Haggie's interview; contradictions, inconsistencies, non-disclosures plus the fact that the incident was not caught on Mr Ballentine's camera as she claimed and then the 'disproportionate force' used to arrest Eve. All this meant that Maloney & Co had the 'case' in the palm of their hands. There was no way Eve could be convicted. But instead of launching their attack, they decided to use a different approach.

Instead of fighting the case on the above points, they decided to ask the Crown Prosecution to drop the case. Instead of listening to the tape; analysing the contents of that 'Interview'; viewing the video; they sent off a letter to the CPS requesting that 'in the interest of the public', the case 'be dropped.'

In it they stated how Eve had a good character; how she was an honest person; how she had worked hard to reach where she was...On and on it went. It read:

> 'Our client is a lady of 62 years of age, of Caribbean origin, who has never been in trouble with the police before.
> She has worked in England for 40 years, studied hard and with dedication had built up her business. She has been deeply upset, not only by these allegations, but also by the manner in which the matter had been handled. The Officer on the case appears to have used 'disproportionate force' to arrest our client and has not been sufficiently

objective in her assessment of the appropriate response to allegations.

The damage alleged is 'minimal'; there is no photographic evidence of it and the 'stated costs' of remedying the alleged damages, stretches credibility.

Our client denies she is 'mentally ill' as had been suggested by both the neighbours and the Officer on the case, on occasions. However, it is indisputable that these proceedings are causing her a great deal of distress and anxiety.

It is our submission that, in view of our client's age, character, the nature of the dispute and the impact the proceedings are having on her, the case should be discontinued.'

How pathetic. Balls! Bollocks! Bullshit! Sad! Mind-blowing! Nonsense!

They had the case in the palm of their hands – there were enough points in this letter to score, to win it. What was stated in the second and third paragraphs alone, was enough to send Eve home a free woman, rejoicing in victory. Yet, Maloney & Co decided to play straight into the hands of the CPS. And from that time on, the case was more or less the CPS's to win.

'Why was Maloney & Co asking the CPS to drop the case, in the "public's interest"? Why would the public be interested in a supposed act of "criminal damage" – worth £75 of pathetic damage – blobs of paint spilt on a neighbour's concrete back yard?'

It was a joke beyond belief! Eve just couldn't understand.

But Maloney & Co had their reasons: reasons which in all her wisdom, the distressed exhausted Eve failed to comprehend; reasons which only they, Maloney & Co knew.

For by some stroke of luck, they had managed to acquire a rich client and there was no way they were going to let her slip through their impoverished fingers without making as much money as they could from her. And so they were playing into the hands of the CPS, playing for time, running up a bill.

The case was adjourned three times, 27th June, 13th September and 31st October 2002; each time, the distressed, worn out 62-year-old Eve had to appear in front of the Magistrate and answer 'the same old questions' over and over again.

"Your name…? Your address…? Your date of birth…?"

The same old questions each time. And to top it all, every time the case was adjourned, a different solicitor from the firm appeared, charging a fee – the cost to Eve forever spiralling.

In effect, Maloney & Co were exploiting the situation, manipulating matters, playing for time, running up a bill for Eve and so making more money for themselves. But it took a while before it sank in – before the naïve Eve caught up with the fact of what they were doing.

There were other unanswerable questions in their firm's behaviour too. For, not only did they play into the hands of the CPS but from the very beginning, Katie instructed Eve at the police station – at a point when she was in such a traumatic state – to accept 'the charge' and not to view the video.

The fact that Haggie had no real evidence to pin a charge on her was never explained to Eve.

In effect if she had refuted the charge, there would be no case for them and so no money to be made, especially from a multi-millionairess.

Poor old Eve! She just didn't understand. Maloney & Co intended to fleece her, squeeze every penny out of her and she just didn't understand.

Bent! Corrupt! Bastards!

It was hard to believe that this was happening. But it was happening alright, right here in England. Practised by a firm of female solicitors who swore on Oath that they were upholding the law – according to the books. That they were maintaining that 'Code of Conduct' according to law.

Eve had read many of John Grisham's novels about corrupt solicitors! Bent, sick, rats, practising out there in America, but she never dreamt that it would happen in England too! And now...'If only Grisham knew, he would have many a tale to tell.'

Sick, female, Bitches! Bent, corrupt Henchwomen!

Being a decent honest-minded citizen, Eve simply did not understand how the sometimes 'corrupt law' works. But when the case continued to be adjourned and adjourned the penny finally dropped! She suspected that something was amiss and sought a 'second opinion' and insisted that the case be tried, once and for all, for the final time.

She made it very clear, 'there was to be no further adjournment.'

And so the date was set. The case was to be tried finally at 9am November 12 2002.

Katie insisted that Eve arrived at Brickwater Magistrates' Court early. 'An hour before the hearing,' she warned, 'so that she could prepare her for cross-examination.'

And so on that cold November's day, having woken up early after a restless night of tossing and turning, she, Sam and a few friends arrived at court at 8am sharp.

But lo and behold, there was no sign of Katie.

Chapter Fifty-Five

In the Waiting Room they sat waiting...waiting and Eve began to panic. She was sweating. Time passed by, then finally at 8.50am a dark skinned Asian guy appeared. He seemed in a hurry.

Introducing himself as Prami Saheed – a solicitor turned judge – he tried to brief Eve, but it was obvious from his conversation that he did not know the facts of the case. He did not study the records.

Speedily they looked at some ad-hoc photos of the scene – photos which their firm's secretary had taken in a hurry. No briefing, nothing! And within three minutes they were ready; ready and waiting, seated in front of the Magistrates' Bench waiting for the trial to begin.

Maloney & Co were supposed to get materials from the police – materials which were 'not disclosed' by the police but Prami told Eve that the police's solicitor concerned was off sick at the time and so they could not get that information.

"The case however must be heard today," he affirmed.

Lies! Lies! Bullshit! For here he was, that very same police solicitor sitting in front of Eve and Prami, looking as healthy and as bold as brass, the learned Judge Prami's black skin shining, his teeth white as the advert from Colgate, both sitting 'as cool as cucumbers' ready for the trial to start.

Eve had never met Prami before and now she sat there sad. She was seething with anger.

The first witness, Miss Ely, took the stand.

"You said that on the day in question, you had seen Mrs Flackerty standing on the ladder, leaning over Mr

Ballentine's fence. Where were you at the time?" Prami asked her.

"In the kitchen, inside my back door."

"And you saw her splashing the paint with her brush?"

"Yes, I saw her"

"I put it to you," Prami continued, "that you never saw anything. You couldn't see anything."

He smiled, the witness smiled too and the lady Magistrate was laughing her head off.

"I did!" Miss Ely replied, still smiling, Mr Ballentine stirring in his seat.

"That's all," Prami concluded, looking at the Magistrates and smiling.

"You may step down," the lady Magistrate said, and 'that was it.'

It was all over, 'within a jiff.'

Like a nursery rhyme, it went. No probing! No deep questioning! No real cross-examination! And before you could say 'Bob's your uncle', it was all over, Eve sitting there unable to believe what she'd just heard; what she'd just witnessed.

She nearly fell off the bench on which she was sitting. She went queasy! She felt sick! She wanted to vomit! But powerless to do a thing, she just sat there, staring at Prami.

Prami did not interrogate Miss Ely. He didn't cross-examine her about the fact that she could not see clearly from a distance of 70' away – she wore glasses and there were overgrown conifer trees which would block her view; the fact that she had left her kitchen back door open, supposedly for the cat, in spite of the commotion going on outside; the question of whether Mr Ballentine was in or out – the police did not check this out. Did Miss Ely see him there? The photos which could have been taken from the wrong angle and so make it inconclusive. The inconsistencies of the tape. So many inconsistencies and contradictions. So many unanswered questions. Yet Prami did not cross-examine Miss Ely on any of these points of blunder.

Seething within Eve stood up. She wanted to hit him in the face; knock the glistening white teeth out of his suave mouth; kick the hell out of him. But she knew if she did that it would be fatal; it would be the end of her and all that she'd worked so hard to build. So she swallowed her pride, summoned her strength and quietly sat down again.

"You may take the stand Mrs Flackerty," she heard a voice saying...her mind still wheeling, working overtime.

"I swear to tell the truth, the whole truth and nothing but the truth, so help me God," she said, as she held the Bible. She was visibly shaking, trying hard to recover from the shock she'd just had.

"There are some photographs in front of you. Look at them," the prosecution solicitor said.

She stared at the coloured photos in front of her, clearly professionally taken, colours glistening to a sheen, the blobs of white paint on the red concrete yard standing out like 'white sentinels on a red stand.'

"Would you say that was a lot of paint on that floor? A lot of damage?" (The photos were enlarged, thus highlighting the blobs of white paint on the red ground.)

For a moment she paused. Still shaking and in a state of shock, she could hardly think straight. But she was brought up to be honest and tell the truth and so, in her distressed state, she answered, "Yes, but..."

She just couldn't think straight.

She didn't get time to finish what she was about to say, when she was interrupted by this young upstart of a prosecutor. Prami the smooth skinned goat, not bothering to intervene at all.

Like a pneumatic drill, the prosecutor drilled, pressing, probing, questioning and examining, until he had 62-year-old Eve sweating. She was almost reaching breaking point, Prami sitting there, his black skin shining, his white teeth glistening

– he never intervened once – the three Magistrates staring the broken Eve in the face as she struggled to answer the questions. Then, after a solid half an hour of cross-examination, Eve was told to step down from the stand, Mr Ballentine and Miss Ely laughing their heads off, having watched her sweat and grilled by the prosecutor.

They had a feast of a day.

From that moment Eve knew she had lost the case and she struggled hard to stop the tears from flowing.

Feeling betrayed, angry, shocked, bewildered, she wanted to jump back onto the stand – tell the Magistrates that 'they would be making a mistake if they convicted her,' drum it home to them, that 'they were making such a fuss about nothing; that this case was costing she and the taxpayer so much money – all for a measly £75 worth of 'so called damage' to a concrete back yard – when there were children and people all over the world starving; people who could not even get clean water to drink and basic food to eat; people who were dying of starvation, malnutrition, diarrhoea, dysentery; people who had no home in which to live.'

'Just think,' she wanted to tell them, 'how the cost of this trial could be put to better use; how this money could be better spent, to help those poor people. Just think!'

She wanted to drum it home to them; let them know 'that somehow, along the line, they had lost their values – the morals which England once stood for; somehow, along the road, they had lost their way.'

Oh how she wanted to drum it home to them. But she knew it would be a waste of time. They were part of the 'system' – a 'new breed' which upheld the very values which the older generation was criticising; values sometimes corrupt, bent, twisted, sick – they were being groomed to maintain it.

'In their quest for power,' she noted, 'human feelings did not come into the equation.'

As she thought of these things... she looked at the female Magistrate sitting in the middle. Forty or so, she was wearing a ring in her nose. She looked so stern, so much in control.

'A single mother, perhaps and maybe homeless and penniless at some stage in her life. Who somehow managed to worm her way out of it, to the position she now occupied.'

'She would do anything to maintain the "status quo",' Eve thought.

As her thoughts gained pace, her face began to drop and her heartbeat quickened.

She knew it would be a waste of time trying to tell these Magistrates, these solicitors, these law people – this 'new breed' – about morals and values of the past. Any such outbursts would surely cost her her future. So she tried hard to calm her distraught feelings, focus on her current situation and sat back nervously waiting for the worst.

The three Magistrates disappeared quickly to the back, but within a few minutes they returned, as swiftly as they had departed.

"The case is adjourned," the woman with the ring in her nose said. "One of the Magistrates had to attend an emergency," she advised.

Yet again, a further date was set – this time for November 20 2002 and so at a crucial stage of the trial, Eve was once again left in limbo.

Chapter Fifty-Six

A week later on November 20 2002, the trial finally resumed. This time to Eve's dismay, Katie appeared on the scene. And this time, she had come well prepared.

She read out a whole list from her well prepared type written letter – about Eve's good character (supplying the reference for the Magistrate to see) plus Eve's medical record (supplying copies of this too), plus her income and testimony from her church, about her good character.

All matters of significance, but truly confidential in nature were read out by her publicly, for all to hear, Mr Ballentine taking note of every detail; Katie, not in the least bit concerned that confidential details about her client, Eve, were being disclosed for Eve's enemies to hear. And they wallowed in it.

In fact, she did not inform Eve that she was going to do this, nor did she give any reasons for so doing.

Eve went mad! But gutted and angry as she was she felt powerless to do anything about it. She felt betrayed – her inner world had just been spied upon. She sat there mute, as she listened to the garbage being spilt about her, the three Magistrates, ears cocked high, taking it all in.

It was as if her world was caving in on her.

Armed with the details they'd just heard, "All rise," she heard the voice saying then the three Magistrates disappeared fast, to consider their verdict.

Within three minutes they were back on the bench. "All rise," the voice said again and everyone jumped to their feet.

"You are found guilty," the Magistrate with the ring in her nose asserted, "of causing criminal damage to the rear yard of 13 Lovell Close... You are placed on 'Conditional Discharge' for two years – that means if you re-offend within the two years, you will not only be tried for that offence but for this offence as well. Do you understand?"

"Y-e-s," Eve stuttered (Katie, too busy typing it all up in her laptop, to concern herself as to whether Eve understood the verdict or not). In fact Eve did not fully understand the implications of it at all.

She looked at Katie, puzzled, but Katie was still bent on her laptop.

"You are ordered to pay costs of £5000. Do you understand? Your solicitor will explain it to you," the Magistrate continued, Katie still head down, busy on her laptop, not bothering even to look at Eve once.

"This court is dismissed!" the Magistrate concluded and Bang! It was all over.

Eve stood there motionless, numb! Dumbfounded! Shaking almost beyond control, as she thought of the verdict. The predicament she was in.

'And we shall set neighbours against neighbours; families against families and their loved ones – to get what we want; for that is our way and there is nothing you can do about it,' she heard herself thinking.

'We shall put up cameras everywhere to watch your every move and there is nothing you can do about it,' the thoughts in her mind were echoing. 'For, you had your way and now it's our turn to have ours,' she could almost hear Haggie and the Magistrate with the ring in her nose and no doubt tattoos on her body, saying.

Her thoughts were playing havoc, ringing in her ears like an alarm bell. But there was nothing she could do but stand there, numb!

'Somewhere along the route, this "new breed" in their quest for power had somehow, lost their way.' Her thoughts were tumbling inside her head.

'They had made the "old" submit to their values – their way – bullied them into submission; bamboozled them into acceptance,' she heard herself thinking, her thoughts whizzing…

'You have lost your membership, your representation,' she could almost hear them echoing, 'and you, the "old" gave in without a fight, meekly and humbly surrendering to our ways.'

'We have won! We have won!' Eve almost heard them rejoicing.

'You are beat! You are beat!' Eve could almost hear them in her subconscious mind, singing, as she stood there frozen, thinking, thinking of the verdict and its repercussions.

She wanted to run, jump, hide anywhere, but there was nothing she could do…nowhere to hide.

She just stood there, numb! Lost for words.

She was beat alright. Beaten to a pulp and she knew it; Mr Ballentine sitting there a happy man, staring her in the face, a broad grin on his wide jaw.

Out of envy, he had her right where he wanted her and he wasn't going to repent, she, almost reading the glow in his heart as she stood there, frozen…thinking!

She felt faint and was just about to collapse when Sam darted forward, grabbed her firmly and led her gently away, she quietly crying her heart out.

They didn't have time to speak to Katie – 'they would speak to her later,' they knew that and as they made their way home that day, Eve's distressed mind continued to work overtime.

'Maloney & Co had this case in the palm of their hands, so what went wrong?' she asked herself.

As she thought and thought in bed later that night, the mysteries surrounding the case began to unravel in front of her – like a jigsaw puzzle, it unfolded.

'They didn't listen to the taped interview which Haggie had recorded – analyse it; they didn't cross examine the witness; they didn't press for "secondary disclosures" and "non-disclosures"; they didn't put Mr Ballentine on the stand and question him; they didn't check to see whether he was at home on the day of the incident; they admitted that the police used "unreasonable force" to arrest Eve but they didn't press charges against the police. And the police did not provide her with a Search Warrant until she was released from Brickwater Police Station. Yet the "Police and Criminal Evidence Act 1984' clearly states that – in the exercise of a power to search premises, police may use reasonable force" to enter the premises and carry out the search.' But that was not the case.

So many inconsistencies. So many flaws. So many questions unanswered.

'The notion that Miss Ely could see – that her back door was "left" of the conifer trees was not questioned – it was not true, but they didn't verify it. The insistence that Mr Ballentine was not in – that he was at work at his property development office was not true either – but no evidence was provided to support that claim.'

So many inconsistencies. So many unanswered questions?

Eve's mind was playing havoc…as she thought of those unjust scenarios.

'You could have said "No. You didn't do it!" she recalls the Magistrate saying to her, when she'd read out the reasons for their decision to convict her.

'They just didn't understand,' Eve thought.

'They just couldn't put themselves in the boots of a 62-year-old elderly lady, who had the traumatic experience of the police breaking her door down, arresting her and putting her in jail.

'They simply didn't understand.

'What a state she would be in. Shocked, traumatised, unable to think straight…to give a comprehensive statement.

They simply failed to comprehend. They simply failed to understand.'

As she reflected on the case on that sleepless night – like a tapestry of patchwork – the answer to the mystery surrounding this case began to reveal itself.

'Maloney & Co didn't act "in the best interest of their client" because they had acquired a very prestigious one. And so, the longer they stretched the case, the more they could bleed money out of their client, Eve.

'They were working with the police too, for, by so doing they were more likely to get referral cases from the police in the future. They had in fact collaborated with the police – "FIX" the case – behind the scenes – simply for their own ends and not those of their client, Eve. No wonder the Magistrate – the woman with the ring in her nose – was laughing her head off during the trial.

'She knew all along the case was FIXED.'

Eve felt sick! She wanted to vomit as the scenario revealed its ugly head that night.

'The whole episode was a sham. A stinking, dirty sham from beginning to end,' she thought 'Grisham did them too much justice when he wrote about them in his novels,' she was almost talking to herself.

She wanted to…? "Sick, dirty, bent corrupted Bastards!" she screamed and screamed and screamed, then finally fell asleep.

When she woke up the next morning, she was in a state of quandary – thinking, for days on end.

Here she was at Lovell Close brooding. 'The neighbours had hated her, not because she had done them wrong, but because they envied her success. They'd put her in jail and now she had a "criminal record" for two years. Two years, the papers which Katie sent her, confirmed. "If she behaved herself for two years," it stated, "her criminal record would be spent".'

But two years was a long time to sit around at Lovell Close, brooding. She couldn't live there, not anymore. She had work to do... She must get moving.

Over the next few days she put her mansion and five of her properties up for sale, leaving Sam to oversee matters. Then she booked a flight for December 20 2002 to take her to the Caribbean, where she hoped to holiday at her villa.

When she'd received the final papers from Maloney & Co, she was so mad at the way they'd treated her that she wanted to throw the whole lot away – burn them – bury them in the dustbin or somewhere, but commonsense got the better of her and she decided to keep them.

Little did she know, that it was to prove 'a gem of gold in a pile of dross', for research on the book, she was later to write.

Chapter Fifty-Seven

After the turmoil of the past few months in England, it was refreshing to watch Eve relaxing under the palm trees by her swimming pool in Trinidad, sipping rum punch and enjoying the cool tropical breeze. She was having a wonderful time in the Caribbean – having fun with friends and relatives, listening to calypso and steel band music drumming away in the background and she didn't want it to end.

But, she had reached the penultimate stage of her life and now there was something else she felt she had to do.

'She had achieved so much in her life; become one of the richest women in England; honoured by the Queen; even had a brush with the Law. And now she was ready to retire in the Caribbean. But before she could do that she must write a book about her life,' she thought. 'Then she could settle in her villa in Trinidad for the rest of her life, sipping rum and coke, enjoying the sunshine, palm trees and blue waters, listening to lovely Caribbean music, eating mouth-watering gourmet food – spoil herself rotten for the rest of her life.'

'The time was right,' she said to herself. So she set about collecting data for her book.

But time passed quickly and before she knew it, it was time for her to return to England to finalise her business plans and collect more research to complete her book.

And so on April 2 2003 she boarded a Virgin Atlantic plane and headed back to England.

Having sold her mansion and some of her properties and banked the takings, Sam booked a suite at the Hilton Hotel, where it was arranged she was to stay.

She had returned – not to stay – but to sell off some of her remaining assets and retire in the Caribbean where she hoped she would spend the rest of her days. And so she got busy!

Plans were quickly put into action to sell five of her '7 Days' charity homes – leaving Sam two to look after – and three of her 'buy to let' properties – which left Sam with enough properties to oversee; enough to earn his living.

Sam would never starve. Eve made sure of that.

But one property held special significance in her heart, so she felt she had to return there – if only to relive the memories she once experienced.

And so early one morning, during the first week of April, she boarded a train onward bound to Castleton and from there she made her way to 5a Mustard Place.

It was a cold spring day, the chilly April winds blowing through the strands of her grey-black hair as she stood outside 5a Mustard Place staring at it, deep emotions welling inside of her; tears ready to flow as she studied the building; its window sills rotting in parts, its worn-out roof signalling to the elements that it was ready for replacement; its chimneys battered in places, almost dancing in the wind.

It was the first flat she had ever lived in, in England…the first flat she'd ever owned, bought on her way to becoming a multi-millionairess and she had special memories of it – special moments; happy time which she, Michael and the children had spent there.

"Goodbye! Goodbye!" she whispered to the flat, blowing a kiss to it as if it were a human being. A passer-by, slowly making his way on his journey home, stopped dead in his tracks when he saw her.

"Are you alright?" he enquired, shocked out of his wits as he watched her blowing this kiss to no one – there was not another soul in sight. He stopped for a split second no doubt thinking, that maybe she was crazy, funny or something!

"I... I'm... OK, OK," she stuttered, trying to hold back the tears as she stood there thinking of the happy moments she'd shared in that flat.

Embarrassed by the incident with the passer-by, she was just about to walk away, when...

"Oh but you are Eve, the millionairess!" he blurted, suddenly recognising her from the newspaper cutting which he'd kept.

"Please can I have your autograph?" he said, pushing a piece of paper under her nose.

She signed the autograph quickly and walked away, knowing deep in her heart that she would never, ever return to Mustard Place again. That little antiquated flat, from which she'd built her fortune – that beautiful, first home, which she'd ever owned, would be gone from her life, forever!

That night she didn't sleep well. She had a lot of thinking to do...

She'd acquired the necessary permission to collect research materials and papers from Brickwater Police Station and she spent a restless night thinking of the task ahead.

The next few weeks or so were spent interviewing personnel from the station, but time was passing by and she needed to collect some final bits and pieces to complete her research work for her book.

'There was one person she must try and see, without whom her work would be incomplete,' she thought. So she decided to make one last visit to Brickwater Police Station to try and locate that person.

Chapter Fifty-Eight

It was Friday 13 May 2003 when Eve marched into Brickwater Police Station for the last time.

She reported to the desk as usual, from where they led her to Sergeant Penny O'Donnel. A big woman she was, 50 or so, she carried about her an air of authority, self-confidence.

"Detective Haggerty? Is she still working here?" Eve enquired. "I would like to meet her please."

"Haggie you mean. Haggie? Didn't you know? Didn't you hear?" the Sergeant recognised Eve.

"Hear what?" Eve replied, her eyes lighting up with curiosity.

"Come!" the Sergeant said, beckoning her on to follow.

Click! Clock! Click! Clock, they went as they marched along the dark, deserted, smelly corridor.

"It was all over the papers, you know."

"The papers...?" (It was all over the papers alright, but Eve wasn't in England. She was in the Caribbean having a nice time and researching her book. And Sam – her beloved Sam couldn't bear to break the chilling news to her.)

"The papers? What...?"

"She knifed her partner to death, you know!" O'Donnel interrupted... and...

Click! Clock! Click! Clock, they proceeded, stopping abruptly at Cell No 2. Then, as quick as a flash... Sl-uu-sh! The peephole opened and Eve's eyes met Haggie's.

Shocked and bewildered, Eve stared hard at Haggie as she lay on the cold hard mattress on the stone floor; a stinking toilet pan in the corner; dirty graffiti words barely visible on the walls. Then... Flop! Haggies' eye-lids closed suddenly.

Whether she recognised Eve or not, no one would ever know.

"She tried to kill herself, you know, so they put her under '24 hour surveillance'."

"What?"

Eve looked at Haggie with pity in her eyes as Haggie struggled to pull herself up. She had lost so much weight; one side of her body crippled: her face deformed almost beyond recognition.

"Are you alright Haggie?" the Sergeant enquired with concern.

"Ar-rr-e-rh." Haggie tried to reply, forcing herself up, her crippled body unable to respond.

"She had a stroke, you know, after she'd tried to kill herself. It left her crippled, deformed on one side. She lost her speech too, she can hardly speak now."

"Ar-r-rrh." Haggie tried to say something, but the words just wouldn't come out.

"It's alright Haggie. It's alright!" the Sergeant said, trying to reassure her then, Sl-s-sh! The peephole closed again.

"Only three and a half hours to go, you know."

"What?"

"Yes! She only has 'three and a half hours' to go."